dark talents

MAX TURNER

dark talents

TWO BOOKS IN ONE

night runner AND end of days

ST. MARTIN'S GRIFFIN
NEW YORK

This is a work of fiction. All of the characters, organizations, and events portrayed in this novel are either products of the author's imagination or are used fictitiously.

www.stmartins.com

ISBN 978-1-250-03862-3 (trade paperback)

St. Martin's Griffin books may be purchased for educational, business, or promotional use. For information on bulk purchases, please contact Macmillan Corporate and Premium Sales Department at 1-800-221-7945, extension 5442, or write specialmarkets@macmillan.com.

Night Runner was first published in Canada by Harper*Trophy*Canada™,
an imprint of HarperCollins Publishers Ltd

First Edition: December 2013

10 9 8 7 6 5 4 3 2 1

Night Runner

For my mother
(gift of life and all that)

Chapter 1
The Visitor

My name is Daniel Zachariah Thomson. Everyone calls me Zack. I live in the Nicholls Ward of the Peterborough Civic Hospital, and this is the story of how I died, twice.

I know what you're thinking: *The Nicholls Ward—isn't that the loony bin? The nuthouse? Where they put people who torture squirrels or think they're Julius Caesar? That explains it. Only a loo-loo would think he could die two times and still be around to talk about it.* Well, the truth is a funny thing. It can be its clumsy self and it doesn't matter what anyone believes. I guess it's like way back in the Middle Ages when everyone and his dog thought the world was flat. That you could sail too far from home and your ship would drop right off into space. The whole planet was wrong on that one, and it didn't change the truth one pinch. My story is sort of like that. Read it and see for yourself. I'm not crazy. I'm here for different reasons.

The other people on the ward aren't all crazy, either. My neighbours all have mental disorders, that's true, but these are never as bad as you might think. Certainly not like the villains in Hollywood movies who turn their victims into wax dummies or serve them up for dinner. Most of the patients in the Nicholls Ward are older people. They need help just to eat. I don't expect to see them appearing in a horror movie anytime soon. They're all pretty harmless.

But I'm different. I stay up all night, for one thing. That's when my whole life happens—when the others have all taken their happy pills and are snoozing away. I do ordinary stuff, like read, or lift weights. And I run every night, usually outside, but I love movies, so if there's a good one on TV, I'll hop on the treadmill instead and watch it in the fitness room. I love video games, too. There's a big-screen TV in the common room. It takes up half a wall. When you wire up a game, the characters are almost as big as you are.

On good nights, my friend Charlie comes to visit. He's my major contact with the outside world, and because of this, and the fact that my schedule is a bit off, the hospital staff usually let him stay after visiting hours have ended, so long as the two of us aren't making too much trouble. Chaos is one of Charlie's specialties. I'm sure he could have a room of his own here. He'd fit right in.

Life in a mental ward is pretty routine. Meals, naps, TV time, medication and lights out—it all takes place according to a carefully crafted schedule. It helps keep everyone stable. I have a little more leeway than the others because I'm the only one awake after ten o'clock, but even my nights follow a regular pattern. You can't exactly set a clock by it, but it never changes very much, either—dinner, free time, exercise, breakfast, reading, sleeping. But all this changed the night a strange old man crashed his motorcycle through the front doors of the lobby and destroyed our big-screen television.

I was in the fitness room when it happened. It was about three in the morning. One of my all-time favourites, *Terminator*, had just ended, but my eyes were still glued to the small television hanging from the ceiling. A woman with hair so perfect it must have been made of plastic was telling me all about the wonders of Miracle Glow hair care products. The way she carried on, this stuff was our ticket to world peace. While she yammered away, interviewing other people whose lives were now fairy tales thanks to Miracle Glow, I pounded the treadmill. My shoes were practically melting. It was a night like any other. Until I heard a noise like an asteroid hitting the building. I felt it, too. A tremor that came right up through the floor. A second crash quickly followed, and the wail of a police siren.

In a flash I was out in the hall, past the reception counter and into the lobby. The whole time I was thinking, *He's really done it this time.* Charlie, that is. But when I saw the devastation, I knew right away it had to be somebody else. Not even Charlie could have managed this. The lobby was a total disaster. There was glass everywhere. The outside doors were blown right off their hinges.

The common room was even worse. The ping-pong table was tipped over and furniture was scattered all over. Actually, this was partly my fault. Well, *our* fault, Charlie's and mine. As soon as everyone had gone to bed we'd set it up that way so we could have a ping-pong fight. Charlie had wanted to celebrate the end of the school year, and so we'd spent a good hour pelting one another with ping-pong balls. Forts of overturned furniture were still set up all around the room. And we'd forgotten to put the ping-pong table back. I could see tire marks on the floor where the driver had swerved to miss it. The black streaks led straight to the wall where the TV used to hang. It was on the floor now in about a million pieces. I could tell right away that no amount of Krazy Glue was going to bring it back from the dead.

Right in the middle of the floor was the driver. He looked about seventy, with long black hair streaked with white and grey. It stuck out in all directions, as if he'd just been attacked by a tornado. He was on his hands and knees. His long overcoat looked too tight, and his mismatched gloves had the fingers cut out of them. Not the best for crawling across broken bits of TV. Sitting against the wall where the television used to be was his motorcycle, though I'm guessing it wasn't actually his since it said "Peterborough Police" on it. The siren was still wailing and the red and blue lights were flashing all over the white walls.

The old man looked up at me with milky blue eyes. He seemed dazed. Like he was trying to bring me into focus but couldn't quite manage it. He looked like a homeless person, or an undercover police officer dressed like a homeless person, in which case, his costume was perfect. On the ground in front of him was an old top hat smushed flat as a pancake, and it looked as though there were about ten layers of clothing sandwiched underneath his coat. That explained why he wasn't in pieces like the television. The padding must have saved him.

I glanced over my shoulder at the reception counter, where Nurse Ophelia, Nurse Roberta and the other overnight staff normally hung out. You could usually spot at least one security guard. Someone had to be there in case the police showed up with a new patient, which often happened just after the bars closed. No one was in sight now.

I made my way over to the old man as quickly as I could. I was worried he might try to get up and fall back into the sea of glass. Down the hall just ahead of me, a door opened and someone stuck his head out. It was Jacob, my red-haired neighbour. I waved for him to come over and give me a hand. He started up the corridor, then turned around. He did this a couple of times, turning back and then turning away again. His hands were over his ears and he was muttering something to himself, so I just let him pace in front of his room and turned my attention back to the old man. His head was shaking back and forth like he was dizzy, and he was mumbling to himself too, so I put my ear closer to his mouth.

"Hurry . . . hurry up . . ." he was saying. I couldn't tell if he was talking to me or to himself. I asked him if he was okay, but he didn't answer. He just shook his head one more time and grunted. Then he took hold of my arm. His grip was strong, which surprised me. I wondered for a second if his fingers were going to punch right through my scrubs. As he stood up, bits of glass fell from his overcoat. I noticed a small cut on his forehead and another across the bridge of his nose. Blood dribbled down his face and into the stubble on his chin, which was grey and black and white, just like his hair. He looked pretty gory, but I couldn't help myself. I just kept staring, I guess because I felt sorry for him. All the Miracle Glow in the world wasn't going to turn his life into a fairy tale. He smelled like the inside of a wine barrel. And, cuts or no cuts, unless he had a good explanation for all the remodelling he'd just done, when Nurse Roberta showed up, he was in for it.

The old man shook his head a few more times, then he looked me over again. It was like he was waking up or something. His eyes came into focus. He stared at my face for a second, then sort of nodded. A smile spread up one cheek. It made his eyes go wrinkly. He clenched his fists, leaned back and turned his head to the ceiling like he owed the man upstairs a miracle-sized favour.

"Thank heavens, boy!" he said. "Finally . . . I've found you."

Chapter 2
Breakout

The old man put a hand on my shoulder and gave it a firm squeeze. Then he glanced down the hall at Jacob, who was still rocking back and forth with his hands over his ears. A door opened beside him, then another farther down. A pair of curious heads poked their way into the corridor. I recognized the Chicago Man and Sad Stephen. With all the noise coming from the siren, we were going to have a lot of company before long.

As soon as the visitor saw the others, he shoved me towards the motorcycle. Now, I was only fifteen years old, but I was tall for my age, and strong, too. Still, I had trouble staying on my feet when he pushed me away. He had a lot of oomph in those arms. By the time I had my balance, he was right beside me again. His head was swivelling every which way. I couldn't imagine what he was looking for. Behind him, through the window, I could see the parking lot was empty. Hardly surprising. Most people wouldn't choose to visit a mental ward at three in the morning.

"Well, what are you waiting for, boy, the Apocalypse?" he said. "You're going to be worm food if you don't get a move on." He looked at me with his eyebrows high on his forehead and a weird expression on his face, like I was supposed to jump on the motorcycle and ride it to freedom or something.

"He's coming," he continued. "He could be here any second." The man put a hand on my shoulder and pushed me gently towards the motorcycle again. He looked back over his shoulder at the parking lot. I got the feeling Darth Vader was about to waltz in and lightsabre us both in half.

When he noticed I wasn't moving, his nostrils flared and an expression of annoyance came over his face. He reached down, grabbed the handlebars of the police cycle and picked it up himself. That was when he noticed the front forks were all mangled.

"Damn piece of garbage!" he shouted. "No wonder the police can't catch anybody." Then he tossed the bike aside as if it deserved a special place in the junkyard for letting us down. It smashed into the wall, and the fierce roar of the siren turned into something that sounded more like the mewing of a dying cat. "We're going to have to run for it," he said.

The wine smell on his breath was so strong I started to gag. He didn't give me time to recover. Instead, he just grabbed my scrubs near the collar and started to sprint. And just like that, I was practically airborne. And I had no control whatsoever over where I was going. The guy must have been bionic or something.

He hauled me through the lobby and out the gaping hole that had once been the main entrance. Our feet made crunching noises on the broken glass. I tried to work his hand free from my shirt, but it was as if he'd tied his fingers into knots. I couldn't budge them.

Then a bunch of things happened, all at the same time. I heard

Nurse Ophelia shouting my name. She was somewhere behind me. About six police cruisers pulled into the parking lot. Two security guards ran into the reception area on our left and started chasing us. And someone shouted, "DON'T MOVE!"

Well, maybe the old man was deaf. Maybe he was so used to hearing strange voices that he'd learned to ignore them. Or maybe he didn't understand English all that well and thought "DON'T MOVE!" meant slip it into overdrive, because that's what he did. And he was fast. Even hauling me alongside him, I bet he would have beaten half the Canadian Olympic team. We almost made it off the lot, but just as we were approaching the street, I heard a sound like a firecracker. The old man slowed a bit. Then a whole bunch of firecrackers went off, and he let go of me, stumbled and fell.

I couldn't keep my balance, so I fell down beside him. I scraped an elbow on the asphalt, and my hands hit something warm, wet and sticky. Then I rolled up onto my knees. The old man was lying right beside me. Blood was pooling underneath him. It was all over my hands and clothes. And it was all over him.

He'd been shot. Many times.

I felt the old man's hand digging into my arm again. He was struggling to speak.

"Run . . ." he said. Then he coughed several times. "Don't let the cops get you. He's coming. Run!"

Chapter 3
The Second Coming

As the blood spread across the asphalt, the old man's eyes went glassy and the strain on his face seemed to go away. A slow smile spread up one side of his mouth.

I didn't know what to do. Smile or no smile, this man was dying. And there was blood everywhere. I started to get dizzy. My eyes spun in quick circles, like they couldn't focus all of a sudden. Everything went red. My teeth started grinding. I was so confused and agitated that all I could do was put my hands against the sides of my head and groan. To be scared or sad would have made more sense, but all I could think was that this was wasteful. I should have been able to do something.

An instant later, police officers were everywhere. Hands took hold of my arms, helped me up and pulled me away. I didn't resist. I just turned my head so I could get one last look. The old man's milky eyes were glazed over. His breathing had stopped. His smile looked wooden now. Frozen on a dead face. Then, just before someone stepped in the way, his head tipped sideways in my direction. One of his eyes twitched and closed. It made him look as if he was winking at me.

I don't remember if I said anything as the police took me inside. I kept trying to look over my shoulder to see what was happening, but a group of officers had formed a ring around him faster than you could say *shoot*, and the two escorting me didn't slow down until I was back inside the lobby.

Nurse Ophelia was waiting there.

"Oh, no . . ." she said when she saw me. I was still covered in the old man's blood.

"It's not mine," I said.

Nurse Ophelia stepped behind the nurse's station and came back a second later with a handful of tiny square packages. She started ripping them open. I noticed her hands were shaking.

"We'd better get that off," she said.

Inside the packages were folded wipes that smelled like medicine. She gave one to me and started wiping at my face. She was a bit more clumsy than normal. Or maybe it was just that I was still dizzy. All this commotion was probably making everyone a little jumpy.

I was just getting down to the business of cleaning my hands when I heard a loud screech. It was the kind of noise a car makes when it stops too quickly—tires skidding on asphalt.

I looked up. A train of police cruisers was pulling out of the lot, and right in the middle of them was an ambulance. It had stopped suddenly, halfway onto the road. It tilted a bit to one side, then the back doors flew open and someone jumped out. It was the crazy old man! He looked around, then his eyes settled on me and he started sprinting back to the ward. A police car was in the way, but he didn't even break stride. He actually stepped right on top of the hood, cleared the roof in a single leap, then jumped off the rear bumper.

The police in the lobby reached for their guns, but the old man obviously didn't care a pinch.

Then he saw Nurse Ophelia and stopped dead.

I couldn't blame the man for staring. Nurse Ophelia was probably the most beautiful woman on the face of the earth. When we were window shopping last Christmas, she caused three accidents just walking from Brock Street to Simcoe. Unless you were blind, she pretty much stopped you in your tracks.

Well, the old man looked at her and his face calmed, but then his brow wrinkled up again, as though he'd just remembered he was supposed to be annoyed. He pointed a finger at her. "Get him out of here," he said. Then he turned to go, and I don't know if it was because of all the police lights or what, but for just an instant, his watery blue eyes glowed red, just like a person in a photograph when the flash doesn't work right. I'm not even certain it really happened, because he sprinted off so fast that no one even had time to take aim and fire.

I looked at Nurse Ophelia and the officers nearby. Some still had their guns out. They looked stunned. I don't think if Santa Claus had flown down in a flying saucer you would have seen more mouths hanging open. One woman started talking into a radio that was clipped to her shoulder.

"Yeah, I think so. The same guy . . ." The way her voice sounded, it was like she didn't believe herself. I didn't hear the rest because Nurse Ophelia quickly took hold of my hand and started pulling me down the hall.

"Where are we going?" I asked.

One of the policemen interrupted before she could answer me. "We have to ask him some questions, ma'am," he said.

Nurse Ophelia barely slowed down. She just looked over her shoulder. "I'm going to get him cleaned up. I'll be right back."

When we got to my room she opened the door. It was dark inside. I like it that way, unless I'm reading.

"I want you to stay out of sight," she said. "Just for tonight."

I didn't really know what to say, so I nodded and took a bunch of the antiseptic wipes from her. I noticed her hands were still shaking.

"I'll get a hamper for your clothes," she said. "They're soaked. Try not to get the blood all over everything."

"What about that man?" I asked.

"Don't worry about him for now."

"Do you know him?"

Nurse Ophelia shook her head. "No. But he's gone. And I need you to focus on getting yourself tidied up. The police will have to talk to you soon." She pointed towards the house phone beside my desk. "You can buzz me after you've had a shower. And you might want to tidy up a little, just so no one gets lost in here trying to find you."

I looked at all the clothes on the floor. It wasn't that bad. There were at least two or three patches of tile that weren't covered.

"Do I have to talk to them?" I asked.

"The police? Yes. I would imagine so, given what's happened. Why?"

"The man on the motorcycle said someone was after me. And he warned me to stay away from the police."

Nurse Ophelia nodded slowly. "Right. Well, if you think this through carefully, Zachary, I'm sure you'll come up with a few reasons not to trust that man's advice."

She had a point. He was a little weird. But then again, so were the rest of us. And when a guy steals a motorcycle for you, tells you to scram, gets blasted full of holes and then comes back to life just to tell you the same thing all over again, well, maybe that guy is someone you should listen to.

Chapter 4
The Interview

I'd just finished kicking the last of my dirty clothes under the bed when I heard a knock at the door. An officer with a round head and big arms was standing in the hall. The badge on his chest said "Officer Cummings." His partner was a brown-haired woman with a pretty smile. Her name was Officer Philips. She asked if they could come in. I said yes and then had to answer a bunch of questions about what happened. I sat on my bed the whole time and pretty much told them everything. Officer Cummings sat at my desk and wrote it all down in a notepad.

"Isn't it a little late to be exercising?" he said when I finished.

"Sunlight gives me hives," I explained, "so I do everything at night."

I looked at him when I said this. I wanted to make sure that he believed me, but he wasn't looking at me. He was looking at Nurse Ophelia, who had arrived from down the hall and was now standing in the doorway.

"Is everything all right here?" she asked.

I thought for just a second that Officer Cummings's eyes were going to roll out of his head and onto the floor, but then he got it together and half stood. His face was a little pink. "Yes. Fine, ma'am. I was just asking a few, um . . ."

"Please sit down," she insisted.

"Isn't it a little unusual for a boy to be up at this time of night?"

"Zachary keeps a unique schedule. It's necessary. He requires very specialized medical attention. It's one of the reasons he's here and not in a foster home. Do you have any other questions for him? I'd like to get him his dinner. And he needs some rest."

"Of course. Just a few more." He sat back down and clicked his pen a few times. Then he cleared his throat. "This guy—did he say anything to you? Did he threaten you?"

"Not really," I said. "He only said what I told you already. That I should run. And that someone was after me." I almost added that he'd told me to avoid the police, but I didn't want to offend anybody.

Officer Cummings smiled. "You don't need to worry about anything. There'll be a car here twenty-four hours a day until we catch him."

I tried to look impressed, but the truth was, the old man had been shot so many times he should have looked like a cheese grater, and it had barely slowed him down. Unless they dropped a building on his head, they weren't ever going to stop him. I wasn't worried about him, anyway. He'd come to warn me. I wanted to know why.

"Was he armed?" Officer Cummings asked me. "Did he have a knife or a gun or anything?"

I shook my head. "Just a top hat."

"Did he offer you anything? Drugs, anything like that?"

"No." I said. "Well, he did offer me a ride."

"And it was just you and the other fellow who saw him? What's his name . . . ?" Officer Cummings leafed back through his pad. "Jacob?"

"Yeah. By the end, other people were in the hall too, but it was mostly just Jacob and me. I doubt he heard very much. He was pretty far away. And he had his hands over his ears."

"Is there anything else you can think of that might help us catch this guy?"

I glanced up at Officer Philips, who was leaning against the wall, then at Nurse Ophelia, who was still in the doorway. She moved her head just a little, like a mini nod, so I knew it was all right to answer.

"He smelled like he'd been drinking," I said.

"No doubt," said Officer Cummings. He flipped his pad closed. "Well, that does it for now. If we need anything else, we'll be in touch." He rose, tipped his head in a goodbye sort of way, then stepped out to wait in the hall.

Officer Philips lingered for a few seconds longer. "Are you going to be all right?" she asked.

I looked at Nurse Ophelia. She nodded and so I nodded.

"Is there anything we can do for you before we go?"

I did have some questions. "Is somebody after me?" I asked.

Officer Philips was about to answer when Nurse Ophelia cut in.

"No," she said quickly. "No one is after you, Zachary. You're perfectly safe here." Then she stepped aside so Officer Philips could leave.

I watched the two officers to see if they had anything to say about that subject, but apparently they didn't. I wasn't finished, though.

"How did he do it?" I asked.

Officer Philips looked confused. Her forehead wrinkled up. "What do you mean?"

"How did that man do all those things? He should have been a splat on the wall after that crash. Then he picked up the motorcycle and threw it. And he got up after being shot. He was supposed to be dead."

Officer Cummings was still waiting in the hallway. He perked up when he heard my question.

"Do you know what PCP is?" he asked.

I shook my head.

"Angel Dust?"

I didn't know that one either.

"Well, he was probably on drugs. I once arrested a guy who was so cranked up on speed, even with a bullet in his shoulder he just wouldn't quit. He had this cleaver—"

Officer Philips put her hand on his arm.

"Yeah. Well, the point is," he continued, "that old guy was probably on something potent. It's not hard to find if you know where to look. Makes you do all kinds of weird stuff. I wouldn't worry too much about it. He won't bother you again. Not with us here."

"So what was he warning me about?" I asked.

The officers looked at each other. They clearly didn't know. Nurse Ophelia answered for them.

"Nothing, Zachary. It was nothing."

Chapter 5
Family Resemblance

Once the officers were gone, Nurse Ophelia stepped into the hall and got the laundry hamper for my bloodied clothes. I still hadn't moved from the bed. She said something to me, but I wasn't really listening, not until she gave my shoulder a squeeze.

"Do you understand what I'm saying?" she asked.

I nodded and said yes.

"You aren't even listening," she said. Then she smiled. "You're going to be fine. I know you better than anyone, Zachary. There's nothing for you to worry about."

It was difficult to disagree with Nurse Ophelia when she smiled at you. And she *did* know me better than anyone. Unlike the other staff, she worked the night shift all the time. She looked out for me. Whenever a therapy session went bad, or if I got irritable with the other nurses, which sometimes happened if I got hungry before mealtime, she always smoothed things over.

"Would you like to go back to the fitness room and finish your run?" she asked.

I didn't know what to say. Running was usually a sure bet with me. And, like she said, she knew me better than anyone. But I knew her, too. And there was something she wasn't telling me.

"*Is* someone after me?" I asked.

Nurse Ophelia sighed. Her eyes suddenly looked very tired. I was hoping she might say something like, "No, of course no one is after you. Who would want to harm you? You're the greatest kid on earth. *Blah, blah, blah,*" but she didn't. Instead, she put her hand over her forehead like I was giving her a headache.

"I should get back to the desk," she said. "The cleanup crew will be here shortly. As soon as this mess is cleared away, I'll check in with you at dinner. We can talk then, okay?"

I nodded and watched while she backed out the door, pulling the hamper with my dirty scrubs behind her. I waited until the squeak of the wheels had faded down the hall, then I flicked on my reading light and picked up my copy of *The Hobbit*.

Of all the books ever written, *The Hobbit* is king. I've read it seven times. Captures, escapes, riddles, battles, magic swords and a magic ring, death and deception, goblins and elves and trolls and dragons, men who turn into bears, and giant eagles and wolves. It pretty much has it all. I think that's why I've always been a bit jealous of the main character, Bilbo. At the start, his life is pretty much the same thing, day after day, just like mine, until Gandalf the wizard knocks at his door. Then, in a snap, he's off on an adventure so grand it can hardly be packed between two book covers.

Well, that was exactly what I needed—a knock at the door and an adventure of my own. But I guess wizards were in short supply. Instead of Gandalf, I got a crazy old man on a stolen motorcycle who smelled like he'd had enough wine to drown a horse. And all he did was trash the lobby.

I opened the book and started reading. After a few minutes, I realized I was still staring at the same page. I started again, but the same thing kept happening. Instead of seeing Gandalf and Bilbo, I kept seeing the old man on the motorcycle. *"I've found you,"* he'd said. Like he'd recognized me. But from where? Nurse Ophelia took me bowling sometimes, and to movies. And, of course, window shopping at Christmas. But I couldn't remember ever seeing him before. How could he know me?

I read slowly for about another hour, my thoughts drifting from the book to the strange incident with the old man. Then I had to get up. I was starting to get hungry.

I'm sure you've had that hole-in-the-stomach feeling that everyone gets when they've missed a meal. For me, it was a lot worse. I'd get pain behind my eyeballs like someone was pinching them really hard, and my throat would get itchy. It might have been because I couldn't eat most foods, and so it was hard for my body to get all of the nutrients it needed. It might also have been related to my blood. I had a degenerative blood disease, so I needed to get transfusions a few times every year. Those were the worst. For days afterwards I felt like I'd been drinking gasoline. If I could have found the right foods or the right medications, my problems probably would have gone away, but that never happened. So I got hungry often. And it always made me irritable. I remember this one time when I was ten years old, the nurse on duty forgot to bring me my dinner. When she showed up just before sunrise to make sure I was safe in my room, I was so angry I tried to bite her. After that, Nurse Ophelia delivered all my meals. She was more dependable.

In the common room, a couple of guys in grey uniforms were sweeping up the glass. They both looked at me as I walked past them, like the mess was somehow my fault. Two policemen were leaning on the reception counter. They were chatting with Nurse Roberta. She was young, and I think most people found her quite attractive. I can't really separate how a person looks from how they treat me, so to me, she wasn't all that pretty. More like cranky and disappointed. I'm not saying she was a bad person, but once she yelled at me for not making my bed, and I was still sleeping in it.

As soon as I got closer to the counter, the two officers stopped talking. They both looked a bit embarrassed, as though they should have been hard at work doing something useful and not chatting up the hospital staff.

"Do you know where Nurse Ophelia is?" I asked.

Nurse Roberta pointed over her shoulder with a pen. "In the kitchen."

I found Nurse Ophelia making my dinner. I sat on one of the metal stools and watched her. She turned and slapped gently at my leg to get me to move out of the way. That was the closest she ever came to showing affection, when she hit people. I slid my stool over and she reached into the refrigerator behind me. She took out a small bag that was full of red syrup. I think it was strawberry.

"Stop scratching your throat," she said.

"I can't help it. It's itchy."

She squeezed the gooey flavouring into the blender with the rest of my dinner and fired it up. Once it was good and frothy, she poured it into a tall cup and stuck in a straw. I always drank my meals. Solid foods just didn't agree with me, so twice a day, it was bottoms up. My friend Charlie called these "brain cocktails." He said they looked like they could bring a zombie back to life. They were the only thing I ever ate. I think they must have had the same thing in them that coffee has, because I got a real jolt from them. And they were filling, too. Nurse Ophelia never made more than two in a night for me. Any more than that and I would have exploded.

My "brain cocktails" also had my meds in them. I wasn't sure exactly what I was taking, but I remember when I was younger having to swallow a lot of different stuff—pills and syrups—and

I got plenty of needles too, and lotions to put on my skin. They all had names that made them sound like they were made on the planet Mongo. Most of them made me sick. That might have been why the doctors kept changing their minds about what was wrong with me. Nothing really worked, and so they had to keep switching drugs all the time. After a while I stopped paying attention. It was too hard to keep track. To make things easier, Nurse Ophelia decided one day just to dump it all into my dinner. It was a pretty simple arrangement for me. She did all the work and I did all the drinking.

The two of us sat in the dining room with the lights dimmed. Nurse Ophelia was very quiet. There was something in her manner that was sort of off. She seemed irritated one minute and sad the next. Her eyes didn't seem comfortable unless they were fixed on the floor.

"What is it?" I asked. I was feeling a lot better with food in my stomach.

"You're looking more like Robert every day," she said.

Robert Douglas Thomson was my father. Just like me, he'd used his middle name, so everyone called him Doug, or Doc, or Dougal or Dr. Thomson. And some of his students used to call him Dr. T. But Nurse Ophelia was the only one who used his first name, Robert. I always wondered if she was right. Did I really look like him, or was she seeing a resemblance that wasn't really there? Since she was the only one on the ward who had known him before he died, I never got a second opinion. I sometimes thought she must have been in love with him, because whenever she mentioned his name, her tone of voice would soften just a bit and the words would come out a little slower, like they were heavy or something. And she would smile differently, too. Like it was nice to think about him, but it was sad at the same time. I guess that's why we rarely talked about him. I don't even know how they met. The most she ever told me was that he'd gotten her out of some trouble when I was just a baby, but I never got the details.

Tonight, she was wearing the same sad smile she always did when she talked about him. Her finger traced a little circle just in front of my mouth. "The nose and chin especially," she said. "Anyone who knew him would recognize you in an instant."

I smiled. As much as I missed my father, I liked it when Nurse Ophelia talked about him. But then she added something strange.

"You look just like him. That's one of our problems . . ." She took a deep breath and shook her head.

So I looked just like my father. She'd told me that before. Big whoop. Didn't most kids look like their parents?

"That must be how that man recognized you," she said. "He must have known your dad." She spoke slowly, as though she was trying to convince herself. Her eyes were staring past me into space.

"I don't understand what the problem is," I said.

Nurse Ophelia put her elbows on the armrests of her chair and started massaging her temples. "So many bizarre things have happened tonight. I just need a minute to clear my head and think things through, okay?"

After a few moments she looked up at me and continued talking.

"Are you feeling all right?"

"I'm okay," I said.

"Are you getting better?"

"I feel fine. I feel *strong*. I *am* strong."

This was true. When you're alone most of the time, you need to have ways to keep your mind busy. Exercise is great for this. And reading, too. I never felt lonely when I was moving, or buried in a good book.

"I know you're strong. But do you think you're getting any better?"

I didn't know what she was getting at, so I just shrugged.

"How did things go with Charlie?" she asked.

"Fine," I answered. "He's always happy when the school year's over."

She smiled, but her eyes still had a far away look.

"What is it?" I asked her again.

She sat up in her chair and focused her eyes on me. I was surprised to see how tired she looked. Not haggard. Just deflated. And sad. She took a deep breath, as though she was gearing up to say something important, but before she could get started she was cut off by a quiet hum and a beep. She reached down to her waist and unclipped her pager.

"What now?" she muttered. She'd barely had a second to read the message when the phone beside us rang. It was the house phone, so the call was coming from somewhere inside the ward.

"That will be Roberta," she said, nodding towards the phone. She clipped the pager back to her belt. "I have to make a call. And I need to get back to work."

The disappointment on my face must have been pretty obvious because Nurse Ophelia reached out and put a hand on my shoulder. Then she gave it a gentle squeeze and got up to leave the room. When she reached the doorway she turned around.

"I'll check in with you as soon as I have a minute," she said. "We can talk then, and if not, I'll come in early tomorrow night. Okay?" She pressed her lips together in a flat smile. I did my best to smile back. Then she slipped into the hall.

I sat there by myself for a few minutes, just looking around the room at all the empty tables. It was strange to imagine that in a few hours everyone would be awake. The room would be packed, and full of the sounds of people eating and talking together. I stood up and started back to my room. It bothered me to be there, all of a sudden. I couldn't say why.

Just before dawn Nurse Ophelia knocked at my door. Four quick raps. She opened it a crack, and light from the hall made a yellow line across the floor. She slipped in quietly and set the rest of my brain cocktail on my desk. I must have left it behind.

"I have to go now," she said. Then she asked me again if I was all right. I'm not sure if I answered. I probably didn't, because she put a hand on my shoulder and gave it a gentle squeeze, just like she had earlier in the dining room. Sometimes you had to do that to get my attention. And it didn't always work.

I often got quiet. It seemed to upset everyone, but I didn't think it was that big a deal. I just had a lot on my mind, that's all. And I didn't always want to talk to other people about it. We all need downtime now and again. I was no different, except that for me it sometimes lasted a while, a few days even. It was one of the reasons everybody told me I needed counselling and psychiatric evaluations and anger management and group therapy and all that other stuff. But I never thought so. I was fine. Just as long as people didn't act like it was the end of the world when I wanted a few moments to myself. And that's how it was just then.

Nurse Ophelia must have known, because she walked over to the window, closed the blinds and pulled the curtain shut. She might have said something to me, but I wasn't listening. I was thinking about my father. He had been a professor of archaeology. I'm guessing he was good at it because he got invited to do lectures all over the world, and digs in places like Egypt and Libya and Turkey. But mostly I remember that he held me lots and read me stories about Jim Hawkins and Captain Ahab and Hawkeye, and he always smelled good and had just enough stubble on his chin that when I got too close it tickled my face.

I missed him. I missed my mother, too. That might sound strange because she died when I was two, and so I didn't really know her, but I somehow missed her anyway. Nurse Ophelia once said it was because I missed the idea of having a mother. I don't really know about that. But I do know that I should have said something to Nurse

Ophelia before she left. Something like "Thank you for dinner" or "I just need to think for a minute" or even just "Goodbye." I should have, but I didn't. I just lay there and stared at the ceiling. And so I missed my last chance to say goodbye. After that night, no one at the ward ever saw her again.

Chapter 6
Charlie

I woke up the next day when I heard the doorknob rattle. I checked my clock radio. It was almost four in the afternoon. Since no one was supposed to bother me when the sun was up, I guessed right away that something was wrong.

My guess was off. It was my best friend, Charlie.

Charlie was my only regular visitor. Dr. Shepherd used to visit me once a week, but that didn't last very long. He wasn't a real doctor, by the way, he was a shrink. Since none of the doctors knew what was really wrong with me or how to fix it, they brought in the brain mechanic to see what he could do. He said my problems were all psychosomatic, which is another way of saying that they were all in my head. Well, if being allergic to most foods and losing half my red blood cells every few months was in my head, Dr. Shepherd was a genius and ought to have won a Nobel Prize. When he gave us his assessment, Nurse Ophelia went off like a car bomb. So he never came back.

Charlie was one of the few outsiders Nurse Ophelia really liked. I think it was because he treated me like I was normal. Ever since we were little, we'd liked the same things. Just like our dads. They were best friends too, so I guess our friendship sort of ran in the family. He was a year older than me, sixteen, but when he let his stubble go he looked about twenty, which meant he could sometimes get into the beer store without being asked for ID. I didn't have any facial hair, so I figured I wouldn't even get into the beer store parking lot.

We often talked about how cool it would be if his family adopted me, but his parents were divorced, and Nurse Ophelia told me that they wouldn't be able to look after me properly, which was probably true. His mother drank more than most hockey teams, and with all my problems, I probably wouldn't have lasted a week with her. And Charlie's dad was a naval officer. He lived in Halifax and was out at sea a lot. He also moved every few years. I didn't think I'd like that. Charlie said he changed schools so much as a kid that he got held back a grade, but I think that was only part of the reason.

I was still a big groggy when he opened the door and burst in.

"Rise and shine, chowderhead!"

Sunlight flooded in and bounced off the floor. I jammed my eyes shut.

"Close the door. Close the door," I told him. I didn't open my eyes until I heard the knob click.

"I love what you've done in the lobby," Charlie said. "It really opens the place up."

He moved over to the window and peeked under the blind. He was more careful this time and didn't let too much light in.

"You're looking awful pasty, Zack," he told me. "What're they feeding you around this place, Elmer's Glue?"

If you ever had a teacher who said that there was no such thing as a stupid question, they'd obviously never had Charlie as a student.

Like chaos, stupid questions were one of his specialties. I turned and sat on the edge of the bed.

"You still wearing that necklace?" Charlie asked.

That might not sound like a stupid question, but my necklace was dangling right out in the open. It was a disc fashioned out of silver, etched and polished so that it made a perfect map of the moon. It even had the Lunar Seas on it. I tucked it back under my shirt. I never took it off, not even when I was sleeping, and so if I rolled onto my stomach it left a perfect circle on my chest. It was a gift from my dad. The last thing he gave me before he died. He told me there was another piece to it and that they fit together, but the other part belonged to my mother. She must have had it when she died, because I'd never seen it.

Charlie handed me the rest of my dinner. Nurse Ophelia had left it on the night table by my bed. I drank until the straw made sucking noises on the bottom of the cup.

Charlie shook his head. "I don't know how you can stomach that stuff. Just the sight of it makes me want to puke. What is it, a lung milkshake?"

"I don't know," I said. "Strawberry, I think."

"It doesn't smell like strawberries."

I shrugged.

"So, what happened?" Charlie asked. "You still upset about the whipping I gave you in our ping-pong fight? Looks like you tore the place apart."

"You mean in the lobby?"

"No, in the ladies' room, you dweeb. Of course in the lobby."

I told him about the old man and the motorcycle, how he annihilated the television, and how he'd gone on and on about me being in danger because someone was after me.

"Get out!" Charlie said. "You? In danger? In danger of dying from boredom, maybe. Why didn't you follow the guy's advice and jump on the motorcycle?"

"I wouldn't have gotten too far. It was mangled."

Charlie pulled out the chair and sat down. "We need to find him," he said.

I didn't think it would be so easy, with the police on his trail. Unless he was hiding under my bed, I wasn't likely to run into him anytime soon.

"Did Ophelia flip?" Charlie asked.

"No."

Charlie seemed surprised by this. No wonder. Weekends in the summertime, this place was a magnet for weirdos, especially after hours. Once, a bunch of high school kids showed up drunk at about four in the morning and tried to get into the building. Nurse Ophelia went out into the parking lot and politely asked them to leave. She was always like that. Polite. No matter what. But you had to be careful, because when she used her polite tone of voice, she expected you to do whatever she told you. Even if she asked you to grab a fistful of bees and jam them up your nose, I'm telling you, if you heard that polite tone, you'd better get on it. Well, one of the kids told her off. He used the *B* word. I almost felt sorry for him. She walked over to the boy, smiled, then picked him up by the scruff of his neck, carried him over to the Dumpster and tossed him in with the trash. *Whoosh.* Like he weighed as much as an empty pop can.

"She didn't toss the old geezer out on his butt?" Charlie asked.

"He was too fast. He ran right over a police car."

"Did they shoot him?"

"About twenty times."

"Wow. There must have been blood everywhere."

"Yup," I said. "It was all over me."

He shook his head like he couldn't believe my luck. "Well," he said, "if someone is after you, I guess we'd better get you outta here. We'll have to plan a breakout."

I laughed.

"I'm serious," he said.

He *was* serious. That's why it was so funny.

"I don't need to break out. I can go for a walk or a run whenever I feel like it."

"So maybe you should go for a long walk? Does three days sound good?"

I shook my head. With nowhere safe to hide from the sun and no way to feed myself, I wasn't going to last that long. But I sensed what he was getting at.

"Have you been up to the cottage yet?" I asked.

Charlie's father had a place on Stoney Lake. He spent most of his summers there, unless he was on a naval mission someplace. Now that school was out, I figured Charlie would be going to visit him there.

"I got a call from the Yacht Club this morning," he answered. "I got the job. There's a meeting early tomorrow, so I'm heading up tonight."

Charlie was a sailing guru. He usually spent his summers racing. I'd forgotten he was hoping to instruct this summer instead. He was saving up for a car. I guess that meant no more ping-pong fights for a while.

"Do you have to go tonight?"

He nodded. I guess that explained why he was here during the day. He didn't usually interrupt my sleep unless it was important. And I think he liked to come at night because Nurse Ophelia was always working. He sort of had a thing for her.

"I'm going to be up at the cottage for the next month or so," Charlie said. "They told me they had work for me in July, at least. August is a maybe. That's why I'm here. I wanted to see if you could come up for a while. My dad's still overseas, so we could pretty much do whatever we wanted until he gets back. It's a perfect getaway place if you're on the run. What do you think?"

Charlie was smiling. I knew exactly why. With his father gone, he was free to stay up as late as he wanted, free to sleep all weekend, free to eat Captain Crunch cereal for breakfast, lunch and dinner, and free to grow his stubble and try his luck at the beer store. Well, that sounded perfect to me. Unfortunately, leaving the Nicholls Ward for so long was probably out of the question. Especially after last night.

"I doubt I'll be allowed," I told him. "Especially if your dad's not there."

"Well, Dan will be up with his kids. He's stuffy enough to count as an adult."

Dan was one of Charlie's older brothers. Or half-brothers. He was from an earlier marriage. I think Charlie's father was working on number three right now.

"We'll pull some strings," Charlie said. "Even a weekend or a Saturday night would be better than nothing. Would you rather sit here all summer watching the paint peel?"

I shook my head.

"What about my allergies?" I asked. It wasn't easy to find food I could eat.

"Can't you take Lactaid or something?"

"What's that?"

Charlie looked at me with a weird expression, like even the dead frogs on Highway Seven knew what Lactaid was.

"It lets you drink milk and dairy products. How else do you get through dinner?"

"I don't know."

"Don't you even bother to ask?" he said.

"Not any more. I just take what they give me."

"Well, is it working? Are you getting any better?"

I shrugged. "I feel fine."

"When was your last transfusion?"

"Three months ago," I said. That meant I'd have another in a few weeks. I wasn't looking forward to it. Days of nausea. But there was no helping it. It was that or keel over.

"Let me see your scars," Charlie said.

I pulled up the right pant leg of my hospital scrubs, and revealed the two circles of scar tissue. It looked as if someone with red paint on their finger had daubed me twice just above the ankle.

"They look better," Charlie said.

"They get fainter every year."

Charlie seemed pleased with this. He'd heard the story of my scars long ago. I'd got them the day my father died. He was on a dig in Libya. Not everyone knows it, but there are a lot of ruins there. It was once part of the Roman Empire. Anyway, my father was working, and late in the day a temple he was examining collapsed on him. He was crushed instantly.

Thinking back, I suppose it was good that he didn't suffer, but at the time I wasn't thinking about that. I just wanted to find him. Since no one could show me his body, I didn't believe he was really gone. And so I took off from camp by myself. I shouldn't have, but it's not every day you become an orphan.

I never found him. I found an angry dog instead. It was hiding in the shadows of a building. Nurse Ophelia once told me that animals will do that when they know they're going to die. They crawl off by themselves and look for a dark hiding place. Well, that dog must have had more diseases than a vet hospital because when it bit me, it made me so sick no one even yelled at me for running away. Apparently I fell into a coma afterwards and stayed like that for a few weeks. I had a high fever too, and a bunch of convulsions.

Because all of my problems started the day my father died, Dr. Shepherd thought the trouble was all in my head. He thought it was just about sadness and loss. But what does a shrink know about Libyan dogs? Five-eighths of sweet diddly, as far as I could tell.

Charlie stayed for another half hour or so. He was a reader, like me, so we talked about books, and that led to movies, and that led to which actors we would want to play us in our life stories. Charlie picked Christian Bale because he was a good Batman. I picked Leonardo DiCaprio, but not because he looked like me, just because he was very good at playing complex characters. Not that I'd have been all that hard to play. I slept all day.

"He's too skinny to play you," said Charlie. "You need that guy . . . what's his name? He played Robin Hood in the old movie."

"Errol Flynn?"

"Yeah, he'd be perfect."

"He was totally skinny," I said. "Plus, he's dead."

Charlie laughed. "Yeah, but you need someone like that."

Then he told me how his classes had ended, and which couples in his grade were doomed to break up over the summer. I didn't know any of the people he was talking about, but I didn't mind. Then he said he had to go, but he'd call the next night and see if I could go with him.

"Try to find out what it takes to get a day pass," he added.

"A day pass? What's that?"

He shook his head. "A day pass out of this place, you numbskull. A 'get out of jail free' card. So you can come to the lake. Don't you want to show off your tan?"

He was backing out the door when he stopped.

"Man, I can't believe I almost forgot." He stepped back in and closed the door. "I met a girl last Saturday. Suki."

"That's her real name, Suki? It sounds like a motorcycle."

"Her real name is Suzanne. God, you are such a dork. Anyway, she has a younger sister, Luna. I told her about you and she wants to meet you. I said you were cool, so you'd better spend the next few days ungeekifying yourself. And you have to find some way out of here."

"How?" I asked.

"I don't know. Can't you chew through the wall or something?"

He opened the door again, then turned back and smiled. "It will be worth it."

Then he left. And although he'd visited me many times before, this time was different because it was the first time he had ever told a girl about me, and it was the first time I'd ever heard of Luna.

Chapter 7
Bad Dreams

It didn't take me long to fall asleep after Charlie was gone. I was good at that, falling asleep. It once happened while I was standing up in the shower. That's how it was with me. When my body needed rest, it was very insistent.

So, I fell asleep and had a dream about my father. This didn't surprise me. I once read that dreams occur because your mind has to reorganize itself when you're sleeping. So much happens during the day that you need to sort what is important from what is not. Some memories you keep close to the surface and others get buried. I think my mind was just trying to keep the memories of my father close to the top, where they belonged.

The dream started back at our old house on O'Carroll Avenue. It's right here in town. An old couple lives there now. They have a big RV in the driveway and the TV is always on. I could tell by the way the light changed in the room when I was running past. I thought about stopping to visit them one night so I could tell them I used to live there, and see what it was like to be inside again, but in the end, I just couldn't do it.

In my dream my dad was cutting the grass. He saw me and stopped.

"Hey, Zack," he said. His voice always had lots of energy in it. Like talking to me was the highlight of his day. And even though I was fifteen, and big for my age, my father was always a lot taller than me in my dreams. Like I was still a little kid. He reached down and mussed my hair.

"You getting better?" he asked.

"I feel better," I said. "I feel strong."

"You look strong," he said. Then he scooped me up in his arms and asked to see my scars.

I pulled up the right pant leg of my scrubs and revealed the two circles of scar tissue.

My father ran his fingers over them. "They look almost better!" he said.

"They get fainter every year."

He seemed pleased by this.

And then, just like that, we were inside the house. I was looking out the window at the snow on the tree branches. It must have been Christmas, because my grandparents were there, and so were Charlie and his dad. I called him Uncle Jake, even though he wasn't my real uncle.

I had lots of gifts to open, but I never got to because my father was suddenly missing. I looked around and caught a glimpse of his pant legs disappearing up the stairs. I ran after him and opened the door to his room, only when I got there it wasn't his room any more, it was an old Roman city. Right in the middle of it was his desk. He was writing in the journal he always kept. He looked at me for a few seconds. Then he closed his journal and stood.

"I have to go now," he said.

I didn't want him to leave. I started to shake my head.

"You don't have to be afraid," he said. "You're not alone."

He waved me over to give me a hug, but the instant I moved towards him he froze. Then he started shouting at me.

"Get away! Run! Run!"

He was gone a second later. Buried in dust and wood and old square stones. I moved closer and looked down into the shadows. Two red eyes were staring back at me. Even though I knew the danger, I couldn't help myself. I had to move closer. And I knew what was going to happen. The shadow darted out on four legs, swift as thought, and bit me hard above the ankle. The pain was very real. When I woke up it was still hurting. And my father's words were loud in my ears.

"Run!"

Maybe I should have. Because there was a man in my room staring at me.

Chapter 8
Family Matters

It took me a moment to figure out what was going on. I usually woke up if someone tried to come in my room, just as I had when Charlie came to visit.

The man was looking at me intently. He was wearing a suit that probably cost more money than an average person would want to spend on their car. It had pinstripes and a perfectly folded hanky in the pocket. His dark hair was perfect too, like a statue's, with just a little grey above each ear, and his face, which wasn't bad as faces go, looked strong enough to crush rock. He shifted so that his elbow was resting on the arm of the chair and his index finger and thumb supported the side of his face. He looked like the next president of planet Earth.

"Are you awake?" he asked.

I sat up and blinked and looked at the door.

"Would you like me to open that a crack? I didn't want anyone to disturb us."

I shook my head. The room smelled a bit funny. Like cigars. It would have been nice to open the door and window to let some fresh air in, but the sun was still up. I didn't want any light spilling in from the hallway.

"Who are you?" I asked.

"I am your uncle, Maximilian."

I looked at him carefully, and then I glanced over my shoulder at the reflection of him in the mirror on the door. He didn't look familiar. It made me wonder if he was lying. Maybe he was the person the old man on the motorcycle had warned me about.

"I don't have any uncles," I said.

"Hmmm," he said, rubbing the backs of his fingers over his chin. "I expected you might say as much."

He stared at me for a few seconds as though he expected me to respond. When I didn't, he reached into the inside pocket of his suit and pulled out a card-sized envelope. He folded it open, then handed it to me.

There were several photos inside. The first was of a young girl and boy sitting on an old fence made of split logs, the kind you might see on a farm. I flipped to the next one, quickly. It was a picture of my father. He must have been on a dig, because he looked dusty and exhausted. His arm was draped over the shoulder of another man, who was more or less holding him up. The photo was a bit blurry, but it was clear enough for me to recognize the other man as the person now sitting in my room. He looked tired in the photo too, but he had a smile on his face like he'd just conquered Everest.

The last one was a group shot. It was from a wedding. I recognized my mother and father, the bride and groom, and Charlie's dad. My grandparents, too. Others I didn't know, mostly women. And this man, smiling again, standing beside my father.

I flipped back to the first photo and looked at it more closely. I'd never seen a picture of my mother as a girl, but this had to be her.

She was wearing a summer dress and her hair was in pigtails. I tried to focus on her face, but my eyes were watering, so it was hard to see.

"My sister's name was Dorothy May. She married your father on our parents' farm, where the two of us grew up together."

I was still looking at the photo of my mother and the boy. It was him.

The man coughed gently several times, as though he was clearing his throat.

"You had no idea, did you?"

I shook my head.

"That means you don't have your father's journal."

"No."

"That's unfortunate. He would have wanted you to have it. And he would have wanted you to know about me. I haven't seen you since you were a baby, but I can see you are growing up to look much like him."

I turned back to the picture of my father in his dusty clothes. I still didn't see the resemblance between the two of us, but it pleased me that others could. In the photo he was standing beside something that looked like a well. There was desert behind him. And large mountains. Or maybe it was rock. I wondered what he had been doing to get so tired.

I tucked the photos into the envelope and reached out to hand them back.

"No, they're for you," he said. Then his eyes widened for a split second. He was looking at my necklace. It must have slipped from beneath my scrubs when I leaned forward.

"You're still wearing his necklace." He smiled. Then his jaw clenched and I saw the muscles there tense for just a second. His eyes looked very sad. "My sister, your mother, had the matching piece. Did you know that?"

I nodded.

"It was a golden crescent that snapped to the side of the one you're wearing. It might be the most beautiful piece of jewellery I've ever seen."

My father had said exactly the same thing.

"We have much to discuss, you and I."

I didn't exactly know what to say. Under other circumstances, I probably would have jumped for joy to discover that I had an uncle—someone who could answer questions about my father and mother. But when a deranged motorcycle thief destroys your television and warns you that trouble is on the way, it sort of puts you on your guard. And I was still stuck in my dream. "You're not alone," my father had said, but he'd also said, "Run." And where had this guy been all these years? The moon?

"Are you really my uncle?" I asked.

He smiled. "Yes," he said.

"Well . . . where have you been?"

He laughed, and I felt myself smile, too. The sound of laughter just does that sometimes.

"Where have I been? Why, I've been many places."

"But I've been here for eight years."

He looked at me and nodded. Then he covered his mouth and coughed quietly.

"I know. At least, I know that now. But I only discovered it recently. I was told eight years ago that you had died after lapsing into a coma. You can't imagine how shocked I was when I got the news you were still alive. Shocked, but very pleased."

I couldn't believe what I was hearing. And yet it made sense. I *had* been in a coma eight years ago. It explained why he hadn't come looking for me.

"How did you find me?" I asked.

"Good question, but the answer is complicated and probably not worth getting into right now because I can't stay long."

He glanced down at his watch. The red numbers on my clock radio told me it was 7:53. The sun would be setting soon.

"Not tonight, anyway," my uncle continued. "And we have more important things to talk about. Like your father, for instance."

He paused. I didn't know what to say. Since I didn't want him to stop talking I kept my mouth shut. Nurse Ophelia had once told me that some people will talk forever if you let them. In this case, I didn't think that would be such a bad thing.

"You were with your father the day he died, I know. I hope it isn't painful if I speak frankly."

It didn't bother me, and I told him so.

"Do you remember what happened?"

"Yes. He was crushed when a temple collapsed."

My uncle nodded almost imperceptibly. He was looking at me intently again.

"That was the official version," he said. "But that's not what really happened."

"No?"

"No."

He put his elbow back on the arm of the chair and propped the side of his face on his index finger and thumb again. This looked like his thinking pose.

"And you probably thought your father was an archaeologist."

"He was," I said. "I went with him on all his digs. After I was two, I did. After my mother died. And when he went to lecture at universities, I went with him then, too."

"Of course," my uncle said. "And the whole world would have agreed with you. Your father was an archaeologist. One of the very best. But he was much more than that. Much more."

Here he leaned forward in his chair. I was sitting on the bed with my back against the wall and I found myself leaning towards him. He looked at the door and paused to cough again, then he turned back to me and spoke in a whisper.

"He was a great believer in truth, your father. He used to say that it longed to be discovered by people like him, people willing to dig it up. He loved archaeology and he admired archaeologists, just as he admired historians and police detectives and other people who search for the truth. But archaeology was a front, of sorts. It was a disguise. It allowed him to conduct his *real* work, the work he did with me."

He looked at the door again and leaned in even closer. His eyes were intense now. Dark and focused.

"Your father was a vampire hunter," he said.

Chapter 9
The Crazy Truth

Well, this guy had certainly come to the right place. He was nuts.

My uncle stared at me for a time. I guess he wanted me to take all of this in. My dad was a vampire hunter.

"That's crazy talk," I said.

He smiled, but then his face went flat and serious.

"Crazy talk? Perhaps." He looked around the room. "But here you are, living in this dreadful place, totally unaware of what is really wrong with you. Isolated and alone. If you ask me, this is crazy, but it is also the truth. The crazy truth of your life. So, who says the truth can't be crazy?"

He moved forward again, his elbows resting comfortably on his knees, his hands clasped together.

"I believe your father was right about the truth. It longs to be discovered. And some truths, once discovered, cannot be ignored. Your father and I hunted vampires. I understand this must come as a shock, but it was vital for your father to keep it a secret—for your protection, as well as ours. It is the reason you and I never met. Sadly, it is also the reason you never learned the truth about your father's death. Or, rather, about his murder. But let me assure you, the truth of this is very important, because the vampire who killed him is looking for you."

My uncle leaned back in his chair, his dark eyes watching me. I was beginning to feel uncomfortable. I almost asked him to leave right then and there, but I wanted to hear him out before I spoke to Nurse Ophelia. She had known my father well, but she had never hinted that there was anything unusual about what he did. And she had never mentioned my uncle. Or vampire hunting. Or murder. It all sounded like hooey. Then I remembered that she'd wanted to talk to me. That she'd been keeping secrets. Could this have been why?

"That doesn't make any sense," I said.

"And your condition, does it make sense?"

I shook my head. "No."

"Well, it makes perfect sense to me. But that is how life is. It makes sense. And if it doesn't, you haven't thought things through well enough. Or you don't have the right information. *That* is your problem—you are lacking the right information. You are fortunate that I am here because I can tell you everything you need to know to make sense of your life and why you are here."

He stood and opened the door. The light was faint now. The day was dying. He checked the hallway and then closed the door again.

"I have to go shortly, and I need to make certain no one will hear any of this. It is for your ears only."

He sat back down and leaned forward, shifting his head to the side just long enough to smother another cough with the back of his hand.

"Your father and I were hunting a vampire, a Baron, who called himself Vrolok. That was why your father spent a few weeks lecturing in Budapest the year before you went to Libya. Vrolok was hiding in Hungary. I discovered him there and brought your father in to help me. Vrolok fled, but none of us knew where.

"When he surfaced in Libya, your father followed. He tracked Vrolok to those Roman ruins. The Baron was using one of the temples as a hiding place. When your father discovered this he moved in. I wish that he had waited for me, but he didn't. Still, he did remarkably well on his own. Vrolok was cornered. It was daytime, and he was weak and tired. Your father nearly finished him, as far as I can tell. But a vampire is not easy prey. Vrolok caused the temple to collapse. It was a desperate gambit, but it paid off. It killed your father. But it also forced Vrolok into the light. He would have perished had it not been for a small boy who happened to run past."

He paused. We were thinking the same thing, my uncle and I.

"I was bitten by a dog," I said. It was barely a whisper.

My uncle shook his head and mouthed a silent "No."

"Perhaps your memory is faulty. The mind can be like that. Tell me what you remember."

I told him. There were eyes in the shadows. I moved closer and the dog crawled out and bit me. It happened so fast . . .

"And tell me," he said, "when you remember this, do you see it as a movie, or do you see it as though it is really happening to you?"

"I don't understand," I said.

"Hmmm." He paused to think. "When you look at me now, you are seeing me through your own eyes. You don't see yourself. You see me, the chair, the desk, the mirror on the door, the wall behind me. When you see the dog in your mind, when it bites you, is it like that, do you see the dog and only the dog? Or is it different? Do you see yourself, as well? As though you are watching yourself in a movie?"

That was an easy one. "I can see us both. Like a movie. We're both in the picture and I'm looking from above."

My uncle nodded. "That means it isn't a true memory. Your mind has recreated the scene and you see the recreation. If the memory were real, you would see only the dog, just as you see only me when you look across the room. Of course, it wasn't a dog, was it. It was the Baron Vrolok. He must have been close to death. Very close. But he drank your blood, and it gave him the strength to survive. To dig deep into the earth and wait for darkness."

When he finished saying this, I stared up at him. It was as if I were seeing him clearly for the first time. There was truth in his words. I could see that. And I also saw another truth. One he had implied. I had been bitten by the Baron Vrolok. I had been infected by a vampire.

And so I was a vampire, too.

Chapter 10
Strange Questions

My uncle was right. Some truths could not be ignored. Not when they rolled over you like the dinner trolley.

I was a vampire. How could I have not known? It was the only thing that made sense. I couldn't go out in the sun. I needed fresh blood every few months. My body didn't like food. It made me wonder what Nurse Ophelia had been putting into those brain cocktails. I began to doubt it was strawberry syrup.

It also made me wonder how much of this she knew. I probably should have asked my uncle about it, but another thought had come to mind—something of much greater concern. After all, this man was a vampire hunter.

"Are you here to kill me?" I asked.

He smiled. His hard features softened and he looked down at the ground for just an instant. "No," he said. "I came here for an entirely different reason. I came here to take you away from this place."

"But don't you kill vampires?"

He shook his head once, slightly, with his lips pressed together. "Not always. In some cases your father and I left vampires alive because they agreed to help us, and because we were convinced they posed no immediate threat to humanity. You must understand, Zachary, vampires aren't very different from normal people. They have choices to make, just as you will have choices to make. They can choose to be good, or to be something that is less than good. I suppose the hunger for blood makes the choice more difficult for vampires, but it remains a choice."

Well, I had no doubt in my mind what I would choose. I would be good. I certainly wasn't a threat to anybody. I didn't even believe in mousetraps. But I was thinking that maybe there was another way out of this.

"Can I be cured?" I asked.

My uncle took a deep breath and put his hands on his knees. Then he pushed himself up and got ready to leave. In a second, an umbrella was hanging over his arm and a briefcase was in his hand.

"There is no known cure for vampirism. Your struggle here is proof enough of that. But there are ways of coping, obviously. You have done a remarkable job of it here, and you ought to be congratulated. In the meantime, I have set about the business of trying to adopt you. It won't be easy. Because medical science can't make sense of your condition, it will be difficult for me to prove that I am capable of taking care of you. But we will find a way . . . assuming that is what you want. You don't have to make your mind up right away. I'll come back, and we can spend some more time talking. I have an appointment right now and I can't be late. I'm on the trail of another vampire, but I'll be back to see you tomorrow. In the meantime, don't do anything to put yourself at risk. I noticed the police outside. I'm assuming there was an accident of some kind?"

"A man crashed through the doors with a stolen motorcycle," I said. Then I told him the rest.

When I was finished, my uncle stared at me for about ten seconds without saying a word. It was as if I'd just disconnected his brain. Then he snapped out of it.

"Tell me again, what exactly did he say?"

I ran through it as best I could.

My uncle looked down at the floor. He was whispering, "Thank heavens . . . Apocalypse . . ." Then he looked up at me with the same intense expression I'd seen on his face before. As though this was the most important thing in the world.

"What exactly did he look like? Describe him to me."

I started with the old man's hair and his top hat and overcoat, and finished with his eyes, but apparently I missed a lot, because my uncle asked me a lot of questions I didn't have clear answers for. Like the shape of his nose and his cheeks and how thick his neck was.

"And his voice, was there anything unusual about it?"

I shrugged. I didn't think so.

"And they shot him twenty times?"

"More or less. It was a lot. There was blood everywhere."

"Did he mention any names?"

I shook my head.

"Well," my uncle concluded, "I think I might know who the culprit is. I'll do some digging and find out for certain. It isn't Vrolok, that's the good news. And the police are here now. I recommend never straying from where they can help you."

"He told me to stay away from the police," I said. I'd forgotten to mention this.

My uncle smiled. "I think you can ignore that part, Zachary. They're usually the good guys." Then his smile tightened and he nodded a quick goodbye. "I'll try to be back before the sunrise. If not, I'll contact you tomorrow."

"Okay," I said.

I suppose I should have stood up and shaken his hand, or said thank you, or done something like that, but I didn't. I'm not sure why. I guess I was still pretty shocked. And truthfully, I wasn't used to that kind of good news—that I might soon be living in a real home with a real uncle. It wasn't as though my life was bad—I wasn't starving in some war-torn country with flies buzzing around my eyes—but it wasn't a bowl of cherries, either. So I just said goodbye.

The moment he was gone I felt a great emptiness inside. I almost jumped up and chased him down the hall. A zillion questions popped into my head. Things I should have asked him. My mother—what was she like, and how had she died? My father and his work. And about Vrolok. Was he really looking for me? Is that why the crazy old man had shown up on a stolen motorcycle? Did he know about Vrolok, too? I felt a bit ridiculous. There was so much to find out and I hadn't really asked him anything. But at least I'd met a person who might have some answers. Maximilian. Uncle Max. I liked the sound of it. And he looked tough enough to survive an alien invasion. I liked that, too.

Chapter 11
Death and Undeath

After my uncle left, I checked the time again. It was almost eight-thirty. I was still expecting Nurse Ophelia to arrive shortly. I was anxious to talk to her about all that I had learned. And Charlie. I imagined his jaw hitting his feet when I told him I was a vampire and that I might soon be adopted by my uncle, Maximilian, the vampire hunter. I had so much restless energy in my bones I could have run to the North Pole without taking a breath.

I paced in my room until the sun went down, then I headed straight for the nurses' station. Roberta was already there with one of the security guards. She was trying to get the Chicago Man to go to bed. He was doing his usual routine, spinning and waving his arms to music only he could hear. He would often stop his dancing to clap out a rhythm and sing, but his voice was just a mumble, and the only word you could ever make out clearly was "Chicago." I guess he was born there. Unfortunately, because the women all stayed on a separate floor, he never had anyone to dance with, except the staff. Nurse Roberta clearly wasn't in the mood.

"Do you know where Nurse Ophelia is?" I asked her.

As soon as I spoke, the Chicago Man turned around and started to spin in front of me, clapping his hands and laughing. I knew just what to do. I took both his hands and we turned a few lazy circles. Then we bowed to each other. It gave Nurse Roberta a chance to slip her hand inside his elbow.

"I'm a little busy right now. Can't you tell?" she said.

After several attempts, she managed to get him pointed in the right direction, and then, with the help of the security guard, started guiding him to his room. "This way, Mr. Butterfield."

I waited for Nurse Ophelia in the reception area for about five minutes. A work crew had been in during the day to replace the shattered doors. Part of the frame had been restored, but the glass was still missing, so tarpaulin had been stretched over the opening. Two policemen were there, and I noticed extra security guards, too. A few were helping the other nurses move people out of the dining hall and into their rooms.

I waited at the nurses' station for another twenty minutes. By this time, everyone was in bed, and Nurse Ophelia still hadn't arrived. With no one around to talk to, I started to get restless.

"Why don't you go blow off some steam in the fitness room?" Nurse Roberta suggested. She was filling in forms behind the counter. "I'll tell her where you are when she arrives."

It seemed like a good idea. I was feeling very irritated. I had to tell her the news. *I was a vampire*! But she must have known. She prepared my meals. Why hadn't she told me?

I suddenly felt very frustrated. How was I going to get answers if she didn't bother coming to work? So I hurried back to my room to get my sneakers. A few minutes later I was on the treadmill, running. It was the one thing I was exceptionally good at. And it didn't matter if I felt lonely, mad or just plain bored. To get my feet moving when the sun was down always did the trick.

I spent most of my time thinking about Maximilian. I imagined telling him everything about my life here. And introducing him to Charlie. As silly as it sounds, I pictured him getting married to Nurse Ophelia so that I could live with them both after he adopted me. I even imagined us hunting other vampires, like Peter Cushing and Anthony Hopkins in the movies. And avenging my father.

Five hours passed this way. By the end, the rubber track on the treadmill was smoking. It smelled like I'd set fire to it. I hadn't really noticed because I was off in my own little world. A world that was now full of vampires.

When I thought more about it, I remembered that we vampires weren't actually living creatures. We weren't dead, but we weren't alive, either. We were *undead*. Trapped between life and death forever. It seemed like a bunch of baloney to me, but in all the stories I'd ever read and the movies I'd watched, that was the word they'd used. And the first step was dying. Once you got infected, that is. Then your human life came to an end and your life as a vampire began.

I wondered when my first death had happened. My human death. It wasn't like I'd been dropped in a pit with a rabid *Tyrannosaurus rex*. Did I die in my coma? Or just after I was bitten? You'd think a guy would remember something important like that. But then again, maybe not. Death might have been so scary, my mind wouldn't let me remember.

In the end, I couldn't figure it out, mostly because the word *undead* didn't really make any sense. I certainly felt alive. But I might have been wrong about that. I'd basically forgotten what life was like for normal people, so maybe I didn't feel alive at all, I just thought I did. Maybe what I felt was something different. It took a while to put my finger on it, but then I figured it out. What I felt was excited. And alive or undead, after eight boring years in a mental ward being spoon-fed one hairball theory after another about what was wrong with me and how to fix it, well, things were looking up.

✦ ✦ ✦ ✦

As soon as my run was over, I tried again to find Nurse Ophelia. I needed to eat. Exercise usually made my appetite go away, but only while I was moving. Now that I had stopped, it was going to come on even stronger. I was in a race with my stomach. Soon it would be freaking out. I didn't see her anywhere, but I quickly found Nurse Roberta outside one of the rooms. She'd been checking up on one of the older patients I didn't know very well.

"Is she here yet?" I asked.

"No. And she didn't call in sick, either. She's a no-show. That means they'll dock her a night's pay." Then she muttered something colourful under her breath about all the work she'd been left to finish on her own. She had a clipboard in her hand. She was checking something off.

"I haven't eaten yet," I said. "I'm starving."

Nurse Roberta's head fell back just a bit and her shoulders slumped. I could tell she felt bad even before she apologized. "I totally forgot." Then she raised the clipboard and tapped it against her forehead, as though she was reminding herself not to be so stupid. "Well, come on, then. We'd better get you something."

We got to the kitchen just in time. My eyeballs were aching and my stomach sounded like an angry bear.

"I haven't done this in a while," she said. "Do you know where everything is?"

While she got the blender ready, I fished in the fridge for what I needed.

"You can't have that," Nurse Roberta said when she saw the box full of syrup bags.

"What do you mean?" I asked. "Nurse Ophelia always puts one of these in."

Nurse Roberta looked confused. Her face wrinkled up and she pointed to the label on the box. It said "Warning: Not for Human Consumption." I'd never noticed before. I guess I hadn't looked that closely.

I took out one of the bags. It suddenly dawned on me what the red syrup was, and it sure wasn't strawberries. My hands started shaking.

Nurse Roberta took the bag from me and gently squeezed it with her fingers. "Must be some kind of gel. Looks a bit like grenadine."

I had no idea what grenadine was, but I wasn't going to correct her.

"Well, sorry," she said, "but I can't let you have that." She closed the fridge and put her hands on her hips. "We'll have to think of something else."

I looked at her very closely. I had been wrong about her. She really was very pretty. But maybe I just thought so because she was trying to be helpful. Or maybe it was because I was hungry . . .

For some reason I got thinking about what Dracula might do at a moment like this. With all his bizarre talents, he was easily the undisputed heavyweight champion of the undead world. He could climb walls, turn into a bat, or a wolf, or mist. He could make himself thin and slip through cracks. He could command rats and other night creatures to do his bidding. He could even go out in the daytime.

I figured that stuff was poppycock. I'd been infected for eight years and I couldn't even keep my room clean.

But some of his talents weren't so unrealistic. And they were certainly better suited for a time like this. Hungry. Alone with a beautiful woman. He certainly wouldn't let himself starve. So I took a page out of his book and made my move.

First, I opened my eyes so they were really wide. Then I sort of raised my hand with the fingers spread wide. "You will let me have my dinner," I said to Nurse Roberta in a slow, commanding voice.

She still had her hands on her hips. Her chin dropped just a little. Then she opened her eyes very wide and raised her hand. "No, we'll have to find you something else," she said. Her imitation was flawless.

And so I learned something very valuable about my power to charm. I guess I still needed a few centuries of practice before I could command humans to do my bidding. Dracula would have been very disappointed.

I put my hand down. I must have been blushing because the skin on my face felt really tight. "I don't think I can have anything else," I told her. "All I know is that Nurse Ophelia mixes one of those in with the rest of my medications."

Nurse Roberta shook her head gently. "Zachary, you aren't on any medications. You haven't been for months. Not since last year. Didn't you know that?"

I shook my head. Then my stomach started to kung-fu my other organs. And my throat started itching as well. Like I had ants crawling around in there.

Nurse Roberta reached out and gently took hold of my hand. "Don't do that," she said.

I'd been scratching at my neck.

"We'd better find you something else," she added.

I shook my head. "Honestly, this is what she uses. I watch her. It's the same thing every time."

"Are you sure?"

I nodded.

She looked a little cross. "You'd better be. If you drop dead on me, and it costs me my job . . ."—she spread her fingers wide and made her eyes bug out—". . . I'll kill you!" Then she cut the bag open and poured it into the blender.

I realized that it didn't look like blood. I'd seen the real stuff when the old man on the stolen motorcycle got shot. This stuff was much thicker.

"We should water that down a bit," I suggested.

A few seconds later, I was drinking. It tasted exactly the same as normal. And it was gone in a blink.

"You gonna be okay?" she asked.

I nodded and smiled. Then I blushed again. I was feeling guilty. I'd been a bit too hard on her, thinking she was cranky all the time.

We left the kitchen and I made my way back to my room. With food in my stomach, I felt a lot better. And so I enjoyed another chapter of *The Hobbit*. Enough to see Bilbo and the gang safely to the house of Elrond. Then I closed my window, lowered the blinds, drew the curtains and went to sleep.

Chapter 12
The Fallen

I woke from a deep sleep around noon. Someone was knocking at the door. The cadence was hurried, but soft. Just to be safe, when I rose out of bed I picked up the chair by my desk and held it up over my shoulder. Then I asked who was there.

"It's your uncle," said a voice. "Maximilian."

I told him he could come in. He opened the door and slipped inside. I noticed his suit was different. He didn't have his briefcase with him, but he was holding a folder in one hand. When he saw me standing in the middle of the empty room, I put the chair back down.

"Redecorating?" he asked. Then his expression changed and he started to cough, worse than before. He had to work pretty hard to clear his throat afterwards.

"Excuse me," he said, thumping his chest with a large fist. "I hope it's okay that I woke you? I was going to slip this file under the door, but I decided that it made more sense to talk face to face, in case you had any questions. I didn't want you to get too worked up, although there is reason for concern."

He tapped the folder against his palm a few times.

"I have been meeting with the hospital admin all morning in hopes of getting you moved out of here," he said, "but because of your condition and your sensitivity to sunlight, they won't give me permission. Not until I become your legal guardian, and that could take some time. I don't think it's safe for you to stay here another night, but at the moment, I don't have the authority to force anyone's hand."

As he spoke, he opened the folder and removed a photograph. It was a picture of a scruffy-looking man in an overcoat. He had a cane and a long, pink scar under his eye.

"I came across some interesting information last night," he continued, "and I wanted to share it with you." He tapped a thick finger on the photo of the scruffy man. "This is Everett Johansson, former Toronto police detective. He retired to Peterborough eight years ago."

I picked up the photograph and examined it closely.

"Ever see him before?" my uncle asked.

I shook my head.

"Your father had a term he used to describe men like this. He called them 'the Fallen,' people who have forsaken humanity and entered into the service of vampires. This man is dangerous. He has eyes all over the city. My contacts tell me that he's looking for you."

I looked at the photo more closely. "Is this why the old man on the motorcycle warned me to stay away from the police?"

"I wouldn't dismiss the idea."

Everett Johansson. The Fallen. He didn't look all that dangerous. Not compared to my uncle. But if he served a vampire, he didn't have to be dangerous himself.

"Does he work for Vrolok?" I asked.

My uncle looked at me, then down at the photograph. "I don't know," he began. "I am assuming he does. Vrolok is in Canada. And as far as I know, he's never travelled to the New World before."

"New World?"

"North America. He's never before risked crossing the Atlantic. He's found out about you from someone. And I suspect that someone is Johansson."

"How would he know I was here? I've never seen him before."

My uncle shook his head slowly. "You wouldn't have to see him. He has many people working under him, in all walks of life. Maybe a delivery person saw you. Or a security guard. Or any one of the police officers who've been here. And there is no way to know, when you see someone, if they are one of the Fallen. They look like ordinary people. They *are* ordinary people. With dangerous friends."

I thought of everyone I came into contact with each day. There weren't that many. But the night the old man crashed through the lobby, there were a lot of different people on the scene, and I was centre stage. It might easily have happened then.

"I think you should stay in your room, just to be safe." Then he smiled and fished into the inside pocket of his jacket. He pulled out a small piece of paper. It had "Maximilian" written across the middle in red letters. Across the top in black was "Iron Spike Enterprises." The *I* in "Iron" was a metal spike. He took out a pen and scribbled a number underneath his name.

"That's my cell number," he said. "Don't hesitate to call if you sense trouble. Or if you get any more strange visitors, like that old man who stole the motorcycle."

"Did you find out who he was?"

"Not yet, but I will. In the meantime, we can't afford to take any chances. Experience has taught me that we should assume the worst. That Johansson knows you're here, and that he's working for Vrolok. I'm betting that's why the old man came to warn you. We'll have to get you out of here right away."

I looked at the window. It was just after noon. I didn't want to go anywhere unless it involved a tunnel or an armoured car.

"What should I do?" I asked.

"Well, sit tight for now. The sun is up. We can't risk moving you in the daytime. I'll do some more legwork this afternoon. Find out what I can, then come back later tonight. Don't worry. We'll get you out of here."

"You can do that?"

He smiled. The muscles on either side of his jaw twitched. He looked strong enough to rip the place apart, brick by brick. "I feel sorry for anyone who'd try to stop me," he said. Then he slipped the photo of Everett Johansson back into the folder. "Pack a bag," he added. "Just essentials. Be ready at sunset. I will get here as soon as I can."

I nodded.

He placed a hand on my shoulder, smiled again, then slipped out the door. I heard him cough again in the hallway. Then his footsteps faded and I was alone.

Chapter 13
Everett Johansson

My uncle had said he'd come back at sunset. *Sunset.* What a beautiful word.

Sadly, that was about eight hours away. I wasn't sure I could go back to sleep, so I started fishing under my bed for another set of clean clothes. They were all hospital scrubs. In the end, I decided the only thing I really needed were my books. I picked up *The Hobbit* and started reading. After some riddles in the dark, my eyes started to droop, so I put the book down and fell asleep.

I woke up in a panic about a half hour before dusk. Something wasn't right. My heart was pounding, for one. And the air just felt wrong. Tense. Sort of like the feeling you get when two people start having an argument.

I sat up in bed and looked about the room. Sunlight was peeking in around my blinds so I had to squint. Everything looked normal, but on instinct, I forced myself out of bed.

Then I heard someone shouting. It was coming from the hallway. If you've ever spent time in a mental ward, you'll understand that this is about as unusual as a cow eating grass. This shouting was different, though. It was the nursing staff who were raising their voices, which was rare. I stuck my head into the hall.

Two police officers were standing in front of the reception desk. A man was with them. With the light behind him, all I could see was a silhouette. He stood behind while the nurses and the officers argued. I tried to get a better look at everyone, but sunlight was reflecting off the floor. It hit my eyes like a handful of pins, so I couldn't see anything. Fortunately, one of the police officers raised his voice.

"I know he's here and I need him up now. He's got to be moved right away. Not tomorrow, not in an hour. Now."

"It's not that simple," one of the nurses explained. "If you don't take the necessary precautions, he could die. He's allergic to practically everything. Food. The sun—"

"I don't care if he's allergic to his own skin. He needs to come with us."

Well, as you can imagine, this got my attention. Even with cottage cheese for brains, I'd still have known they were talking about me. Then the man I couldn't see very well stepped closer to the others. He was dressed in an overcoat and he had a cane in one hand. He turned around and saw me. For a split second we stared at one another. When he took two steps towards me, I noticed that he walked with a limp. And even though the sun was bright enough to melt my hair, I could see the scar under his eye. It was like a thick, pink stripe. His eyes widened for just an instant, and then they narrowed as we acknowledged one another.

It was Everett Johansson. And he had the police with him.

I slammed the door shut and backed away from it. My hands and face were hurting from the sunlight that had been bouncing off the floor and walls. Ten seconds' worth, maybe twenty, and already every inch of my exposed skin was covered in red spots.

I started looking for my uncle's business card. I couldn't remember where I'd left it. As I was rummaging through my bedsheets, I realized it wasn't going to do me any good. The only phone I could have used to call him was at the nurses' station. The house phone in my room worked only inside the building. I was done for. The police were just outside the door, and I had nowhere to hide but under my bed. I was a little too big for that.

I pushed the bed in front of the door and threw my chair on top for good measure. The door opened inward, so that would slow them down for a few seconds. But I had to find a way to hold out for at least a half hour or so. Then, once the sun was all the way down, I could run away. Or maybe I wouldn't have to. My Uncle Maximilian had said he would be here. But the bad guys weren't going to wait, and there wasn't anything between us but a few inches of wood and a single bed. So I did what a lot of people do when they get into trouble and don't have a clue what to do. I looked up.

Footsteps were right outside my door now. I heard a knock.

"Zachary, are you in there?" The voice belonged to Nurse Roberta.

"Zachary," said another voice. It sounded all crackly. "It's the police. We know you're in there. Please open up. We need to have a word with you."

The next knock was loud and hard.

"I hope you're decent," Nurse Roberta said.

I was too frightened to say anything. A few seconds later, someone tried to push the door. It opened just a crack before the bed got in the way. One of the police officers said something in a loud voice and tried to force the door while Nurse Roberta asked me to "Please open up" over and over again. A few seconds later they had pushed the bed back far enough that one of them could slide it completely out of the way. The chair toppled to the floor. Everett Johansson was the first one in.

"Where is he?" I heard him say.

But Nurse Roberta didn't know. None of them did. I was gone.

Chapter 14
Emergency Exit

Perhaps you don't believe that I really am a vampire. It is a stretch, I'll give you that. But if you do believe I am a vampire, well, you can't be a numbskull about it, either. I'm not a storybook vampire like Count Dracula. I can't do supernatural. My escape wasn't all that impressive. Check the ceiling of your school someday. Or an office. If it's like mine, it's really a false ceiling. It's made of rectangular foam tiles that sit on a plastic frame. You can poke them up with a broom. Up above, you'll find the plumbing and ducts for heating that run every which way.

That's it. That's how I got out. I just stood on my desk, pushed up the tile, slid it backwards, jumped up and grabbed one of the black pipes hanging overhead. Then I pulled myself up and slid the tile back in place underneath me. *Ta-dah*!

Are you impressed? Maybe not. But I tell you, it was awfully nerve-racking hanging there, hoping the police would leave.

Everett Johansson was furious. "Where did he go?" he asked again.

"I don't know," the nurse answered. "There's no way out of here but the window, and it's barred."

The bed was moved and moved and moved again. The mattress was lifted and the sheets pulled off. The room was only about eight feet wide and twelve feet long. It didn't take them long to search it.

"I'll check the next room," the nurse said.

"No, he's in here somewhere. There's no way he could have gotten out."

I listened while they moved the bed again.

"Wait a minute," Johansson said. "Give me that chair."

I heard the sound of people shuffling around, then the tile underneath me popped up just a hair. That got a reaction. I had to get moving. Pipes ran in every direction. So did the metal heating ducts, but they didn't look as strong. I took my best guess and slid, hand over hand, foot over foot, along the pipes in the direction of the kitchen.

"Get me a light," Johansson continued. "I can hear him. He's in the ceiling."

An instant later the tile disappeared. Johansson's head and shoulders rose through the space. He had a small flashlight in his hand.

I got lucky. There was dust everywhere, and the beam of his flashlight didn't penetrate very far into the darkness. He scanned straight ahead first, then on one side and the other. By the time he looked behind him I was even farther away.

"He's heading that way," Johansson said.

A tile to my right popped up and then disappeared. Then another one off to my left. The two police officers joined the search. The beams of their flashlights lit up the dust all around me.

"Over there," said a voice. I tried to speed up, but it wasn't easy hauling myself along. Unless I found a way to turn invisible, they were going to catch me.

I kept moving in the direction of the kitchen. I was starting to slow down because my wrists were getting tired. I was breathing heavily. All the dust made it difficult to get a full chest of air. I couldn't hang on much longer.

Then a tile popped up right in front of me. I waited for the officer underneath me to look up, but he didn't, because someone started yelling at him. It was Nurse Roberta.

"You can't do this!" she shouted. "This is a mental ward. Anything out of the ordinary throws these people for a loop. Our job is difficult enough. Tearing the ceiling apart like this is out of the question."

I could have dropped to the floor and kissed her. Instead, I slid, as quietly as I could manage, back the way I'd come.

The officer ignored her. He tossed the tile to the floor and removed another. It gave me a better view of him. He was standing on something. A chair, or a ladder, maybe. I thought he might turn his flashlight on me, but he didn't even have it out any more. I scanned the darkness above the remaining tiles. The other officers must have stopped using theirs, too. The beams were no longer shining through the dust. They were simply tearing down the ceiling one tile at a time. Soon, the whole network of ducts and plumbing would be exposed. And so would I.

The officer removed another tile, and another. As the tiles disappeared, more light danced up through the dust. I was going to be in plain view very soon.

Then I heard another voice shouting, "He's in here! He's in here!"

It was Jacob, my red-haired neighbour from across the hall. I could hear him giggling.

The officer in front of me stopped pulling out tiles. A second later, I heard the heavy sound of his feet as they hit the floor. Then he ran off in the direction of Jacob's room.

This bought me a few precious seconds. I considered what to do. The dining hall would still have a few patients lingering in it.

So would the kitchen. So would the common room. There was nowhere I could drop where I wouldn't be seen.

Another voice started shouting, too. It was Sad Stephen. He had chronic depression and came in a few times a year for shock treatment. Sounds horrible, but it might have been working, because he was laughing too, just like Jacob.

"No. I see him. He's in my room!"

I nearly started laughing myself. A few seconds later, every person on the floor who could talk was shouting.

"He's in my room!"

"No, my room!"

"He's in here!"

". . . right behind you!"

In the end, it didn't make much of a difference. Johansson told his men to go back and keep pulling out the tiles. I felt a twinge of panic until I realized that what he was doing was ridiculous. The ceiling of the first floor was huge. It was going to take them too long. They were never going to be finished by nightfall. But, of course, they didn't know my uncle was coming to save me. They must have thought they'd have all night.

I scuttled back in the direction of the kitchen. My wrists were starting to burn. I couldn't hang on much longer. A few feet away was a heating duct. The metal strips that held it in place looked flimsy, but I was out of options. I slipped my leg over it. The duct seemed to handle the weight just fine. Then I slowly shifted my whole body over until I was settled neatly on top. It made some noise, but with everybody shouting, I don't think Johansson would have heard me if I'd torn the whole thing loose.

Soon the ruckus came to an end. I guess the thrill of screaming "He's over here!" only lasts so long. Shortly afterwards, security and the nursing staff started herding people back to their rooms for lights out.

Johansson and his men continued their work. The bedrooms, the lobby, the reception area, the nurses' station, they were all being done systematically. I didn't care. Dusk was approaching, and my uncle was coming. Or so I thought.

As the police moved closer, I heard the dining room clearing below me. Soon it was quiet, and I decided to make a drop. I slid a tile all the way back and looked down. It was at least twelve feet to the ground.

What was I afraid of? I was a vampire now. Couldn't most of us fly?

I let go and hit the ground with a soft thud. No broken bones. Not even a tingle. I crept towards the kitchen. A few night staff were cleaning up after dinner, rinsing dishes and putting them through the wash. Their backs were to me. Still, I watched for a few seconds to make certain they weren't glancing around. They seemed pretty busy, so I managed to crawl over to the refrigerator without being seen. I opened the door as quietly as I could and grabbed the box of food Nurse Ophelia used to make my brain cocktails.

My uncle had said to pack the essentials. Well, this would have to do. It was time to get going.

I crept back into the dining room, grateful that the lights were off and the area was empty. But the only doors that could get me outside of the building were in the lobby. If I climbed there above the ceiling, which would have been almost impossible with the box I was carrying, I still would have had to drop down right in front of Johansson and his men, assuming they hadn't finished that section completely by now. That wasn't going to get me very far. And even though there were exits at both sides of the building, they were unlocked only if there was an emergency. I had to think of something else.

So I walked to the wall and pulled the fire alarm. Instant emergency.

As soon as it started ringing, I ducked under a table and waited.

Almost right away, the two kitchen staff made their way through the dining hall. Neither saw me. Then I snuck back into the kitchen, grabbed an apron from the wall, tied it around my waist and walked out myself. I thought if I looked casual enough, with all the traffic in the lobby, I'd get out one of the side doors, no problem. I just needed my luck to hold.

It didn't.

They say timing is everything. Well, I don't even wear a watch, so mine could have been better. I strode out of the dining hall expecting to merge with a crowd of people, but the lobby was nearly empty. I hadn't waited long enough for everyone to figure out what was going on and leave their rooms—assuming they could do all of this without an instruction manual or a personal attendant. To make matters worse, Everett Johansson was arguing with Nurse Roberta at the reception counter, so I practically bumped into him.

"Zachary, stop! It isn't safe!" he shouted.

I ran for the closest exit, the lobby doors right in front of me. The police were close behind.

Did I mention that I was pretty quick on my feet? Running for a few hours every night is apparently very good for this. I'd never actually been in a race before, but as it turned out, none of the officers inside had a chance. I bolted through the outside doors so fast, all they could do was shout. I looked back over my shoulder for a second, and that's when I collided with the officer waiting in the parking lot. I was so surprised, I dropped my box of food and tripped to the pavement. I'd totally forgotten there were men posted outside.

I tried to stand up, but someone had taken hold of my wrist. As I twisted away, a heavy weight pressed down on my back, flattening me against the asphalt. Someone started shouting at me, telling me not to move. At the same time, I felt another officer grab one of my legs. Then a third pinned my arm. And just like that, I was in the hands of the police.

Chapter 15
The Vampire

I wrestled with the three officers as best I could. It was hard because I was on the ground and they were all sitting on me. Then they weren't. The first officer, the one on my back—he flew off into the air like he'd been fired from a catapult. He landed on the hood of a police car. The second one—he was trying to pin my legs—he flew off an instant later. Unfortunately for him, he missed the car. I heard him grunt as he landed on the asphalt.

The last guy was kneeling on one of my arms. The look on his face was one of total astonishment. He half stood up and put his hand on his holster. Then he got hauled off the ground.

"You won't be needing that gun," a voice said.

I expected it to belong to my uncle. It didn't. It belonged to the crazy old motorcycle man. He was standing in the parking lot in his top hat and overstuffed overcoat, with the police officer in one hand and the officer's gun in the other. He was actually holding the guy a foot off the ground. The old man stared at the pistol for a second, then tossed it into the Dumpster beside us. Then he ripped a set of keys from the officer's belt. "Thanks," he said. And officer number three was airborne. "Have a nice evening," the old man added as the officer soared away.

I was so stunned I couldn't move. When he looked down at me, I thought for just a second he was going to pitch me out with the rest of them, but he didn't. He reached down and helped me to my feet. He must have been as strong as an elephant.

"So . . . didn't bother fixing the motorcycle I left for you?"

I couldn't speak.

The old man started walking over to the police car near the new lobby doors. It was a Ford Mustang. "Don't forget your box," he said over his shoulder.

I picked up the carton of food, then took a few uncertain steps towards the car. The old man was trying to unlock the door with the keys he'd stolen. None of them seemed to work.

"Oh, hang it," he said. Then he tossed the keys over his shoulder and just ripped the driver's-side door off the car. No joke. Like it was made of wet newspaper.

He was climbing into the driver's seat when I heard a man shout "Stop!" It was the first police officer. The one who had landed on the car. He was back on his feet and had his gun drawn. It was pointed right at us.

"Hands on your head. Back away from the car," he shouted.

"Hurry up, boy!" the old man snapped.

My door opened from the inside and I ducked in. The cover of the steering column had been ripped off and the old man was rubbing two wires together.

"Don't move or I'll shoot," shouted the officer.

The old man turned to me and smiled. "Time to slip it into overdrive."

I smelled a spark and the engine turned over. Then I heard several gunshots. The sound made every muscle in my body jump.

"Hang on," the old man said. He was talking through clenched teeth like he'd just been punched in the stomach. A dark stain was spreading across his chest.

Blood. The smell of it filled the car. I felt the muscles in my jaw begin to twitch and my head got all dizzy. It was exactly the same way I'd felt when I first saw him bleeding, the night he'd crashed into the lobby of the Nicholls Ward. I felt agitated, too. Almost angry. There was just a flash of it, but enough that I had a fleeting urge to rip his coat off and help myself to what he'd spilled so it wouldn't go to waste.

He threw the car into reverse and spun into the cruiser behind us. The officer with the gun was standing right beside it, so he had to jump out of the way to avoid being hit. We slammed into the car and the front end caved in over one of the tires. Without a tow truck, it wasn't going anywhere. Then the old man slipped the gearshift into forward and tore out of the parking lot.

"Buckle up," he said.

I had the box of food in my lap. I was fighting with the seat belt when I felt his hand pushing down on the top of my head. An instant later, several shots hit the back windshield and pebbles of glass flew all over the back seat.

"Are you hit?" he asked me as we raced down the street. He had to shout because there was so much wind coming in through his open door.

"No," I answered.

"Good."

I noticed he was still grinding his teeth. He looked into my box of food. "Toss me one of those, will you?"

I reached into the carton and pulled out one of the square bags. When I handed it to him, I noticed his teeth. Two of them in particular. You know the ones I mean. They were twice as long as they should have been, and pointed, like a wolf's.

"You're a vampire," I said.

"Well, give the boy a cigar. What were you expecting? A cherub?"

"What's a cherub?" I asked.

"What's a cherub? Don't young people go to Sunday school any more?"

I shrugged. I had no idea what young people did.

"Of course I'm a vampire," he continued. "Did you think you were the only one in town?"

"You mean there are more of us?"

The old vampire laughed. "More of us! Vampires are everywhere. Why, I'll bet you half the bureaucrats at City Hall . . ." He bit into the bag and took a sip. A look of total disgust came over his face and he spat everything out the open door. The wind blew half of it back inside. "What is this crap?"

I looked at the box to see if it said anything other than "Warning: Not for Human Consumption."

"Blood," I said. "At least, I think so."

"Are you nuts?" he said. Then he laughed. "What am I saying? I just helped you escape from Crackerbox Palace." He held the bag under my nose. "Does this swill smell like blood to you? If this is the real deal, I'm the Master Chief and you just got powned."

The bag looked fine to me.

"Must be from an animal," he said. "Probably a pig or a cow." He went to toss the bag out of the car, but I stopped him.

"Don't, I'll have it."

"Your funeral."

He handed the bag to me. I drank it. It wasn't as filling as one of my brain cocktails, but it tasted just as good. I waited a few seconds to see if my stomach was considering any acrobatic routines, but I didn't feel so much as a cramp.

"Don't you have any of the real stuff?" the old vampire asked me.

"What real stuff?"

He looked at me like I was too stupid to be alive. I noticed his eyes again. Watery blue. "Human blood, of course. What did you think I meant?"

I was shocked. "You drink human blood?"

"Once you start, there's only one way to stop."

"How's that?"

He spun the wheel and we skidded around a corner. "You get killed," he said.

So vampires could die. Of course they could die. Wooden stakes and holy water and all that. I stared at the old vampire for a moment, wondering how much of what I'd read in books and seen in the movies was true.

"Do you hunt people?" I asked.

He looked in the rear-view mirror. It had a bullet hole in it, so he took a quick glance over his shoulder, then he started driving with one hand.

"Not unless they really get on my nerves," he answered.

I wasn't sure if he was lying or not. But he was weaving all over the road.

"What's the matter?" I asked.

"What's the matter? I got shot three times. That's what's the matter. Here, take the wheel."

I'd never driven a car before, but I'd played my share of racing games. As it turned out, driving a car in real life and driving in a video game weren't quite the same. Especially, holding the wheel in one hand from the passenger's seat. I side-swiped a parked car and knocked over a couple of garbage cans, but I didn't get us killed. I guess that was the main thing.

Meanwhile, the vampire was frantically digging underneath his coat. I couldn't tell if he was on fire or had a bumblebee in his shirt. Then he took out a bag that looked a bit like the one I'd given him, only this one was bigger. It was rectangular and had a red cross on it. It also had a bullet hole in the side, so half of the blood was gone.

The smell of it was strong, but I didn't get as worked up this time, I guess because I'd fed already. But a part of me still wanted to grab the bag from him and drain it myself.

"Damn," he said. "This was my last one." He put his mouth over the bullet hole in the side of the bag and finished the rest. By this time we were approaching Water Street, the main road running through town. I could hear police sirens behind us.

"Are you okay?" I asked.

"I'll be fine. Vampires heal very quickly, boy, much faster than people, especially if they get fresh blood. The good stuff, not that bovine crap you were pushing earlier."

He must have been telling the truth—that vampires healed quickly—because he actually managed to keep the car straight for a whole block.

"Where are we going?"

"To the river. I know a place we can hide."

"Isn't the police station this way?" I said. This didn't seem like the best route.

The vampire didn't answer. Instead, he stepped on the gas, ran a red light, then turned onto Water Street. The tires made so much noise when he rounded the corner that I was surprised they didn't fly off the car. A few blocks up the street in the other direction was the police station. I looked out the back. There were so many flashing red and blue lights, every officer in town must have been in on the chase. As it turned out, not all of them were behind us. A group appeared very suddenly around the bend. They had a roadblock in place. Several cars were parked end to end across the street.

The vampire jumped the curb so we were cruising right on the sidewalk. We were lucky—nobody was out for a stroll, just a few ducks that had wandered up from the river. Fortunately, we missed them. Unfortunately, we hit the back of a cruiser that had moved to intercept us. The hood flew off our car and the windshield crumbled into a spiderweb of broken glass. Then the engine started making clunking noises.

"That's the problem with these damn Mustangs," the vampire said. "A couple of high-speed collisions and they just fall apart."

I was gripping the handle above the door so firmly I nearly pulled the roof down on us. I expected the car to fall to pieces, but it didn't. We kept charging forward.

"What are you doing?" I shouted.

"I have a plan," he answered.

I wondered if it involved checking him into the Nicholls Ward. I was about to tell him that my room was free, but he turned and asked me a question.

"Are you warm?"

This guy really was a loon. His door was missing. The car was like a wind tunnel. With his hair whipping around, it was a wonder he could even see the road.

"No," I said. "I'm actually pretty cool."

"Well, that's too bad. I thought if you were warm, you might like to go for a swim."

I looked out my window. Like I said before, we were driving down Water Street. It had that name for a reason. The Otonabee River was flowing beside us. It looked like a giant shadow.

He cranked the wheel over. We left the sidewalk and started spinning on a strip of grass that sat between the river and the road. We did a slow three-sixty, then went over the bank. I heard myself shouting in surprise. For a moment we were airborne. Then the back of the car slammed into the river. Water splashed everywhere. The car stopped dead and the Otonabee started pouring in through the rear window and the open door.

The vampire calmly undid his seat belt. "So, did I pass my driving test?" he asked. Then he gave me a quick wink, turned and dove into the water.

Chapter 16
Creatures of the Night

As soon as the vampire disappeared out the car door, I frantically undid my seat belt. Half a dozen police cruisers were screeching to a halt where we'd left the sidewalk and spun into the river. There was no time to lose. I started to push my door open, then I realized it would be easier to swim out the driver's side, so I jumped over the gearshift, took a deep breath and pushed off against the sinking car.

The river was freezing. If you've ever jumped into cold water, you know exactly how shocking it can be. The chill goes straight to your bones and makes it hard to move. And the water was loud. That meant it was moving fast. It took me totally by surprise. The instant I was clear of the car, the river pulled me straight under.

I hadn't been swimming since my father died. I could sort of picture how the whole thing was supposed to work, but making it happen was another matter. The water tossed me back up and I managed to sneak another breath, but a half second later I was under again. Then I banged my shins against a rock and lost all my air. I tried rolling onto my back so I could keep my face above the surface, but the current made it too difficult. My head came up, slipped under again, and I took in a mouthful of water. The next time I made it up for air, a wave splashed into my face. By this time I was coughing like a pack-a-day smoker. My arms were flailing and I kicked with both legs. I might just as well have had rocks in my pockets.

I heard a muffled voice off to my right. Someone was shouting at me. With all the noise of the river, it sounded like it was coming from twenty miles away. I took a quick look around for the vampire, but with the water in my eyes I couldn't make anything out.

"Stand up," the voice shouted. "STAND UP!"

It sounded like the vampire, but I couldn't be sure. It also sounded like good advice. I put a leg down and touched bottom. The water was about four feet deep, shallow enough to touch, but deep enough that the strong current pushing at my back made it impossible to stand in place. I got knocked off balance right away, but I just put my other leg down and so managed to keep my head above water.

Eventually I got the hang of it, bounding from leg to leg as I drifted with the current. I must have looked like those guys who landed on the moon, springing up and down like I didn't weigh a thing. The only difference, aside from the fact that I wasn't in outer space, was that I couldn't see where I was stepping. There were rocks on the bottom and so I lost my footing a few times and wound up swallowing more water. But with the current pushing me so quickly, I covered a lot of ground. Enough that I could no longer hear or see any signs of the police.

I spied the vampire off to my right. He was about a hundred feet away, moving towards the shore, which was steep and high and covered in trees. From the street, he'd be pretty much invisible. I followed as best I could. By this time, I'd swallowed half the Otonabee and could see the edge of Little Lake up ahead. In a relatively short time, we'd managed to travel back up Water Street, past the police station and most of the downtown. The vampire waved me over, and as I approached, the water got shallower and shallower, so my moon-jumping changed rather abruptly into normal walking. Or at least normal stumbling.

"We should keep moving," the vampire said. "They'll have the dogs out soon."

"Where are we going?"

He nodded over his shoulder. "I want to get to the far side of the river," he explained. "It's a bit ironic, really." And he looked at me as though he'd just told one of the funniest jokes in the history of comedy.

"I don't get it."

"Don't you read vampire books or watch the movies? We aren't supposed to be able to cross running water. It's a bunch of baloney, but in this case, it's sadly true."

I still didn't get it. And I wasn't keen on the idea of leaving our hiding spot. But another minute with this kook was going to be the death of me. I was tired. What I wanted most was to collapse into a warm bed. Even a coffin would have done.

"Well, this is no good," he said at last. "There's a place we can hide on the far side of the river, but we can't get across this way, and we're still too close to the heat." He peered over his shoulder again, as though expecting the police to appear any second. Then he looked me over and smiled. "You all right?"

I nodded, shivering. "Who *are* you?" I asked.

"I have had many names," he said, pulling his tattered overcoat up around his face so that it looked like a cape. He spoke with only his eyes and matted hair showing. "But you may call me . . . *John*."

If this was supposed to be a joke, I didn't get it.

"John Entwistle." He paused, like this was supposed to mean something to me. "You know, like the bass player from The Who."

"Who are The Who?"

"*Who are The Who*? You gotta be joking! Rock band. Late '60s early '70s."

I still didn't get it.

He started shaking his head again, then he looked up at the sky. A sliver of moon shone through the thin layer of clouds overhead. He took a deep breath and let it out slowly. "Man, time moves quickly."

I'd heard other people say that, too. I'd noticed they were never young.

"How old are you?" I asked.

"Six and a half." I thought he would say more, but he didn't. At least not right away. He kept his face to the sky. His eyes were closed. It was like he was soaking up the starlight. Then he fixed me with a steady stare. "When you're as old as I am, boy, you start counting by the century."

That took a few seconds to register. Six and a half centuries. Six hundred and fifty years old?

"You're joking." I said.

Mr. Entwistle reached into his coat and pulled out a silver flask. It had a bullet stuck to it.

"Of course I'm joking. I'm really only thirty. I've just lived hard."

At this point, I really didn't know what to believe.

He pried the bullet lose and tossed it into the river. Then he uncapped the flask and held it up. "To our escape," he said. He took a swig and offered it to me. I accepted, but as soon as I got it near my mouth, my whole system recoiled.

"What's wrong?" he asked.

"I thought it was blood!"

He shook his head. "No. There's the good stuff. And then there's the *good stuff*. I guess you're a little young for Crown Royale." He took the flask back, put down another swig, then tucked it away.

"How did you do it?" I asked.

"Do what?"

"Get up after being shot so many times? That first night at the hospital, they shot you about twenty times. There was blood everywhere."

"The blood wasn't mine," he said. "I'd stuffed my coat with Red Cross bags, thinking you'd be hungry."

As soon as he said this, I remembered something I'd forgotten.

"I left that box of blood in the car," I said.

"That swill. Leave it. You'll never reach your potential drinking that crap. I almost feel sorry for the fish."

I'd never had anything else. "I don't want to kill anyone," I said.

"You won't have to. There are other ways of getting blood. I'll show you. Stick with me and you'll be fine."

I looked him over. He was a disaster. Still, he wasn't freaked out like he had been the night he remodelled the Nicholls Ward. It made me wonder what had spooked him so badly.

"Why did you steal that motorcycle?" I asked.

He scratched at his stubble and thought for a second or two. "I was in a bad headspace. But that was two days ago. I'm better now, as you can see."

I could see that I needed to get in touch with my uncle, or I was probably going to end up in jail, or worse.

"Do you have a cellphone?" I asked.

He laughed. "Yeah, I left it in my Porsche. Now we should get going. The cops are after us. And someone else is after you. Another vampire. A powerful one. With some dangerous friends." He looked at me closely. I wondered if he was testing me to see how much I knew already.

"The Baron Vrolok," I said. "And the Fallen."

Mr. Entwistle raised his eyebrows and nodded slowly. "The Fallen. Interesting term. I like it. It fits. But as for Vrolok, well, we can talk about him later. For now, we need to disappear. And I know just the place." He nodded towards the heart of the city and reached out with a hand to help me up the bank. "Come along, boy. Time for your first lesson."

He raised his upper lip just enough on one side to reveal the long canine tooth underneath, then he bounded off. I did my best to follow. If this was my first lesson, at least it was about something I understood. Running.

✦ ✦ ✦ ✦

That night we were like a pair of wolves. Fast. Tireless. The hours drifted by. We dodged through backyards. Over fences and hedges. Across the rooftops of downtown apartments and single-storey row houses. Mr. Entwistle was light on his feet. Nearly invisible. And he didn't really run like other people. He bounded. He loped. Half the time I couldn't see him or hear him. I think he must have been testing me to see if I could keep up.

I couldn't.

But whenever I lost track of him for more than a few seconds, he'd appear on a rooftop overhead or leap out of the darkness so that our chase could continue. He stuck to the shadows, and I followed. Up and down fire escapes. Into trees. Along the edges of buildings and rows of parked cars. I felt alive. And, as weird as this will sound, I felt as if I was somehow part of the night. That my body was just a shadow, an extension of the darkness.

After we'd put a few miles behind us, Mr. Entwistle began to speak.

"You've lived a half life," he said. "Like a caged animal, alive but not free. But you feel differently now, don't you, boy?"

I nodded. I did feel different. Excited. Uncertain. I was being hunted by another vampire, my father's killer. And his minions. An avalanche of trouble was headed my way, but I was strangely unafraid.

It was true that I had no idea what was going to happen to me, but there are many kinds of uncertainty, and uncertainty about the future is just one of them. There is also the uncertainty of where you fit in. Where you belong. Until my escape with Mr. Entwistle, I never felt as though I really belonged anywhere. My parents were dead. I had no brothers or sisters. No home of my own. And as much as I loved Nurse Ophelia, I certainly didn't belong in a mental ward. But those days were over. At that moment, I knew my place. I knew what I was. The problems that had made my life miserable back at the ward—my reaction to the sun, my food trouble, my transfusions, my bouts of anger, the need to be alone—these things had always been shrouded in mystery, because no one could explain why I was like this, why I was so different. I'd been waiting for an answer. For a cure. Well, the waiting was over. I was a vampire. A creature of the night. Inhuman. Beyond human. Stronger. Faster. Tougher. And the certainty of this gave me a profound confidence. I was finally where I belonged. In the darkness.

"To run, to hunt with another vampire, is to realize your true self," Mr. Entwistle said. "You realize how you were meant to be." He stopped to sniff the air, then glanced at me from the corner of his eye. "But be cautious. It is at moments like these that your desire to kill will be strongest." He turned and scrambled over a tall wooden fence.

We were in the old west end, a neighbourhood of century-old homes. I can always tell when I'm running in an older neighbourhood. The houses all have wide porches, whose whole point seems to be to welcome guests to the front door. It's way different in the new areas of town, where the houses are all the same and the garages jump out at you like the cars are more important than the people. Whenever I imagined living a normal life, in a normal home, it looked a lot like the one in front of me. It was set well back from the street on a large lot with huge trees all around.

And even though it was dark and a bit rundown, it had a strangely inviting feel.

"Are you ready?"

I didn't know why Mr. Entwhistle was asking me this, but I said okay anyway.

"Well then, let's go." And he started up the lane.

Chapter 17
The Safe House

While I walked beside Mr. Entwistle, our feet scuffing on the paving stones, the world of the night opened up like the pages of a book. Something—probably a cat or a squirrel—was moving quietly through the hedge off to our right. Bats hunted overhead. I could even hear the beating of moth wings; dozens were circling under the street lamp behind us. I sniffed at the air and noticed a faint trace of wine.

"Whose house is this?" I asked.

Mr. Entwistle laughed. "Mine."

He turned towards a carport on the far side of the house. There was a Porsche underneath. A cherry-red convertible. He took out a set of keys, unlocked the door and reached inside. When he resurfaced, he was holding a cellphone to his ear.

"Just need to check my messages."

I had to smile. I guess he wasn't such a disaster after all.

He led me up onto the porch, then through the front door and into the hall. I was curious to see what he'd have stored away in a house so old, so I was surprised to discover that it was nearly empty. No shelves or carpets or pictures or lamps. Only the living room had any furniture—just two wooden chairs that sat near the fireplace. There was a small, round table between them with a half-empty glass of wine on it. An overturned bottle was lying on the floor, accounting for the smell I'd detected on the walk.

"I must have been in a hurry," Mr. Entwistle said. "Never leave a glass half full."

He walked over to the table and drained the glass. I stared at him dumbly.

"Oh, sorry," he said. "Did you want some?"

I shook my head and raised my hands so he wouldn't bring it any closer.

Mr. Entwistle sat down, then he kicked the other chair over to where I was standing. The echo was loud in the empty room.

"Most vampires can't take anything but blood," he said. "The instant you're infected, a rapid metamorphosis takes place in your body. The pathogen isn't well understood, so no one knows exactly what happens. But you know the results. Most things you can do better—run, hear, see, smell, heal. But some things you can't do at all. Eating is one of them. Cells can no longer make digestive enzymes to break food down into substrate. It takes about thirty years to reactivate those portions of your DNA that produce enzymes for metabolizing alcohol."

I didn't know what he was talking about and I didn't ask. Half his words sounded made up. He bent over and retrieved the bottle from the floor. Then he peeked down the neck to see if anything was left. Apparently there was enough. He tipped the neck over the glass and a thin red stream dribbled out. Less than a sip.

"Thirty years, so you've gotta be committed."

He offered the sip of wine to me. I took the glass and sniffed at it. The smell made me think of mouldy fruit, rotten and sour. The expression on my face made him laugh. I handed it back. There was no way I was putting that stuff in my mouth.

"Thirty years to be able to drink wine again. Thirty years . . . seems like a short time to me now. But not back then." He snorted. It might have been a laugh had there been any trace of humour on his face. "Those were the plague years. The time of the Black Death. Took my wife. My son, too. But not my daughter. She lived—for about another ten years. Soldiers killed her. Burned her as a witch. Edward's men. Edward III. Ever heard of him?"

I shook my head.

"Well, that's not terribly surprising. He wasn't very popular by the end. But things were different back then. Life had no value."

He looked at me, and his eyes were smouldering.

"The place is pretty empty, isn't it, boy?"

"Yeah," I said.

"Surprised?"

I nodded, then shrugged. "I guess."

"Well, I've learned not to get mired in the past. I don't collect things. I don't need things. I have faith, and I have a purpose, and that's what matters."

He held up the last mouthful of wine so that the crimson liquid glistened in the moonlight streaming in through the back windows.

"To finding purpose," he said.

He upended his glass while I stepped over to the chair across from him. My shoes were still a bit damp and they made squelching noises on the floor.

I sat down and felt myself drifting away. I had never concerned myself with purpose. I'd spent most of the last eight years wondering what might be wrong with me and whether anyone could make it better. I had been waiting to be fixed. And while I'd waited, my only concern had been how to spend my time so that I didn't die of boredom. I tried to explain this as best I could, and I think he understood me.

"The biggest problem was that you didn't know yourself. But you're on track now that you've discovered the truth."

He looked at his empty wineglass with a sad expression. Then he stood and walked into the kitchen. When he came back he had another bottle in his hand.

"What is *your* purpose?" I asked him.

He used his teeth to pull the cork from the wine bottle and poured himself a glass.

"I help vampires," he said.

"Only the good ones, I hope."

He laughed and raised his drink. "Not usually," he answered. "It's the bad ones that need the most help."

Mr. Entwistle sat and stared at his glass of wine. After seeing him all paranoid in the nuthouse, it was odd to see him so relaxed. Odd and reassuring. Of course, he could have used a few hours in a hair salon and about a gallon of Miracle Glow shampoo. And with his mismatched gloves and overstuffed overcoat, he still looked the part of the crazy motorcycle man. But it didn't matter now. I trusted him.

"You know that my father was a vampire hunter?" I said.

"No," he answered. "But I can see another lesson in irony tucked away there someplace. God has quite a sense of humour."

He seemed to doze off for just a second or two, then his head jerked up. "So he's gone, your father? Or retired?"

"He died."

"I'm sorry for your loss," he said. "But perhaps it will prepare you for your life as a vampire. You will outlive everyone you know. It isn't easy."

Then he stood, removed his overcoat and held it up so that the silver moonlight shone through many finger-sized openings. They were bullet holes. When he tossed the coat to the floor, I saw what he was wearing underneath. It wasn't ten layers of clothing. It was like something out of a video game.

"What's that?" I asked.

"Body armour," he said. "Platinum." He thumped his chest. "Sewn inside a double Kevlar weave. Cost me more than my car, but it's worth it. Stops most small-arms fire. A bullet still feels like a sledgehammer, but it keeps the blood where it belongs."

That explained it. I'd watched him get shot so many times that all the wine in his stomach should have been streaming out onto the floor.

"Do you have another set?" I asked.

He shook his head.

"So, what do we do now?"

Mr. Entwistle looked around. "You don't have to decide on anything at the moment. Just relax. You're in a safe house. No one knows you're here. You can rest and get used to being a vampire. It's no small thing. Then, once you're ready, you can start testing yourself. See how strong you are. How fast. What it takes to exhaust you. How well you recover. How quickly you learn. What your strengths are. And your talents."

"What do you mean by 'talents'?"

"That's a loaded question." He picked up his wineglass and spun it in his hand, then he put it under his nose and inhaled deeply. "All people have talents. Things they're naturally good at. But when it comes to vampires, that word has a special meaning. You know, most people who get infected, they don't become vampires. The body's immune system fights it off, as it would any other disease. I think that's why, in all the old stories, people had to be bitten so many times."

I remembered that from *Dracula*. It seemed to take three bites.

And you had to lose a lot of blood too, which I guess made you weaker. It made me wonder: if you were healthy, how many times could you get bitten and still stay human?

"I only got bitten once," I said.

Mr. Entwistle's eyebrows rose in surprise. Then his face relaxed. "But you were young. Maybe that had something to do with it. Vampires don't usually bite children."

I nodded.

"You are the only child vampire I've ever seen who has survived," Mr. Entwistle continued. "But that's not what I'm getting at. The whole talent thing has to do with the pathogen. From what I can tell, it's like a kind of retrovirus. Do you know what that means?"

I shook my head.

"It means it's a kind of virus that alters the DNA of the host. Sometimes the results are bizarre, the sort of stuff that fills fantasy stories. Witches. Wizards. I've met vampires that could breathe underwater, walk through fire, pass through walls, make themselves as light as air, rip steel, travel out of their bodies, change their shape, read people's thoughts. There are as many talents as there are vampires. We are unique, after all, like the rest of God's creatures."

"What's your talent?" I asked him.

"I can drink," he said, and laughed. Then he stopped abruptly and cleared his throat. "Well, that's more of a hobby than a talent, really. No, I see things. Visions. Snippets of the future, the past, the present. That's what led me to you. I had a vision of a boy. Oh, it was months ago now. A child vampire. I was amazed at first. Then saddened. He was starving and lonely. Then I had one again last month. And another. And another. Just about every night, come to think of it."

"What did you see?"

"I saw you alone most of the time. Reading. Running. Boy, for a young blood, you've got some speed."

I looked away, a bit embarrassed, but the tone of his voice drew me back.

"I saw you chased from your room by the cops. And I saw . . ." He stopped to clear his throat. "I saw what is hunting you."

Chapter 18
The Boogeyman

Mr. Entwistle let out a deep breath. His head tilted sideways but he kept his eyes on me. "You mentioned a name earlier," he said.

"The Baron Vrolok."

He shook his head. "That can't be real. *Vrolok* is the Slavic word for vampire, or werewolf. Centuries ago, they were thought to be the same creature. Perhaps they are. But Vrolok is an assumed name. An alias. No one would be called 'Baron Vampire.'"

"But you've seen him?"

"Yes, if we're talking about the same vampire. Glimpses of the past, mostly. Atrocities we won't speak of. He's old, boy. And insane. They call him 'the Impaler'—for good reason. I have a book on him upstairs. Grim reading. When I saw that your paths were destined to cross, it nearly undid me. I couldn't sleep. For weeks I was haunted because I knew the danger, but I didn't know where to find you. I got frantic. Then I had another vision. You were talking to a nurse, the same one you were standing with a few nights ago. Pretty little thing."

I remembered the expression on his face when he saw Nurse Ophelia that first time—a flicker of recognition.

"Well," he continued, "once I knew you were in a medical facility, it was enough to start a search. And so it has ended." He smiled, but there was something in his eyes that made me doubt my troubles were over.

"What is going to happen to me?" I asked.

His hands moved apart just a bit. It was a kind of shrug. "Who knows?" he said.

Was he drunk already? He'd just told me he could see the future.

"I thought you said you have visions."

This made him laugh. "Yes, but I don't get to choose. I only see bits and pieces of what might happen. Possibilities. The future is never set. It moves. It changes. Most of what I see never comes to pass . . . thankfully."

He leaned forward and his head tipped up, as though what he was about to say was particularly important. "You have my protection now, which is no small thing. You'd have to dig your way to China to find another vampire as old as I am. Don't worry about the future just yet. Do what is right, for the right reasons, and the rest will take care of itself."

He got up and walked towards the stairs in the front hall.

"Time for sleep now," he announced. "I haven't done this much talking since the Nuremberg Trials."

He waved for me to follow him up the stairs, then led me to a guest room. Inside was a canopied bed. The window beside it was boarded over. A pile of magazines sat on the floor.

"You'll be safe in here," he said. Then he turned to go.

"Wait," I said.

"What is it?"

"My uncle was supposed to come and get me," I said. "That's why I ran outside when I did. I thought you were him at first."

"He'll be worried, no doubt."

I nodded. "He was coming to break me out."

Mr. Entwistle turned his head just slightly, as though he needed to look at me differently to see if this was true.

"To break you out?"

"Yes. He was worried, just like you were. He told me about Vrolok. And about Johansson."

"Who's Johansson?"

"One of the Fallen," I said. "He's with the police. I was running from him when you arrived."

"And who is your uncle?"

"Maximilian," I said. "He's a vampire hunter. Like my dad."

Mr. Entwistle looked at me with an expression of disbelief on his face. He put a hand against the wall as if to steady himself.

"Maximilian is your uncle?"

"You know him?"

"Know him? Know him! He's like the Boogeyman to us. *Maximilian.* And I practically kidnapped his nephew. Great. Just great." He pushed his hair back from his forehead and looked down at the floor. "Wait a minute," he said. "He must know you're a vampire."

"Yes. He was the one who told me."

"And he didn't kill you for it. Well, that's promising." He walked to the hall window and looked outside. "We'll need to get in touch with him. But not right now."

"Why not?"

He raised his hand and gestured towards the backyard. "The sun will be up soon. If I've learned anything in the last six hundred and fifty years, it's this: don't tempt fate. Your uncle is a vampire hunter. The most feared man in the western world. He has contacts everywhere. And he kills people like us. You'll have to forgive me for not inviting him into my house just before the sun rises."

I was surprised to hear him talk this way. And embarrassed. I'd always thought I read people very well. I trusted my uncle. Truth is, I trusted most people. But in his case, I believed he had a genuine interest in my safety. If he'd wanted me dead, I'm sure he could have managed it quite easily by now.

"Sorry," Mr. Entwistle said. "We can talk more about it tomorrow night. There will be a way to get in touch with him, but I'd rather err on the side of caution. For vampires, this is a sanctuary. No one can know about it. Especially not people like your uncle." He leaned forward and raised his eyebrows. "Or it won't be safe."

I nodded. Then we said good night.

A few minutes later I was stretched out on the guest bed. It was the first time in recent memory that I'd spent a night outside of the ward. I wasn't exactly nervous, but it did feel a bit weird. And not just because the room was different. My mind was muddled. Mr. Entwistle's comments about my uncle had made me see things differently. I guess I couldn't blame him for being worried. I hadn't really seen Maximilian from a vampire's point of view. Things were obviously more complicated than I'd thought. My life had been so simple before. And easy. But not any more.

Chapter 19
The Vampire Problem

I slept late the next day, probably because of all the running Mr. Entwistle and I had done the night before. The sun had been down for about an hour when he came to wake me. He was dressed in his body armour.

"Sleep okay?" he asked. He had his hand on the doorknob and was leaning in from the hallway.

I stretched and yawned, then clamped my eyelids down to try to wake myself up.

"I have to go out," Mr. Entwistle continued. "I'm going to try to get us some blood."

I sat up. "Good," I said. "I'm starving."

Mr. Entwistle looked at me funny. "Starving?"

"Yeah."

He stepped into the room. "You're starving?"

I nodded again.

"But you drank yesterday. I watched you."

"So did you," I said.

"Yes. But I won't need blood again for another week, at least. I'm just getting more because I've run out and some might be available, not because I need to drink it right now."

Well, this was weird.

"I usually drink twice a day," I said.

He looked at me like I had two heads. "Twice a day?" He thought for a moment. "Must be that cow swill you were drinking. Vampires don't need that much blood. Not when they get the real stuff."

"Really?"

"Haven't you seen the movie *Dracula*? He drinks a woman dry and sleeps for a hundred years."

"I thought that was just a story."

"Well, it is. Or that part of it."

"Have you ever slept for a hundred years?"

"Well, no. But . . . but you can't do that nowadays. The world changes too quickly. If I'd fallen asleep a hundred years ago, I wouldn't know what a car was. Or an electrical appliance. Or airplanes, movie theatres, radios, televisions, push-up bras, computers, telephones, Velcro. Why, I'd be useless. But that's not the point. A vampire should be able to drink and coast for a while. Twice a day!"

I guess as a vampire I didn't quite have my act together yet.

"So you're going out?" I asked. "Should I come?"

He shook his head. "No. Too dangerous. You need to relax. Think. Sleep some more. Start writing the great Canadian novel. I won't be long. An hour, tops."

"Where are you going?"

"Blood donor clinic. They're closing in another half hour, so I've got to hurry." He turned to the door, then stopped. "By the way, I've been thinking about your uncle."

"What about him?"

"I think it's time for Maximilian and me to sit down and settle our differences."

"What differences?"

He took a deep breath and let it out slowly. "There are a lot of opinions about how to solve the vampire problem."

I sat up and swung my legs out of the bed. "You mean that we exist?"

"More or less. Some people want to see us wiped from the face of the earth . . ."

"I don't think my uncle is one of them," I said.

Mr. Entwistle cleared his throat. "Maybe not. But it is how he deals with the rogues."

"The bad ones."

"Exactly."

I think I understood this. After all, weren't most vampires evil? "How else are you supposed to deal with them?" I asked.

"In a word, forgiveness. 'Am I not destroying my enemies when I make friends of them?' Abraham Lincoln."

Abraham Lincoln. I'd heard that name somewhere. "Is he that guy with the beard?"

Mr. Entwistle shook his head in disbelief. "Guy with the beard? Guy with the beard! Is that what they're teaching you kids in school these days?"

I shrugged. "I don't know. I've never been to school."

This seemed to stump him completely. He was speechless for about ten seconds.

"Never been to high school?"

I nodded.

"It's the most important time of a young man's life!"

He must have seen that this bothered me, because he flipped his hand through the air like it didn't matter at all.

"So what? I never went either. And I'm richer than Bill Gates."

"Really?"

"Well, rich in memories." He smiled again, then his face flattened out and his voice got a little more serious. "Don't worry, boy. There's a reason for everything. Why my wife and son died. And my daughter. Why we have this contagion. And if there is a reason for your being here, it might just be so that your uncle and I can find a way forward without having to declare war on each other."

I was scratching my head when he said this. I stopped and looked at him carefully. What did he mean? I was afraid to ask. In his body armour, he looked more formidable than anyone I'd ever seen. But it was more than that. He had a kind of inner strength. A confidence. My uncle had it, too. I didn't want them to be enemies. And I didn't want to be stuck in the middle. It was bad enough that Vrolok was after me.

"Where does the Baron Vrolok fit into this?" I asked.

"That conversation will have to wait." He pulled up his sleeve and checked his watch. "Yeah. I need to boogie. Clock's ticking." He stopped in the doorway. "We'll get in touch with your uncle when I get back."

"Is that a promise?" I asked.

"I make no promises. My word is my bond." He smiled a tight-lipped, goodbye kind of smile, then nodded. "And until I get back, you're grounded."

"What does *that* mean?"

"You can't leave the house. That's the way it is when you go underground. You have to stay out of sight until the coast is clear."

"For how long?"

"No idea. But the library's down the hall. That should keep you out of trouble for at least a few centuries. Hopefully, by then your troubles will be over." Then he grunted a goodbye and slipped out the door.

Chapter 20
Collision

After Mr. Entwistle left, I lay in bed for a few minutes flipping through magazines and thinking over what I should do. My brain kept taking me back to the vampire problem—about the rogues, the bad ones—as though that was somehow the secret to figuring everything out. I was going to have to ask Mr. Entwistle more about it. And about Vrolok, in particular. If that wasn't his real name, I had to find out who he was and what powers he had. Talents, Mr. Entwistle had called them. Was he a shape-shifter? Could he walk through fire or breathe under water? It made me wonder what *my* talents might be. Before long I was out of bed and pacing the room.

Walking up walls. That would be cool. Just like Spider-Man. Maybe I could build my own web-shooters, too. Of course flying would be better, but I couldn't really imagine how that would work. I mean, if you were light enough to fly, wouldn't you sort of float around all the time? Maybe there was more to it than that.

I'd never even had any flying dreams, so I wasn't exactly qualified to say. Charlie got them all the time, so if he became a vampire, maybe that would be his talent. Then he'd never have to worry about getting caught. Of course, if I could turn invisible, that would pretty much solve things, too. And getting blood wouldn't be a problem. I could just sneak into the civic hospital and drink it out of bags.

As I pictured myself gorging on a huge stash of blood, my stomach rumbled. A hollow spasm followed. It was time to feed. I stepped out into the hall to have a look around. I thought there might be a supply of blood hiding someplace. And if not, then at least I was moving. That might take my mind off my hunger.

I started my search in the kitchen, but the only thing in the fridge was wine. The cupboards were empty, too—nothing but dusty plates and a box of light bulbs. I went down into the basement. Three doors opened off a central hall. The first room had padded walls and a padded floor and ceiling. I'd seen a couple of these back at the ward, although I didn't remember the ceilings being padded. I guess when vampires got put in time-out, they were a little more jumpy than normal people. Next to the padded room was an office. The computer on the desk wouldn't have been out of place on the Starship *Enterprise*. Newspaper clippings were tacked to the wall beside it. Most of them had to do with people disappearing. The last room was full of filing cabinets. They were all locked.

I went back upstairs. There was nothing in the bedrooms but magazines and closets. Then I found the library. It stretched the whole length of the house and was lined with wall-to-wall bookshelves. Other volumes were piled in stacks on the floor. The room was practically groaning from the weight of them all. Mr. Entwistle wasn't kidding—it would have taken centuries to read them all. Most of the books were old. *Very* old. And even though I've heard a lot of people say you shouldn't judge a book by its cover, well, you sort of can with an old book, because if it was crummy someone would have thrown it out a long time ago. So you can bet I was pretty excited.

The only light in the room came from a gas fireplace that was set in the wall opposite the door. Two windows sat on either side, and through these I could see the yellow glow of a streetlight outside, and the dark silhouettes of leaves and branches. It was like they were waving to me, begging me to come outside and join them. Plunging into the darkness for a long run would have to wait. Without Mr. Entwistle, I wasn't going anywhere.

I was just deciding where to begin my search for books about vampires when something fluttered across the window. I caught a glimpse of a dark shape out of the corner of my eye. When I turned it was gone, so I moved closer, to get a broader view of the yard outside. The night air was so thick with fog you couldn't see the sky. It made the neighbouring houses look hazy and ghostly. Bats were diving under the streetlight in search of food. That must have been what caught my eye. In the shadows below, two green, glowing eyes blinked up at me. It was a raccoon. We stared at each other, then it bolted from its hiding place and disappeared. As I watched the fog roll past, the porch lights across the street faded to a soft white. The street lamp all but disappeared. So did the bats. I thought at first that they were just hard to spot in the haze, but when I listened for them, I couldn't hear anything. A chill went through me and I shuddered. A cold had settled into the room. And a quiet. I held my breath, but all I could hear was the sound of my heart and the wooden floor creaking under my feet.

I backed away from the window. I probably shouldn't have been so close to it anyway, in case someone saw me. Then I realized I was being silly. With all the fog, anyone in the yard would have needed X-ray vision to see up here. Still, I couldn't shake the feeling that something wasn't quite right. I snuck back to the window and edged one eye past the frame. Something flew past and I jumped back again. It was a large bat. The biggest I'd ever seen.

I hid behind the rocking chair so that the back of it was between me and the window. The flapping of large, leathery wings returned. This time it didn't go away. And it was much louder than it should have been. I peeked around the edge of the chair. The bat was hovering right outside the window. Wait a minute—hovering? That wasn't right. I was hardly what you'd call an expert, but I'd spent enough time running the city streets after midnight to know that bats darted. They were always on the move. You'd never see a bat soar like a hawk, that's for sure. They sort of flopped through the air, instead. They could do it pretty quickly, but you'd never call it graceful. This one just . . . *hovered*. It was unnatural. And it raised goosebumps on my arms and neck.

I stayed hidden behind the chair until I heard the sound of tires crunching on gravel. Someone was pulling into the driveway. I stiffened at the sound. Then I noticed that the flapping had stopped. A car door slammed. Then another. I didn't want to risk going to the window to see who it might be, not with that bat outside. It looked big enough to tear the beak off a bald eagle. It didn't take a genius to figure out what that meant. Not after listening to Mr. Entwistle's description of vampire talents. Some were shape-shifters. He'd said so himself, and the stories were full of things like that. It seemed crazy, but then again, three days ago I'd been nothing more than a kid with a bad sun allergy. I couldn't take anything for granted any more.

I quickly tiptoed out of the room. I reached the top of the stairs just as several sets of feet climbed onto the porch. The old planks creaked. I heard whispers. I hesitated. There was no way I was going to go down into the hall. But I had to know who it was. A sinister thought had taken form in the back of my mind. Dracula, the same vampire who could turn himself into a bat, couldn't enter a stranger's house without an invitation. That usually meant having a human servant break in first, then open a door or window. Once he'd even got a dog to break in for him, or maybe it was a wolf. I couldn't remember.

I bent down so I could see through the hallway onto the porch, but there were no windows set in the door and none beside it, either, so there was no way to see who was lurking outside. I did notice that a steel bar had been set across the back of the door, sitting in a pair of brackets. I didn't remember Mr. Entwistle barring the door when we came home. He must have set it up that way before he left.

I strained to listen, then something crashed against the door. It sounded like a wrecking ball. The whole place shook. A crack appeared in the middle of the door and bits of plaster dropped from the hall ceiling.

The people outside were smashing their way in!

I tore down the stairs just as another crash sounded from the porch. The door broke apart, but the bar remained in place. Through the opening I could see two policemen. They were holding something between them that looked like a small battering ram. Off to one side was a man in an overcoat with a thick, pink scar under his eye. Everett Johansson. Somehow, he had found me.

I ran out of the hall, through the living room and into the kitchen. I had to find a back door. It was on the far side of the stove. I could see another pair of brackets and a steel pipe lying on the counter. Since this door wasn't barred, I figured Mr. Entwistle must have left this way.

I could hear voices shouting behind me, then a loud clank, which I guessed was the steel bar on the front door falling to the floor. The men were coming inside, only seconds away.

I yanked on the handle of the back door, but it didn't open.

"Come on," I shouted. I kept pulling, then noticed it was locked. None of the rooms in the Nicholls Ward had locks, so I'd sort of forgotten about them. I twisted the deadbolt and pulled the door open. Then I grabbed the steel bar, just in case, and darted outside.

Men were entering the kitchen as I cleared the landing. In four steps I was around the side of the house. I coiled my body for a mid-stride leap, then launched myself up onto the lower branch of a tree. I used this as a springboard and cleared the neighbour's fence. I couldn't tell if anyone had seen me, but I wasn't taking any chances. I just kept running through the fog. Full blast.

I jumped another fence, and another. It made me think of men running hurdles at the Olympics, only these were six feet high. When I reached the last property on the block I ditched the pipe. It was slowing me down. Then I tore across the road and into the next yard. I wanted to stay off the streets. There was too much light. I ran through people's yards instead. Dogs barked. Lights came on. People shouted. I didn't stop, not for anything. My feet were moving so quickly that, if the earth had opened up below me, I would have run through the air. And the whole time, I had only one thing on my mind.

Vrolok had found me. My father's killer.

Wasn't that place supposed to be a safe house? And where was Mr. Entwistle?

I laboured on. All I could hear was my own frantic breathing. I thought it best to hold a straight line and put as much distance between me and the bad guys as I could manage. Soon, it was like I was running in a tunnel. My eyes took in nothing that wasn't right in front of me. So I didn't react when I heard a loud roar and a scream. It took me too long to sort out what it was. The roar turned out to be a car horn, and the scream was skidding tires. It was a police van. I'd reached the end of someone's property and had run onto the street without looking. The police must have been searching for me. They were moving quickly. And so there was little I could do. I just lifted my feet and curled up into a ball so that my legs hit the grille and my shoulder hit the windshield. And then I was airborne.

Chapter 21
Homecoming

I remember an explosion of light. Pain followed. Then a sharp snap from inside my body somewhere. And more pain. Then darkness.

When my eyes started working again I was lying on my back with my arm twisted underneath me. It was broken. My stomach was bucking. Even though it was empty, it still wanted me to throw up. The whole world was spinning around me. Even when I closed my eyes.

I managed to sit up. The pain in my broken arm made my vision go black and for a few seconds I think I was unconscious again. Then I put my one good hand against the side of my head and rocked back and forth, moaning.

I was vaguely aware of people approaching. I didn't know who. I didn't care. I just wanted them to go away. I wanted to be back at the ward. To have my dinner with Nurse Ophelia. And ping-pong fights with Charlie. And I wanted the pain to stop. What I got instead were two voices just above me.

". . . not your fault. Came out of nowhere."

". . . kid move so fast!"

". . . never seen anything . . ."

"Are you okay?"

". . . look like anything's broken?"

"Can you hear me?"

". . . neck seems fine . . ."

". . . at his arm . . ."

". . . kid from the ward . . ."

Then one of them touched me. That was a big mistake.

I'd always suspected that I was much stronger than other kids my age. This wasn't just a vampire thing, it was also because I lifted weights every night. Turned out my strength was off the charts. I didn't really understand that until I felt the policeman's hand on my shoulder. He was wearing a bulletproof vest. I think they all wear them now, which is good. It probably saved his life. I balled my fist and smashed it into his chest. I didn't even see where he landed.

Then I screamed. It wasn't a shrill scream, the kind of sound a person makes when they're afraid. It was more like something you'd expect to come from the mouth of an angry predator. I was furious. Then I was back on my feet, running. I can guess that the police tried to catch me. They never got close.

In time, maybe an hour, my rage started to subside. I slowed and listened. Cars. Distant voices. The hum of electricity. Feet shuffling on the sidewalk around the corner. Rustling leaves and creaking branches. Nothing out of the ordinary. I was alone. And I had no idea what to do. I should have asked Mr. Entwistle before he left where the blood donor clinic was. If I had, maybe I could have figured out why he hadn't come back.

I decided to keep running.

More time passed. I looked at my arm. It was black just below the elbow, and it had a crook in it. I'd been cradling it in my other hand. It didn't feel as painful now. More itchy than anything. And it throbbed as I ran.

What I needed was blood. According to Mr. Entwistle, that would speed up my healing. But I also needed a safe place to hide. So I kept running, oblivious to the houses and blocks as they passed, until I found myself in familiar territory—my old neighbourhood. I turned a corner and just like that, I was standing in front of our old house on O'Carroll Avenue.

I don't know why I chose to go there. Maybe a part of my memory decided for me. I think it must have remembered that I'd once been safe there. And loved.

I stood at the end of the front walk, uncertain. Now that I wasn't moving, I felt very exposed, so I dashed over to the neighbour's place and hid behind a tree. Then I just stared at the house, thinking. The lights inside were off, but it was late. Maybe eleven o'clock. The older couple who lived there now must have been sleeping. I crept out from behind the tree, then I noticed that the big RV that was usually parked in the driveway was gone. It probably meant that they were away. I'd just have to chance it.

I sprinted into the backyard. I hadn't seen it in eight years and it was totally unfamiliar. Everything looked smaller than it should have been. Our old apple tree was gone, and instead of the hedge there was a fence. I crept up to the back door and tried to open it. It was locked. Even with one arm broken I probably could have torn it off the hinges, but I didn't want to damage anything if I didn't have to, so I tried the basement windows. The first one was locked too, but the second one wasn't. It was one of those sliding windows. The wide and short kind. It made a hissing noise as I opened it, and it seemed so loud to me that I was afraid the whole neighbourhood might wake up.

I had to slide in feet first. There was a huge laundry sink underneath, the kind that's made of cement and looks like a big feeding trough, so I didn't have far to go. Fortunately the sink was empty. As soon as I was inside I turned around, slid the window shut and locked it behind me. Instantly, I felt safer. I could actually breathe without worrying about all the noise I was making. After a few deep breaths, my heart began to settle. As it did, the throb in my arm returned.

There was a washing machine beside me. The floor was covered in stuff, mostly boxes and clothes. The room didn't seem familiar, especially the smell. It wasn't foul, but it wasn't a clean smell, either.

I stepped out of the sink and listened. Nothing. To my left was a set of wooden stairs that led to the back hallway. It didn't look as familiar as it should have. Too small. Too worn. I climbed them slowly, cringing each time the old wood creaked. At the top of the steps was a door. I tried to push it open quietly, but it was stuck at the bottom, so when I put some weight behind it, it opened with a pop. And that's when I discovered what the strange smell was. It was a dog. A big husky. It was waiting for me in the back hall. And it didn't look happy.

Animals are a bit like people. You meet some nice ones and some that are a little prickly. This dog was a walking cactus. Its eyes didn't even get along—one was blue and the other was green. But I could see right away that all of his teeth were alike. Long and sharp and white. The way he showed them off, you could tell he was very proud of this.

He snarled, took a few quick steps and lunged at me. I was just fast enough to back up and close the basement door. My heart started pounding again.

The dog was now barking loudly and scratching at the door. With the luck I was having, the neighbours were probably going to show up any minute with torches and pitchforks. There was no way I could stick around with Barky making so much noise, so I ran down the steps and climbed into the sink again. I was aiming to crawl out, but my broken arm was still useless, and the window was too high for me to manage without something taller to stand on. The lights were still off, so I had to fumble around looking for a chair or a stool to put in the sink. In the end, I found something else, and I decided to go upstairs instead and try my luck with Barky.

I'd once read a book by Jack London, *The Call of the Wild*. Actually, my dad read it to me. And we watched the movie on TV. The story is about a dog, Buck. In one scene, he gets thrashed by a man with a stick. Apparently, that's how you establish who's boss. Well, I figured there were lots of ways of showing someone who was boss. And whoever heard of a vampire running away from a dog?

Barky was still scratching at the door when I hit the top of the stairs. He was making more noise than a police siren. I turned the door handle and pushed it open with all the strength I could muster. It wasn't easy. I was carrying an awkward load in my one good arm. But even with all my heavy breathing, and Barky's barking, I could still hear his claws scraping over the tile floor as I forced him backwards. The door opened just enough for me to lean my shoulder in. That was all the space I needed.

I leaned over and dumped my awkward load onto the floor. It was a big bag of dog food, one of those fifty-pounders that old people buy because it probably saves them ten cents. Kibble spilled everywhere. About ten years' worth. And just like that, Barky was my best friend. I didn't even need a stick.

I waited behind the door while he filled his belly. I was feeling jealous. Without a blender and a bag of blood, I wasn't going to be eating anytime soon. And that meant my arm was going to be useless for a while.

After a minute, I stuck my head out and said hello. Barky ignored me completely. He wasn't eating the kibble so much as he was vacuuming it up with his mouth. This gave me a chance to look around. And that was when they hit me. Old memories. I guess it happened because my nerves were a little more settled, but a flood of things I'd forgotten all about came back from some part of my brain I hadn't talked to in a long while.

I could hear my father's voice calling me for dinner. I remembered how he hummed or sang whenever he cooked. Just bits of songs. Never a whole one.

Other things came back. The sound of the back door slamming, all the times I'd gone crashing out into the yard. Coming in from the cold and kicking off wet winter boots. How my dad used to straighten them all the time so that they were always waiting in a row. The vent we dried our mittens on.

My stomach began to tighten.

I left Barky in the back hall stuffing his face. There was a door separating the back hall from the rest of the house, so I closed it to keep him from following me, then I made my way to the stairs. I didn't bother going into the living room or exploring the rest of the house. You would think it might have made me happy to be home after so many years, but it wasn't like that. I felt like an intruder. Or a ghost. Like my body was in the present, in the house as it was now, but my mind was stuck in the past, in my home as it used to be. It made me feel very lonely. Like my life was gone somehow.

At the ward, when I felt this way and got all quiet, it wasn't really because I didn't want to talk to anyone, it was because I only wanted to talk to my parents. My father, as I remembered him. And my mother, as I imagined her.

So I was talking to them as I climbed the stairs and turned down the hall to my old room. I opened the door and stared inside. It looked like a guest bedroom now. Right in the middle was a tall brass bed. It smelled dusty. Unused. I sat on the edge of it and looked out the window at our neighbour's house. Its two front windows loomed on either side above the door. As a kid, I thought it made the house look like a face. And there it was, staring at me again. It was the only familiar thing there.

More memories came back. I couldn't turn them off, even though I was tired and my head felt thick, like it was full of jelly. Mostly I remembered stories my father had read to me. When I couldn't sleep, I'd creep into his room across the hall. Sometimes he'd have fallen asleep watching the news, so the TV would still be on. Other times, after we'd been watching a movie, the room would still smell like buttered popcorn. I thought it was funny that he always cooked it in a pot on the stove even though we had a microwave.

I didn't sit still for very long. I was exhausted. I couldn't feed, so I decided the next best thing was to get some sleep, even though the sun wouldn't be up for a long time. I considered lying under the bed, but then I remembered my dad's closet. It was big, the kind you could walk right into. But more importantly, it had no windows, so when the sun came up it would be pitch black in there.

My dad's closet had always been off limits. One time, I snuck in just before Christmas to see if there were any presents hidden there, but I didn't find anything. Just the same, when he found out, he exploded. It was the only time I remember being afraid of him. He was furious.

Like everything else, the closet was much smaller than I remembered, but it was deep enough for me to lie down flat. There were two rows of clothes hanging inside, and everything smelled like mothballs.

I lay on my back and rested my broken arm on my stomach. The bone might already have mended, I couldn't be sure. The black coloration was gone. It was yellow now. And the odd crook in it had fixed itself somehow so it didn't have that funny bend to it.

I was feeling beat, but I wasn't really sleepy, for some reason. My body was certainly happy to be resting, but my brain was still going sixty miles an hour. I wondered what Charlie would have made of all this. And Nurse Ophelia. Chases and escapes and more chases. And vampires and giant bats. I wondered if they were all right. If they knew I was in trouble. If they were worried.

I let out a deep sigh and turned my head to the side. There wasn't much to look at, just a baseboard running along the wall, so I ran a finger over the cool wood, tracing the pattern in the grain. Then I noticed there was a seam in it that was nearly invisible. Just a thin, vertical crack so slender you'd have needed eyes like a hawk, or a vampire, to see it.

I lay there for a time, rubbing my fingers over the seam in the baseboard. It was strange that my father never wanted me to see the inside of this closet. There was no way it was just about Christmas presents. This place was off limits all year round, even in mid-July. Who does their Christmas shopping in the summer? As I was thinking this over, my finger kept rubbing the seam, until I got a sliver. I don't know if it was because I was still hungry or what, but I got angry again, so I banged my fist against the wall.

A piece of the baseboard slipped forward. I thought at first I must have broken it. Then I noticed that it had separated where the seam was. A little farther down was another. The board was obviously meant to come loose. I rolled carefully onto my side and pulled it free. In behind was an empty space. I stood and turned on the closet light so I could see better. Then I got down on my knees and reached in. The space wasn't even two feet wide, but it was deep enough to hold a box about the size of a chessboard. I pulled it out carefully and set it on the closet floor. It was covered in dust and looked to be made of tin. I blew the top layer of dust off, then pried up the top and looked inside.

Chapter 22
The Journal

Money. The tin was full of it. Some old. Some new. And it was from all over the place: England, Germany, France, Spain, Italy, Hungary, Nigeria, Libya, Turkey, even Malaysia. Sadly, none of it was Canadian. And there were passports. Four of them. All of them had my father's face, but the names were all wrong: Charles Montagne, Jean Levasseur, Frederick Steinke, Thomas Richardson. There was an empty holster, too. It had been folded and the leather had dried so that it was too stiff to be useful. I guess this didn't matter because there was no gun, but there were several boxes of bullets inside. Many of the bullets had spilled out and were rattling around with all kinds of coins and tokens. No wonder my father never wanted me to go in the closet. If I'd found this stuff as a kid it might have been a disaster, especially if the gun had been there, too. I don't remember my father ever having one, but he must have had a weapon of some kind when he went hunting for vampires.

On the bottom of the tin was a notebook. The cover was a collage of coloured squares. Some of them had neat designs that reminded me of far-off places, like India and Egypt. I recognized it right away. It was my father's journal, the one he wrote in when I was a kid. He always encouraged me to keep one too, but I never got in the habit.

I carefully removed it. The cover was soft and a bit pliable. I lifted it to my nose. It had a musty smell. I flipped it open to the first page. It was dated September 14. I started reading.

Out for Chinese with Jake. Michelle was furious when we got back. Charlie had fooled her into answering the door. By the time she realized nobody was there, he'd locked her out on the porch. We found him and Zack asleep on the sofa watching Invasion of the Body Snatchers. *If we can't get these kids to behave, we're going to run out of babysitters . . .*

I tried to remember what this was about, but I couldn't. Charlie and his father were over a lot when I was a kid. And Michelle? That must have been the babysitter's name, but my mind couldn't dig up a face to go with it. Still, it was kind of funny. Charlie was always getting into trouble as a kid. Not much had changed.

I kept reading, hoping to find something about vampire hunting. It was slow going. My father's handwriting was terrible, as though he'd done most of his writing in the back seat of a car. I had to guess at every fourth or fifth word. And my arm was still throbbing. Still itchy. I had to stop frequently so I could find a position that would make it more comfortable, or just flex my other muscles and try to drive the dull ache somewhere deep where it wouldn't distract me. So that first night I didn't get very far. Although I did discover this one gem. He'd been writing about some work he was hoping to do in Kashmir, and then his writing style became choppier.

Got an emergency call from Mutada in Damascus. N spotted outside village near Kandahar. Will fly out tonight with Max.

The next entry was a few days later.

Cornered N at dawn in a cave. Max flushed him with a gas bomb. Mutada immobilized him perfectly with a Taser. N refused amnesty. Chose to watch the sunrise. Recommended scattering ashes but Mutada took them to villagers instead. They mixed remains with cattle urine and lime dust and painted village gates. Evil to ward off evil, Mutada said.

This was about a vampire. It had to be. I put the book down and tried to picture it. Chasing a vampire from a cave. And a gas bomb. That sounded cool. So did the Taser. I'd seen them on television. They give you a whopper of a shock. I guess they worked on vampires, too.

I read some more, but the next few entries were about a lecture my father was preparing to give on European megaliths. Still, it was better than lying in the dark with nothing to think about but my troubles.

I fell asleep well before the sunrise. I next remember being in my old room. My Spider-Man poster was back on the wall. Toys littered the floor. I was looking over the edge of the top bunk at Charlie, who was just waking up below. Everything looked just as it should have. Only the smell was off. Like mothballs.

"Rise and shine, lazybones," I said.

In an instant the two of us were standing shoulder to shoulder, looking out the bedroom window, only we were in Mr. Entwistle's house, in the library. And Charlie had turned into my dad. He was wearing the suit he usually wore when he gave lectures. It was grey and had flecks of white and black in it.

"Look at all that fog," he said. He reached down and put a hand on my shoulder. "It's like a werewolf movie."

I could hear the flapping of large, leathery wings.

"We should get away from the window," I said. I knew the bat was coming. And I knew what it would turn into.

My father shook his head. "Those aren't bats. Look!"

I pressed my face closer to the glass. A wind was blowing up. It cleared the fog away. Instead of Mr. Entwistle's yard, there was an open field below us. The ground looked charred, as though all the crops had been burned. And it was stained with the blood of dying men and women. As far as the eye could see there were bodies impaled on long stakes. Some of the people were still alive, screaming and quivering. Birds pecked at their eyes and lips.

My father started to laugh. It didn't sound right at all. I turned to look at him but he was gone. In his place was a shorter man. He was thick, like a bear. He stared at me with large, deep-green eyes that were wider apart than they should have been and set above hard cheekbones. Under his pointed nose was a dark moustache. He was wearing a fur cloak, and a red shirt with big gold buttons. Over his heart was a brooch in the shape of a dragon. The dragon had a cross in its mouth. The man's hair was long and flowed from under a hat that reminded me of the spires you see in pictures of far-off churches. But what I noticed most was his mouth. His lips were thick and blood-red. And when he smiled at me he had the teeth of an animal.

I was too scared to move. He reached out and took hold of my arm. Pain ran up my elbow and into my chest. When I tried to pull away, the pain intensified. Then I snapped awake.

There was nothing around me but darkness. And the smell of mothballs. I was back in my father's closet. All I could hear was my heavy breathing. In my sleep, I'd rolled onto my injured arm and it was throbbing painfully. I sat up, grimacing, and tried to cradle it as best I could. It was as if the man's thick fingers were still digging into my skin.

I wondered who he was. And about the bodies. I'd never seen anything like that. My head shook for just a second. A quiver of revulsion. Then I stood up too quickly. My head went dizzy for a few seconds and I had to lean against the door. I needed blood, badly. But the only food in the house was doggy kibble, and I wasn't about to go three rounds with Barky just to get his leftovers. He would have chewed me into Spam.

I decided the best thing was to get moving. Put some distance between me and my nightmare. Those awful images, the bodies and the vampire, had left me feeling nauseous. My belly was empty too, and screaming for blood. Running would cure that, at least for a time. And I still had to find out what had happened to Mr. Entwistle and why Nurse Ophelia hadn't come in to work, and I needed to get in touch with my uncle. It wasn't going to happen if I stayed hidden in a closet.

I turned the light back on and started repacking my father's box. Once all the phony passports and money were in place, I hid it behind the baseboard again. I kept the journal for myself. Then I straightened things up as best I could and went downstairs. I had just decided to go out the front door and risk being seen, rather than go out the back and risk being bitten by Barky, when someone opened the front door.

Chapter 23
A New Plan

I was standing face to face with an elderly man. He was bent slightly at the waist and looked so frail that a gentle breeze might have swept him off the porch. He stared at me for a second. His glasses were so thick they were probably bulletproof. They made his eyes look humongous.

"Who are you?" he asked. "What are you doing here?"

He didn't sound angry, but he was obviously surprised. Since he didn't seem like a mean person, I decided to tell him the truth.

"I was just feeding the dog," I said.

"Oh!" The man looked surprised. Embarrassed, even. He peered back over his shoulder for an instant as though he wasn't sure if he should be there.

"Well, Bert asked me to feed Chaucer. I've been doing it for the past few nights." He cleared his throat. "Who did you say you were again?"

I raised my hands to show him the hospital duds I was wearing. "Just a guy who escaped from the nuthouse," I said.

He laughed.

"I have to be honest," I added. "That dog makes me very uncomfortable. I've fed him, and I was thinking he should be let out, but I don't want to go near him. Do you mind doing it? There's no way he dislikes you as much as he dislikes me."

The older man moved past me into the front hall. "Ah, he's not so bad. He just has to get used to you, that's all." He held out his hand. "It's Al," he said.

"Zachary," I told him. "I'm Dr. Thomson's son."

We shook hands.

"A doctor's son. That would explain the clothes," he said.

I smiled, raised my hand in a quick wave, then slipped out the door. As soon as I hit the street, I felt my lungs expand with a huge breath of relief. Then I started off again.

A plan was taking shape in my mind. I would need food soon. And a safe place from the sun. For that I needed help. I needed my uncle.

I headed to the Brookdale Plaza. It was a strip mall on the edge of my old neighbourhood. There was a bowling alley in the back where Nurse Ophelia took Charlie and me once in a while, and a handful of stores and restaurants. There was also a phone booth near the corner gas station. If I could get a number for Iron Spike Enterprises, my uncle's business, I'd be set. Maximilian would know what to do.

I searched the phone book but found nothing. Then I dialled 411 and got an automated voice. It asked me for the person I was looking for, and the address. When I said I didn't know, it kept asking me to repeat myself. Eventually I got transferred to an operator.

"Iron Spike Enterprises?" she said. Then she asked me what city. I had no idea, so we tried Peterborough, then Toronto, then Ottawa, then Kingston. We found nothing.

"I think the best thing would be to try an Internet search," she said.

I almost bit the end off the phone.

Then I thought of Charlie. He was at his cottage on Stoney Lake. He might have a computer there. I managed to find the number for his cottage in the phone book, but since I had no money, I had to call the operator again. Unfortunately I got a different person and had to go through this whole song and dance about how I was in trouble and needed to make a local person-to-person call. Charlie had once told me that his older brother Dan drank too much wine one Christmas Eve and tried to call the Pope that way. He probably had an easier time of it than I did.

Charlie picked up the phone and the operator asked him if he would accept the call. He didn't seem a bit surprised to be hearing from me.

"I'm glad it's you," he said. "You won't believe what happened. My mom called. She said the cops came to her house. They were looking for you."

"I know," I said. Then I corrected myself. "I mean, I'm not surprised. They came looking for me at the ward, too. I had to run away."

"Wow. The cops. That's sick! What did you do, switch everyone's medication?"

I didn't feel like explaining it to him right then and there. You don't feel terribly safe in a phone booth. The walls are see-through, for one thing. And I kept expecting to hear the sound of oversized bat wings.

"Can I explain later?" I said. "I just have to get out of here. I'm at the Brookdale Plaza. Is there some way you can come and get me?"

"I don't think so. I'm here by myself. Dan won't be back with his kids until tomorrow. He's off riding the roller coaster at Canada's Wonderland."

"Well, I need a place to hide," I said. "I'm in a lot of trouble. I need to get to a computer. I need to call my uncle."

"You have an uncle? Wow! Where's he been all this time? The moon?"

"That's what I thought. It's a long story. Can you come and get me? I don't feel safe here. And I'm starving."

Charlie took a moment to consider.

"Suki might have a car, but it's a bit late to wake her family up . . . Could you take a cab or something? I could pick you up at the marina."

I'd forgotten for just a moment that his cottage was on a small island.

"I don't have any money," I told him.

"It's okay. I've got some. Just get here."

Chapter 24
Charlie's Cottage

The scariest part of that night was waiting for the cab. I suppose it took only two minutes or so to arrive, but every second felt like the tense moment in a horror movie. All that was missing was the creepy music. I hid behind a Dumpster until the cab arrived. Once we got moving, I felt a lot safer, which is usually about that time in the movie when the bad guy jumps out with a chainsaw or something and hacks you to bits. Fortunately nothing happened, and the cabbie got me there in about twenty minutes.

When I climbed out of the car, Charlie was waiting on the dock. He saw me, waved and came over to pay the fare.

"How much is it?" he asked.

I don't know what the cabbie said, but Charlie pulled a wallet out of his back pocket and took out some bills. He handed them through the window to the cabbie and then pushed me roughly on the shoulder.

"Run," he shouted, stepping past me.

I didn't move right away, so he pulled me forward.

"Run!"

I don't know why it is that I don't always do what I'm told. I suppose it's because I usually want to understand what is going on before I make a decision to do anything. It seemed strange that my friend was pulling me towards the dock and screaming in my ear like that guy with the chainsaw had just appeared, but when I saw the cabbie open the door and get out, well, the look on his face told me everything I needed to know. It was pure rage. There's probably a picture of him in a dictionary somewhere under *maniac*. I can picture the words underneath it: "Don't ever, ever cheat this man of his cab fare!"

Charlie must not have had enough money.

I ran. Fortunately, Charlie was ahead of me by quite a bit and had untied the boat. It was a small tin boat with a bright orange engine that made me think of a pumpkin. He didn't bother trying to start it. He just pushed off from the dock. I had to leap.

I was excited, so I jumped too far. Fortunately, I had the presence of mind to drop my father's journal into the boat as I flew over it.

My feet hit the water on the far side, but I managed to turn and grab hold of the boat as I dropped past. An instant later, the coolness of the water seeped through my pants. I kicked my legs and tried to pull myself over the side, but Charlie didn't give me the chance. He fired up the motor, put it into gear and took off. I could hear the cabbie swearing at us from the dock, but I didn't look back for even a second. As soon as the boat started moving it was all I could do to hang on. After my adventures on the Otonabee, I was so scared of drowning that I dug my fingertips into the metal. I could feel it bending from the pressure.

Charlie didn't slow down. Even though there was water spraying everywhere and we were too far out for the cabbie to get us, or even hit us with a rock, he kept the throttle turned up to full. I'm amazed I didn't tear the boat in half. Finally I started shouting at him to slow down, and he cut the engine. He was laughing hysterically.

There must be something contagious about laughter because a second later I started up, too. We were a pair of hyenas. The whole time, I kept trying to climb into the boat, but I was laughing too hard. After a minute, Charlie reached over the side and helped me in.

A second later we were heading down the lake again. I was clutching my father's journal against my stomach, which was grumbling so angrily I'm surprised it didn't crawl out and attack me. And I was getting cold. My clothes were soaked right through. So was the journal. I'd splashed so much water into the boat that it was drenched. I hoped I hadn't wrecked it completely.

Charlie must have known I was really bummed out, because he didn't say a word to me once we were moving. He just let me shiver. All I could think about was how awful things were. My life had gone from painfully dull to totally out of control. And I felt ridiculous because it was what I'd always wanted—an adventure just like Bilbo's. Well, I imagine you've heard the saying "Be careful what you wish for." The wise guy who came up with this one must have had a brain the size of a watermelon. My own adventure had arrived like a kick in the pants. Baron Vrolok and his servants were after me. I was soaked, freezing and penniless, with no way to feed myself. I didn't even have a change of underwear. If there was an adventure survival guide out there someplace, I'd already broken every rule in it. And that wasn't all. While I was screwing up left and right, the people I needed most were disappearing, one at a time. First Nurse Ophelia. Then Mr. Entwistle. It made me really nervous because I was with Charlie now, my best friend. If things kept up the way they were going, well, we were both in for it.

The boat ride to Charlie's cottage was mercifully short. I was shivering so much I'm surprised I didn't chip a tooth. But Charlie's place was warm and cozy. I'd never been in an old-fashioned cottage before, but I'm sure if you ever have, you know exactly what it's like to walk into one for the first time. It has this wonderful smell, like old, sun-baked wood. The design was simple: just a porch, a kitchen, a living room and a master bedroom, all laid out in a row. I'm betting it was just what the survival guide would have recommended.

"I'll get you a towel and some clothes," Charlie said. He disappeared into the bedroom. While he was gone, I sat on the kitchen floor against the cupboards and tried to figure out what to tell him, but it was hard for me to concentrate. The hunger was coming on. Pinched eyes. Churning gut. Itchy throat.

I didn't notice that Charlie was back until he grabbed my wrist.

"What are you doing?" I snapped, jerking my hand away.

"Relax. You want to scratch a hole in your neck?"

I don't know about you, but whenever someone tells me to relax it always has the opposite effect.

Charlie tossed a dry shirt and pair of pants on the floor beside me. "Man, who's pulling on your tail?"

I closed my eyes and took a deep breath. I even tried counting to ten to settle myself down, but I only made it to three. Blood. I swear I could smell it right through Charlie's skin. It made my teeth grind together.

"I need to eat." I kept my eyes closed when I spoke. I was sure if I looked at him, I'd bite him.

"What do I have that you can keep down? You're allergic to everything but air."

"I need blood," I said.

There was a long pause after this. I opened my eyes just to make certain Charlie was still there.

"Blood?" he said.

I nodded. "Yes. Blood. Now. Like, *right now.*"

Charlie was sitting in a kitchen chair. He stood up so that he was looking down at me.

"Oh, blood. Right. Of course, blood. What was I thinking? Well, we just happen to have a huge barrel of it in the back. Do you want some fries with that?"

What should I have expected? But I did need to eat. I didn't want some part of my mind taking over and forcing me to do something unspeakable to my best friend, so I told him the truth.

"I'm a vampire. I got infected eight years ago. I need blood."

We stared at each other for a few seconds, then Charlie started shaking his head.

"You lucky duck," he said.

Chapter 25
Food Trouble

Charlie kept staring at me. I couldn't tell if he was stunned or jealous.

"You believe me?" I asked.

He put his hands on his hips and flashed me a grin like he heard this sort of thing every day. "What do *you* think? I told my dad I thought you were a vampire years ago."

He walked across the kitchen to where I was sitting on the floor, then he reached down and offered me his hand. He was very trusting. If he'd known how much I wanted to help myself to what was flowing through his wrist, he might have run for his boat.

I took his hand and stood up. Then I started changing out of my wet clothes and into the dry ones he'd brought.

"I can't help you with the blood," he said. He started digging through the refrigerator, then he stopped to look at me. I was hopping up and down trying to get my foot through the second pant leg. It was tough because my skin was wet and the material kept bunching up. I bumped into the counter and slipped to the floor.

"Aren't vampires supposed to be super-coordinated?" he said.

What could I say? I was having an off-day.

He turned back to the refrigerator. "What have you been living on?" he asked.

I had to answer him with my teeth clenched. I had never been this hungry. Not ever. "Animal blood of some kind. I don't really know. From a cow, maybe? I thought it was strawberry syrup."

"Would Nurse Ophelia know?"

I nodded. "But she's gone. She never came back to work."

"What do you mean, she never came back?"

"I mean she never came back. The night before I left, she didn't come in. I think something happened to her."

Charlie walked over to the telephone. "I hope not," he said. "Maybe she just got sick."

"She never has before."

"Well then, she was overdue." He picked up the phone and started dialling.

"Who are you calling?" I asked.

"You," he answered.

He waited, then started speaking.

"Hi. It's Charlie Rutherford. I'm calling for Zack Thomson or Ophelia. I was hoping someone could let me know what is happening. If someone could call me back as soon as possible, I would appreciate it. My family is very worried. Thanks." Then he left a number and hung up.

I slipped back to the floor and put both hands over my stomach. I was so hungry I nearly bit myself. I couldn't move. I couldn't lie still. It was worse than being hit by that van.

"Do you know her home number?" Charlie asked me. "Or her last name?" He must have meant Nurse Ophelia.

I shook my head and grunted a no.

"Damn . . ."

Charlie walked over to the fridge and opened the freezer. He took out something that hit the counter like a big block of ice. I heard scraping noises. When I looked up, he was jabbing something with an ice pick. Then he reached down and handed me a cold chunk of pink stuff that looked like part of someone's brain.

"What is it?" I asked.

"Frozen hamburger," he answered.

I knew better than to eat it, so I just sucked on it. It didn't do much. At least, not right away.

"So, you can drink animal blood?"

"I guess so." I waved my hand like I was hailing a taxi. "Keep 'em coming."

For about an hour or so, he fed me frozen hamburger, then frozen steak, then frozen pork chops. I didn't chew on them, I just did my best to drain every bit of moisture from each piece. It helped pass the time while my stomach went nuts.

We talked the whole time. I told him everything, starting with Mr. Entwistle's motorcycle stunt and ending with my flight from Al and Barky.

"I've got an idea," he said. He handed me another piece of frozen pork, then he slipped on his windbreaker and headed for the back door.

"What are you doing?" I asked him.

"Ordering breakfast," he said.

I waited while Charlie did something behind the cottage. He was making a lot of noise. The sound was metallic, like someone shaking cymbals. Then I heard footsteps on the roof. A few minutes later, Charlie came back.

"What was that all about?"

"Squirrel traps," he said.

I fired the last piece of frozen pork into my mouth. "You've gotta be kidding," I said.

"Hey, I'd rather rid the island of squirrels than watch the neighbours' dogs disappear one at a time. Unless you have plans to rob a blood bank?"

He had a point. "Do you think it will work?" I asked.

"What, the traps? Yeah, better than throwing rocks . . ."

"No," I said. "I mean squirrel blood. Do you think I can drink it?"

"I have no idea." He threw up his hands. "Who do I look like, Anne Rice?"

He didn't look a bit like Anne Rice, but I didn't think there was any point in saying so. Instead, I just sat on the floor and held my stomach.

"Here, try sipping this," he suggested. He handed me a glass of water.

I shook my head.

"Blood is mostly water," he said. "If you can drink cows' blood, you should be able to handle this."

That made sense. I put a few drops in my mouth and let them slide around. Then I swallowed. Nothing happened. Nothing bad, anyway, so I took a few more sips. I nodded to Charlie. I was going to be all right. At least for a while.

"So, what will you do in the morning?" he asked me. Morning was about two hours away.

"I need to get in touch with my uncle."

"I was thinking more about the sun," Charlie said. "What are you going to do when it comes up and you can't be in the light?"

"Have you got a place I could hide?" I asked. "Somewhere that's dark?"

"There's the tool shed."

"Won't anyone look in there?"

Charlie laughed. "Dan's a pencil-pusher. Do you think he knows a hammer from a hamster? He spends so much time at the office he barely has the energy to lift a mug of coffee when he comes up. I don't think he's ever been in the shed. But if I tell him there's a vampire in there, I'm sure he'll steer clear of the place."

Chapter 26
Bad Press

I suppose I should have been happy about sleeping in a shed. It was better than turning into charcoal when the sun came up. But there were two windows—one in the door and one above the workbench—and they made me very nervous, even though Charlie had taken a staple gun and nailed garbage bags over both of them.

Around noon the next day he knocked and walked in. I refused to come out of my sleeping bag until he'd closed and locked the door.

"What is it?" I asked from behind my pillow. I was using it like a shield.

Charlie didn't answer, but I heard a racket, like someone dropping a whole bag of silverware down a flight of stairs. I peeked out from behind the pillow. Charlie was holding up his traps, with a triumphant smile on his face. Each had a red squirrel inside. They were making more noise than a marching band.

"What am I supposed to do with those?" I asked.

He shrugged. "Hey, this is *your* thing. What did you expect? Was I supposed to serve them up with some spider goulash?"

He said he'd come back after sunset, and closed the door behind him. I tried going back to sleep, but the squirrels were trying to escape. I was worried the sound of their frantic scurrying would reach the far end of the lake. I considered putting them outside, but I couldn't risk it. The summer sun was strong. And now that I was awake, and there was food in the room, my stomach started barking orders.

You can guess what happened next. I don't want to go into detail, but if you've ever eaten meat, you can't hold this against me. And if you are a vegetarian, well then, I'm really, really sorry. I cried afterwards. I couldn't help myself. I'd never hurt anything before. I'd seen nature shows on TV. Survival of the fittest and the law of the jungle—these weren't new to me. I needed blood to live. And to heal. But knowing this stuff didn't help. Reaching inside a cage to kill a defenceless animal just felt wrong. I swore right then and there that I wasn't ever going to fish for my dinner in a rodent trap again. Preying on the helpless was out. There had to be a better way.

I fell asleep feeling distraught.

Charlie came back just after the sun went down. He was carrying a flashlight and a newspaper. When he opened the door, I could hear other voices coming from the cottage, but I didn't recognize them.

"Dan's back with his kids," Charlie said. "He said there were cops all over the marina. They were passing around photos."

"Of me?" I asked.

"Probably. Dan just said it was a kid. I guess it's lucky he hasn't seen you in a while or he might have told the cops you were a friend of mine."

"How did they get here so quickly?" I asked.

Charlie shrugged. "Must have been the cabbie," he said.

It made sense. If he'd called the police after we took off without paying, he might have identified me.

"Did you hear back from the ward?" I asked.

"No," he said, "but I'm going to try again. I thought I'd wait until Dan is asleep. It won't be much longer. I'll come back when the coast is clear." He passed me the newspaper and smiled.

"What's so funny?" I asked.

Charlie crouched down in front of me. I was sitting with my back against the shed wall. He reached over and opened the paper. Several pages in was a caption that read "Escaped mental patient still at large." There was a small photo of me beside it.

"Zack," he said, "you've been stuck in the nuthouse for eight years. You're out on the weekend for the first time in your life. Did you think you'd be this famous already?"

I folded the newspaper up so that the article was easier to see. Charlie handed me the flashlight.

"Try not to get too bent out of shape about it. Suki's family is here. You can meet Luna. There'll be a party somewhere we can crash. It's time for you to live a little. Have some fun. Whatta you say?"

I nodded. I sure needed something good to happen.

"I'll be back in a bit," he said. Then he slipped quietly out the door.

I turned on the flashlight and read under my sleeping bag. The article was short on detail. It explained how I had escaped from the Nicholls Ward with the help of another man who was involved in a suspected arson downtown. It referred to a second article. I made a mental note to look at that one too, then kept reading. Apparently, I was pretty much guilty of every crime but treason. I'd stolen a car, some hospital supplies, assaulted police officers, resisted arrest, destroyed private property and been an all-around bad person.

I flipped to the other article. "Fire levels Salvation Army: Arson suspect killed in blaze." There were before and after pictures of the Salvation Army. The first one showed a red-brick building with flowers blooming in beds near the door. The second one was a photo of the charred remains. Beside these was a thumbnail sketch of Mr. Entwistle. It made him look like a drugged-out hobo. Underneath was a caption that read, "Do you know this man?" along with a number for Crime Stoppers.

According to the paper, the fire had started shortly after nine o'clock, about the same time Mr. Entwistle had left the safe house. The fire had spread quickly to all four corners of the ground floor, so the Fire Department was pretty sure an accelerant was used. I figured that meant gasoline or something. The article didn't say. But it did say that a few witnesses saw Mr. Entwistle entering the building just before it caught fire and collapsed. He was one of three people crushed or burned. The other names I didn't recognize, but they were apparently Red Cross volunteers.

I read and reread the article, hoping there was something in there that would say for sure what had happened to him. I had to know if he was really dead. But there was nothing in there about finding his body. And no one had actually seen him die. At least, it didn't say so. They didn't even know his name. But there was a reference to the first article about my escape from the Nicholls Ward and his role in that, so they knew something about him.

I couldn't believe he was dead. A man who'd lived for six hundred and fifty years wasn't going to die in a fire. What was the point of having visions if you couldn't see when the building you were in was going to collapse?

I put the paper down and lay back. I didn't want to read any more. I needed to take my mind off things. I was getting sick of getting bad news everywhere I turned. Fortunately, Charlie came back less than a half hour later, so I wasn't stewing by myself for too long. Even before his hand touched the door I could smell something funny. It was either cologne or bug repellent.

"I have some good news and some bad news," Charlie said. "The good news is, I have Dan's BlackBerry. We can use it to get a number for Iron Crown Enterprises."

"Iron *Spike* Enterprises," I said.

"Whatever."

"What's the bad news?" I asked.

"We're out of squirrels," he said. "Just kidding. I got in touch with someone from the Nicholls Ward. Nurse Ophelia hasn't been to work since you left." Then he said something about the woman who'd answered the phone that I won't bother repeating. "She said if Ophelia doesn't show up today she's getting fired."

"Has she called in?" I asked. "Has anyone spoken to her or called her house?"

Charlie shrugged. "The way it sounded, no one has spoken to her."

"What about her last name? Did you find out what it is?"

Charlie shook his head. "No. That stuff is apparently confidential, and the woman wouldn't tell me. Maybe if you called she'd tell you. I don't know."

I tipped my head back against the wall. My heart must have known what my brain was thinking, because it started to pick up the tempo. "I think something's happened to her," I said.

"I hope not. I'll call again tomorrow and see what I can find out." He sat down and let out a long sigh. "Does she know you're a vampire?"

I shrugged. "I think she must."

"I wonder why she didn't tell you."

I wondered that, too. But mostly, I wondered if she was okay.

Charlie put his hand on my shoulder to push himself back up to his feet. Then he offered me his hand and pulled me up from the floor.

"Why would she go back there anyway?" he said.

"What do you mean?"

"Think about it. If she knew you were missing, she'd look for you. She wouldn't go in to work knowing that you might be in trouble. As long as you're gone, she'll be gone."

This made sense. Sort of. Nurse Ophelia wouldn't go back if I were missing. But she'd disappeared before I had, so she might not even have known I was gone. I didn't mention this to Charlie. I figured it would only make him worry more.

"My uncle can help," I said. "Mr. Entwistle said he's the most feared vampire hunter in this part of the world and that he has contacts everywhere. If anyone can find her, he can."

Charlie took out Dan's BlackBerry and started searching for my uncle's business number on the Internet. We tried all the major cities we could think of. Charlie eventually got a hit in Montreal and dialled the number. As soon as it started ringing he handed me the BlackBerry. No one answered. It made me wonder if he'd disappeared too, just like Ophelia and Mr. Entwistle. Then his voice came on and told me I could leave a message.

"It's Zachary," I said. "I'm at a friend's cottage. Please call back as soon as you can. There's been a lot of trouble, and I need your help." Then I left Charlie's number.

"Now what?" I asked.

Charlie took the BlackBerry from me and crammed it into his pocket. "Now?" he said, clapping me on the back. "Now it's time to experience the true joys of having no adults around."

Chapter 27
Meeting Luna

Charlie and I snuck down to the water and climbed into his boat. Within seconds we were speeding off to Suki's cottage. Fortunately, my hunger was gone, which was a relief to both of us, but neither of us had any idea how long that would last. Charlie had brought a couple of the squirrel traps with him. I didn't think it was necessary—I was more or less decided on the rodent issue—but nothing I said would change his mind.

Suki's place turned out to be a house-like cottage on the mainland. I didn't get a look at the inside of it because Charlie didn't think it was a good idea for me to come up to meet her family. Even though it was very unlikely that they'd been to the marina and seen the photo the police were passing around, there might have been something on the news. So while he visited Suki, I sat on the dock and swatted at mosquitoes. It made me wonder what happened if any of them got infected with my blood. Could a mosquito be a vampire? What difference would it make, since they all sucked blood anyway? And what if it delivered my blood to someone else? Could vampirism be spread through mosquitoes, like malaria? It seemed to me that it wasn't too likely, or there would have been a lot more of us around.

About ten minutes later, Charlie came back down to the dock. "We're going to an island party," he said. "Unless you want to try your luck with the cops at the marina?"

An island party sounded like a pretty dangerous idea to me. After all, if you want to avoid attracting attention, bury yourself under a tree or something. Don't go to a party. But I wasn't about to argue. I didn't have anywhere else to go. I was like a guy on a train. I could ride it to wherever it was going or I could take my chances and jump off somewhere along the way. An island party sounded pretty stupid, but it also sounded like fun, so I wasn't quite ready to jump.

Suki came down to the dock a few minutes later. She didn't really walk, she sort of bounced everywhere. Charlie introduced us.

"So you're the famous Zachary," she said.

I didn't know if this meant that she'd read about me in the paper. All I managed was a limp smile.

"Charlie's told us all about you," she continued.

Well, that was awfully nice of Charlie. I sure was hoping he hadn't mentioned the squirrels.

"It's nice to meet you," I said. And it was. She had a friendly way about her. Sometimes you can tell that about a person straight off.

I didn't notice Luna until she was practically on the dock. She crept down as Suki and I were talking. The way Charlie had talked back at the Nicholls Ward, it was as though we were destined to be the next Romeo and Juliet or something. Well, if you were picturing a romantic first meeting like the kind in the movies where two people gawk at each other because their brains are melting from too much happiness, you're way off. She looked at me and said, "Hi."

That was it. I might have been a fence post. I'm not sure what I'd been expecting myself. That she'd be so pretty my jaw would dislocate when I saw her? It didn't. She looked pretty normal. Two arms, two legs, one head. Long copper curls. Then she looked at me. Her eyes were an emerald green. They suited her.

"We've come to fix your squirrel trouble," Charlie said. He held up the two traps like they were God's answer to the rodent crisis.

Suki laughed so loudly I thought all the squirrels on the mainland might lose their hearing.

"I'm just going to leave these out back," said Charlie. "Nothing like a good bit of roast squirrel to start the day, eh, *Zack*?"

"You said it."

As soon as Charlie disappeared around the edge of the cottage, the rest of us fell quiet. I stood there feeling very foolish because I had no idea what to say, so I just helped Suki climb into her boat, which looked a lot like Charlie's except the motor was newer and less pumpkin-like. I offered her my hand.

"What a gentleman," she said. Then the boat lurched and she kept herself steady by grabbing my arm. She gave the muscle there a squeeze.

"Wow," she said.

I was really glad it was dark because I'm sure I lit up like a Christmas candle. Then I helped Luna in. Too bad, her balance was a little better.

Finally Charlie came back. He hopped into his boat and asked the girls where we were going.

"Elephant," said Suki. Then she and Luna sped off.

"What's Elephant?" I asked, stepping into the boat.

Charlie fired up his motor. "It's an island," he said. Then he twisted the throttle and we bounced down the lake, chasing the girls.

✦ ✦ ✦ ✦

Driving down the lake was like navigating through a dark maze. Islands and rocks and buoys were scattered around like they'd just dropped from the sky. Soon the channel opened up, however, and I could see where we were going: a small shadow of an island that looked like it was on fire.

It *was* on fire. Apparently, this was the whole point of an island party. You made a fire so big the rocks practically melted. As we got closer, I could see the boats and the silhouettes of a few people walking around. Woodsmoke hung in the air, mixing with the odours of gasoline and what I later discovered was beer. But the focus was the bonfire. People orbited around it all night, some sitting, some standing. It was strangely alluring. Curls of orange, red and yellow light, and even small flashes of green and blue leapt from the wood, popping and sparking.

Charlie had beer in his boat, which made him as popular as the ice-cream man. He was generous and fun and everyone knew him, so I was considered all right just because of that. I showed up like his sidekick, and if Batman and Robin had followed us in, I doubt anyone would have noticed. We were that cool. Honest.

Luna sat across from me. She seemed to know everyone, too. And when she laughed, I laughed with her. They were real moments. I'd never really understood that word, *real*. As in "Get real." Or "He was so real." I understood it that night. I was undead, but I was alive, too. And nervous. This was probably a good thing. It kept me from opening my mouth too often, which would have crushed all my coolness to smithereens.

"So, Charlie's one of your friends?" someone asked me.

I decided that when people spoke to me, I'd just answer honestly. "He's my *only* friend," I said.

Everyone thought this was funny.

It was much later at this point, and there were only six of us still sitting around the fire: Charlie, Suki, Luna and me, and twins whose names I've totally forgotten. All I remember was that they had a place on the same shore as Suki and Luna. And one of them had dark hair and the other had bleached his so that the tips were yellow. It was the only way I could tell them apart.

"How did you get to be so . . . ?" Suki held her breath and flexed her arms in a circus-strongman pose. She had downed a few drinks by that time and was speaking very frankly.

"I used to live in a mental ward," I said. "They have a great fitness room there."

She thought this was hilarious.

And so the party continued pretty much like that. It was almost perfect. I didn't get to talk to Luna alone, which would have been nice, but we did talk. At one point, she saw my necklace and asked me what it was.

"It's a full moon," I explained. "It belonged to my father. There's another piece, a gold crescent that fits along one side, but my mother had that part. I've never seen it."

She was sitting beside me. When she spoke she had this habit of reaching out to touch my arm, as though she needed to get my attention every time she had something to say. It made my insides tumble.

"May I?" she asked.

I didn't know what she meant until she reached around my neck. She undid the necklace clasp at the back and pulled the chain free. For just a second her face was so close I could feel her breath on my cheek. Then she sat back down and held up the necklace for a closer look. Although the moon charm was made of silver, the red and orange flames of the bonfire made it look like burning gold.

"It's beautiful," she said.

"I think so, too."

"And you never saw the other part?" she asked.

"No."

"But your mother had it."

"She died when I was two," I said.

"Oh, that's so sad," she said. But she dragged the "so" out for about five minutes, which I guess meant that it was *sooooooooooooooo oooooooooo* sad. Then she asked me how my mother had died.

I wasn't sure what to say. Once, when I was a young kid, I'd asked my father about it, but he never really answered. He just said that sometimes people go away and you never get to see them again. It upset him so much to talk about her that I never asked again after that. I think he would have told me, eventually, if he had lived longer.

"I don't know how she died," I said.

Charlie was surprised by this. "What do you mean, you don't know?"

"I never got the chance to ask my father again before he was killed."

"Your father was killed?" The question was asked so quietly, I don't think anyone heard it but me. Luna spoke in a whisper. She cleared her throat. "Someone killed him?" She was louder the second time.

I nodded.

"Do you know who it was?"

I don't remember who asked this question. Everyone was suddenly part of the conversation. I think it must have been one of the twins.

"Yes," I answered.

"Did they ever catch him?" Suki asked.

I shook my head. "No."

"You must just want to kill him," the blond twin said.

I wasn't sure if it was a question. If it was, I didn't answer it. I didn't even want to think about Vrolok.

"If anyone killed our parents, and I got my hands on them, I don't know what I'd do," Suki said.

This started a conversation between the twins about what they would do if they caught their parents' killer. It sort of turned into a competition. They carried on for a while, until Luna interrupted.

"You don't know what you'd do," she said. I can't remember which twin she was speaking to. It might have been both of them. "Until you're really in a situation," she continued, "you just don't know."

The blond twin disagreed. "If someone killed my parents, they'd have it coming."

Both twins seemed to agree on this. But Luna wasn't finished. "Killing is killing. If it's wrong, it's wrong."

At this point Charlie stood up and heaved another log on the fire. A fountain of sparks exploded into the air. "Enough already," he said. "If you can't agree to disagree, I'm going to have to start chucking people in the lake."

And that was the end of it. For a few quiet minutes, we all just stared at the fire.

I thought about what Luna had said. That killing was wrong. I couldn't imagine arguing against it. But a part of me understood what the twins were saying, too. Vrolok *should* pay for what he'd done. Still, if I got my chance and took revenge, would it make me just as bad? I couldn't decide.

When the blond twin got up for another beer, it seemed to wake everyone up. "Anyone else want a drink?" he asked.

"No thanks," said Luna.

"Come on," said Suki. "One won't kill you."

"I don't like it."

"I don't either," I said. "It smells like water someone boiled running shoes in."

Luna smiled when I said this. I'd seen her smile before, but this one was different. I guess I'd just gotten her off the hook, so this smile was just for me.

Not everyone looks better when they smile. Everyone looks worse when they frown, but not everyone is fortunate enough to have a really good smile. Luna would have given Nurse Ophelia a run for her money. When her lips came together and turned up, her face widened just a bit and her eyes kind of squeezed shut. It was perfect. I guess I must have been staring, because I stopped paying attention to everyone else until Charlie slapped me on the shoulder.

"You get used to it," he said.

"Used to what?"

"The beer. You get used to it."

"Apparently, it takes thirty years," I told him.

He looked at me funny, then nodded over to the dark twin. "You want one?"

The dark twin shook his head without taking his eyes from the fire. He was thinking about something, you could tell.

"What kind of a nutcase kills someone, anyway?" he said to no one in particular. It seemed an odd remark from someone who had just spent the better part of a half hour defending his right to take revenge. I almost told him to go examine his reflection in the lake.

"Luna could tell you about some nutcases," said Suki. "She used to work with young offenders."

Luna had her arms folded across her knees. They made a cradle of sorts for her head. She looked ready to fall asleep. "None of them ever killed anybody," she said.

Charlie took a haul from his beer, then spoke as if he was holding in a burp. "Still, you must have met some headcases."

Luna shook her head. "Not really. But some of them were pretty rough."

"Pretty rough?" Suki said. "One of them robbed a bank with a shotgun."

"Is that true?" asked Charlie.

"Yeah."

"And your parents let you work with people like that?"

"It was a summer camp, not a mercenary camp," said Luna. "It was totally safe. And the kids were great."

"They sound great," said Charlie. The twins laughed. Charlie clapped me on the back. "Well, we've found the way to her heart, Zack. All you need is a shotgun."

I think I must have blushed when Charlie said this, like the whole point of the night was to set me up with Luna. I guess in his mind it was.

Suki tried her best to look miffed. "I think it's very brave that my sister worked with young offenders."

"It's not that big a deal," said Luna. "They aren't much different from any of us."

Charlie wasn't buying it. "Has anyone here robbed a bank lately?" he asked.

"That's not what I mean," said Luna. I could tell she was frustrated. She looked as if she were about to say more. Then she changed her mind.

"I know what you mean," I said. I hadn't spoken in a while. It seemed to surprise everyone. "I used to live in a mental ward," I added, and everyone went quiet.

The twins looked at each other and then at Charlie. They laughed. He didn't.

"I thought you were joking about that," said Suki.

I shook my head. "I was seven when my father died," I explained. "I got really sick and went into a coma. When I came out of it, I was angry all the time. And there was no one around to look after me. I guess I had nowhere else to go." I talked a bit about how nice everyone there was. Jacob and Sad Stephen. Even the Chicago Man. "They don't have easy lives either," I added when I was finished.

Luna was looking at me. She must have understood. I guess the same was probably true for the kids she worked with. Their lives weren't easy. But you can find a reason to like just about anyone. You just have to do a little digging sometimes.

"You seem pretty normal," Suki said to me.

"He's anything *but* normal," said Charlie.

Suki laughed. She had her arms around his waist. It looked very comfortable. She gave him a squeeze.

And that led to a discussion about what "normal" is, which led to families and home life and whatever. I guess that's when I learned that talking in groups is really hard because everyone has to have their turn, and so you don't always get to say what's on your mind, and you have to listen to everyone when you really only want to listen to one person. I kept asking Luna questions about her old job and the kids she worked with, and other things, but with four other people chiming in, I didn't get as much from her as I would have liked.

Then suddenly it was time for everyone to go.

Charlie and I escorted Luna and Suki home, which basically meant we followed them in the boat. Luna and I did the driving because neither of us had been drinking. I'd never driven a motorboat before, but it was a little easier than steering a Ford Mustang at eight hundred miles an hour from the wrong seat. Charlie helped me navigate so I didn't hit a rock or an island, and that was the main thing. As I got close to their dock, I didn't know what to do, so I just cut the engine and we drifted in.

"That was a lot of fun," said Suki. Her voice was so loud, I noticed, that even the bats in the air turned away from us. Luna must have been worried about waking up the rest of the lake because she put her arms around her sister, then shushed her by lifting a finger to her lips.

Suki started giggling. "Sorry," she whispered.

Charlie climbed out of the boat. I was amazed he didn't fall in. "Gonna get me some squirrel meat," he said.

"What's with the squirrels all of a sudden?" Luna asked.

"We've run out on the island," Charlie explained. "It's thrown off the whole food chain. We have to restock before the ecosystem collapses." Then he burped, waved his hand in front of his face and walked into the dark.

"He's the one who should have been in the mental ward," said Suki.

I was about to disagree. Then he came back to the dock with a trap in either hand. It would have ruined my argument. Inside one trap was a red squirrel. The other had a chipmunk in it. Each was trying frantically to find an exit. It sounded like a circus. Charlie held them up like trophies.

"You're taking our chipmunks, too?" said Suki. "You should be taking deer instead. They're all over the place this year."

"No room for deer. Just rodents. Rodents of every variety."

"Why?"

"I just bought a pet fox," said Charlie. "You don't want him to starve, do you?"

"You're joking," Suki shouted. "You wouldn't dare." She tried to grab one of the cages. When she put her hands on it, the squirrel inside nipped her fingers, so she shrieked. That's when the light came on in the cottage.

"That's our cue," said Charlie. "Time to run." He yanked the traps away and scrambled into the boat. Then he leaned out to give Suki a kiss, which ended when Luna yanked her sister away by the arm.

"On behalf of the island, I thank you," Charlie said. "In fact, the whole ecosystem thanks you. No, the whole *planet* thanks you."

The two sisters were running away. Actually, it was more like Luna was dragging her sister away by the arm.

"See you tomorrow at the Yacht Club," Suki said over her shoulder. "And bring your friend with you."

I was glad she'd added that, even though I wouldn't be able to go.

As soon as Charlie sat down, I pulled the ripcord on the motor and we puttered away.

"So, what do you think?" Charlie asked me.

I was thinking that his pet fox was hungry, but that wasn't what he was really asking me.

"They're nice," I said.

Charlie threw up his hands. "You say that about *everybody*!"

Chapter 28
A Warning from My Father

When we got back to the island, Charlie went to bed straight off. Since it was at least four or five hours before sunrise, I decided to sit down on the dock and read more of my father's journal. The pages were all crinkled now because they'd gotten soaked from my first boat ride when I'd jumped into the lake escaping from the cabbie, but at least I could still read the writing.

My father talked about some archaeological work being done in England along the Fosse Way, which sounded like an old road. I was skim-reading at this point. Then a short entry caught my attention. I was pretty sure it had to do with another vampire, because my father stopped using proper names.

I received an urgent call from Dr. Q regarding one of his patients, a recent carrier named C. He is having difficulty adjusting to the contagion. I have called Max in for support.

My brain went into computer mode when I read this. Carrier? What did that mean? A vampire? Could it have been something else? I didn't think so. I quickly skipped ahead. After an entry about a trip to the Tower of London, the story continued.

C has gone missing. We suspect he is responsible for the recent deaths of two women near Hyde Park. We have several agents posted in the neighbouring boroughs. I hope this will be adequate.

Well, any doubts I had that C was a vampire were gone. And agents? Did that mean my father had people working for him? Perhaps he and Maximilian were part of a much larger organization. I read on. There was nothing for a week, then this.

Got a call from Dr. Q near midnight. One of our agents discovered C's body near the rail yard in Egham. Most of his bones are shattered. Suicide is the likely explanation.

I felt my stomach sink when I read this. Who ever heard of a vampire committing suicide? I started to close the journal, but as the facing page turned towards me, I noticed another entry with the initial *C* at the bottom. I guess the story wasn't over.

C is recovering well. His damaged tissues have completely regenerated. (Ratio 1kg:5L is consistent with past cases.) The process was completed in less than 2 days.

Two days. Wow! Vampires really could heal quickly when they got the good stuff. A person with shattered bones would have spent months in a hospital getting better, if he lived at all.

There was more on the following page.

With the hunger issue resolved, C's rationality is returning. It confirms my deep suspicion that without adequate nutrient and guidance, few carriers adjust well to the symptoms of their infection. C has agreed to assume a role in a donor clinic. Max is skeptical, but Dr. Q has every confidence that C will not regress.

And that was it. But it was plenty.

The first thing I thought was that my father was dead-on about feeding. It *was* difficult to be rational on an empty stomach. It explained why I'd been so angry eight years ago when I came out of my coma. And why I'd bitten that nurse when I was ten. My hunger issue hadn't been resolved. But that might not have been the most important idea buried in these entries. It was clear that my father didn't see himself as just a vampire hunter. He helped them find their way. I should have guessed as much. My uncle had suggested that not all vampires were bad. I guess this meant my father helped look after the good ones. It was comforting. And a bit alarming, because it sounded as if they needed lots of help. C had more or less gone off the deep end. It made me wonder how many vampires had similar problems. I suppose I should have been grateful that I'd been living at the Nicholls Ward. When I'd needed help, Nurse Ophelia and the rest of the staff had been there. I might not have managed so well anywhere else.

I decided to flip through the journal to see if there was anything else written with capital letters instead of names. I scanned each page as quickly as I could manage, but the writing was so messy, and the pages so wrinkled, it took a long time to find anything. Then about three months later there was this short entry.

Flew in to Heathrow. One of our agents is missing. There are three other victims in the Dartmouth area, all women. Evidence suggests possible WW.

"WW." That had to be something special, or my father would have just spelled it out properly.

The next entry was short.

Met Max in Torquay. Tracks outside of Plymouth confirm our suspicions. We set bear traps and doubled the watch.

I skimmed a whole page that described a boat trip up the Dart, which I guessed was a river. Then I found this.

Success and disappointment. The bear traps have ended our hunt.

Bear traps? I tried to imagine the kind of creature you would catch with one of these.

Identity of WW impossible to determine. Dr. Q determined his psychosis is incurable. Despite availability of nutrient, killing urge cannot be suppressed. Hemlock administered. Body cremated. Ashes scattered in the Dart.

Was this about a werewolf? I flipped quickly through the pages ahead, searching for another WW, but I didn't find any more. Then I put my hand against my forehead and closed my eyes. If only my father had told me what he was doing when he was still alive. If we'd just been able to talk about it. There were so many things I might have asked him that could help me now. But I guess I was way too young back then. And I probably wouldn't have believed him. Werewolves? It was nonsense. Then I laughed. I was a vampire now. It was sort of like a doctor not believing in a dentist. Of course, I *would* have believed my father.

I reread the last few lines: "*His psychosis is incurable . . . killing urge cannot be suppressed . . . Body cremated . . .*" I was noticing a very disturbing trend in these entries. Insanity. And death.

My father had had no way of knowing what I would become. And still, he had left a warning for me that was probably more important than anything he'd said to me when he was alive. If I wasn't careful, I might turn out like these others.

I started reading again, then my stomach grumbled. I was getting hungry. After all this reading about vampires going crazy, I wasn't about to let my belly complain without doing something right away. The journal would have to wait.

The squirrel traps were still in the boat. I reached in and lifted them onto the dock. Mr. Chipmunk was eyeing me from the farthest corner of the cage. He could probably guess what was coming. So could Mr. Squirrel. I don't think any of us were happy about the arrangement, so I opened the cages and let them go. There seemed to be no point in killing two rodents when an army of them wouldn't have satisfied my appetite for very long. And I didn't want to have to cope with the guilt of killing something so small and helpless.

Still, I had to feed. I didn't want to turn into a monster. I decided it was time to follow Mr. Entwistle's advice and test myself. And I needed to stretch my legs. I was used to burning lots of fuel every night. All this sitting around was making me restless.

I zipped on a life jacket. I felt a little nervous about being on the water by myself, so I put a second one on overtop. It was snug, but if the boat decided to flip over on me, I didn't want to end up as fish food. Then I untied the boat and pushed off. When I was far enough from the shore that the sound of the motor wouldn't wake anyone up, I pulled the ripcord and took off for Luna's cottage.

As I made my way past the lights along the shore my thoughts returned to the bonfire. What I'd said and heard. I forgot about carriers and agents and werewolves and psychosis and just enjoyed replaying the evening in my head. Then I started changing a few things. Mostly, I just stole a lot of Charlie's jokes and made myself a lot funnier. And I imagined supporting Luna in her argument with the twins about revenge. I shouldn't have stayed so quiet when she was really arguing on my behalf. After all, both my parents were dead and I hadn't done a thing about it. By the time I was halfway down the lake, the whole episode was completely altered. I came out looking like a saint. And a genius. And a stand-up comedian.

Then I imagined telling Luna the truth about myself. Everything. In this version, everyone had left the island but the two of us, so no one got to interrupt. I started with my father's real profession. And my condition. Then Vrolok. I think a part of my mind was preparing me for when this conversation might happen for real. It was also preparing me for disappointment. It seemed that, even in my imagination, no matter how I sugar-coated things, she just wasn't going to be interested in a guy who got angry when there was no blood to drink and who couldn't go out in the sun. We could never be like Charlie and Suki, which was too bad. They obviously liked kissing a whole lot. But who would want to kiss a vampire? It was like I had fifteen diseases rolled into one.

I stopped the motor about fifty feet from the shore in front of Luna's cottage. The water made soft lapping noises against the hull as I drifted in. I took my life jacket off, tied up the boat and slipped quietly onto the dock. There was a gentle breeze blowing over the water. I put my nose to the air and stopped breathing to listen. It wasn't long before I heard something rustling just past the cottage. I snuck through the shadows and into the laneway. Then I discovered the source of the noise. A raccoon was nose-deep in a garbage can on the back of the porch. When it saw me approach it scampered off. There must have been no shortage of garbage cans on the lake, because this one waddled like an overstuffed house cat. It was lucky. I hadn't come all this way for blood that was made from recycled garbage. I had come because of what Suki had said about the deer.

Chapter 29
The Killing Urge

I followed the driveway from the cottage to the main road. Between domes of grey and pink granite, tall evergreens grew in clumps. Most of them were cedar, I think, and pine. Where it was rocky there were clearings, and it was in one of these that I picked up the scent of something wild. Fur, I guess. Then I saw the deer. A buck with arm-sized antlers.

I approached from downwind so it didn't hear me until I was close. It bolted just as I sprang. I was fast, but the buck was faster. He outdistanced me in a few seconds. Still, I wasn't worried. Way back before bows and arrows and farming and the wheel, our earliest ancestors practised exhaustion hunting. I'd seen it on a nature program once, and it worked like this. Your great-great-great-whatever-grandfather and his buddies followed an animal for six or eight hours until it ran out of energy. Then they stabbed it with sharp sticks. It apparently worked because running on two legs is more efficient than running on four legs, so even though the animal was faster over short distances, in a long race it eventually ran out of juice and collapsed. Exhaustion hunting. Not a lot of fun. I think it was the main reason farms were invented.

Well, I didn't have six to eight hours. And I didn't have my friends with me, or a sharp stick. What I had instead was a running speed much, much higher than any ordinary human's. I was hoping this would matter, or I was going to have to consider putting rodents back on the menu.

The buck ran deeper into the woods. I followed. I'd never run in the forest at night. I wasn't sure I could manage it. My arm was better, fortunately. I hadn't really been paying attention to it, so I guess it had sort of fixed itself. That was a bonus. But the ground wasn't even. It kept throwing off my stride. There were roots and rocks lying all over the place just waiting to trip me up. To avoid these I tried bounding from one open patch to another. It seemed to be working, until I hit a clump of moss. It swallowed my foot and I nearly pitched head over heels. There was a lesson in that. Avoid the moss. I learned to spot it quickly.

Fortunately, I could see well. And my eyes could focus in a snap. I had to trust them. Look down when I needed to, but keep mapping out the best way ahead.

Rocks and roots. I'd been jumping over them. Time to fix that. It was slowing me down. I started using them as launch pads so I could cover greater distances between strides. I took powerful steps. Long and fast and smooth. I would have made Mr. Entwistle proud. It was awesome. I was where I belonged. In the dark. In the wild. And my powers of survival were being tested.

I pushed the buck over trails that wound through the forest. It was faster than I was. Over a few hundred feet it wasn't a close race, but it couldn't keep the same pace after a few miles. Gradually it slowed down. Then it stumbled.

My body went a bit haywire. It started in my mouth. I felt a sharp pain in my upper gums. Something moved against my front teeth. The taste of blood, my blood, was in my mouth. The same thing had happened during my first disastrous meal back in Charlie's shed, so when I ran my tongue over the area, I knew exactly what I'd find—two long, sharp teeth that seconds before had been the short version you would see in a normal person's mouth. These were my canines, the vampire's teeth, the ones we use for feeding. They had descended. And with them came a feeling that I could only think of as *the killing urge*. My father had mentioned it in his entry about the werewolf. It was a lust for blood so strong that once it took hold, there was no turning back.

My eyes locked on the buck's neck. An instant later, it was dying with my fangs in its throat.

I have heard people say that the best part of the hunt is not the kill but the thrill of the chase. Well, I'd bet my last pair of running shoes that none of them ever killed anything larger than a housefly. Sure, the chase was fun, exercise and all that, good for the heart. But the meal at the end was tops. It frightened me, actually, how intense it felt to surrender to that killing urge and feed.

As the warm blood coursed down my throat, it was as if my senses were waking up. Everything was magnified. Nothing moved around me that I didn't see in the clearest detail. Bats, moths, rustling pine needles. And I heard every sound. The buck's failing heart. My own heart pounding in my chest. Heavy breathing. The drone of mosquito wings. I could pinpoint every one of them. And the smells. Evergreen boughs. Musk. Fur. Damp leaves and old needles. The soil. I could even smell the lichen and the granite rock around us.

The sense of being watched was very strong—as if all the creatures around me in the forest were aware of what I had done and were afraid.

I fed like a predator. And I had no remorse. None.

I look back at this moment with a mixture of sadness and something else. Understanding, maybe. Or acceptance. I'm a vampire. Sometimes I wish I could live on tofu and alfalfa sprouts, but I can't. And I understand that I'm not consistent. I don't always act the same way. I'm a nice guy as often as I can be. As my Uncle Maximilian said, I have a choice. And I choose to be good. Until I get hungry. Then I'm something that is less than good. Then I'm a killer.

Chapter 30
Marshmallows

Charlie came to get me just after sunset the next night. "You sleep all right?" he asked.

"Yeah." I stretched and blinked my eyes. It felt good to tense every muscle.

Charlie tossed a dark bundle into the shed. It landed on the sleeping bag I was using.

"What's this?" I asked.

"Your scrubs."

"They're soaked."

"Yeah. You can thank me later. I had to clean them in the sink. You must have run about fifty miles in those things before you got here. The smell was killing all the birds."

"What's wrong with these?" I said, pulling at the collar of my shirt.

"You wore them to the bonfire last night. You want to spend the rest of your life stinking like a chimney?"

"Do you have something else I could wear?"

Charlie shook his head. "Do you want to wear a bedsheet? My clothes would never fit you."

"Then whose clothes am I wearing?"

"Those are Dan's. I scoffed them the night you got here. He was at Canada's Wonderland, remember? Well, he's in his room right now, so there's no way I'm going to be able to borrow any more. You want me to tell him an escaped lunatic is living in our shed and needs another set of duds?"

I stood and unrolled the shirt and pants from the ward. Charlie had obviously tried to wring them out because there were crease lines all over them.

"I can't wear these!"

"You can if you *believe* you can."

The boat ride was freezing. I endured it thinking about how nice the bonfire was going to be. I was disappointed when we arrived at the girls' cottage and Charlie announced to everyone that we were going sailing instead.

"I left a window in the Yacht Club unlocked so I could sneak in," he said, climbing out onto the dock. "I'll open up the doors and we can rig up a boat."

"I don't think that's such a great idea," said Suki. "If someone saw us, we could lose our jobs."

"Well, you don't have to come," said Charlie. "I just thought it would be cool to take Zack out for a sail. He's never been."

Unless he was planning to light some part of the boat on fire, I didn't have any great interest in sailing, especially if it was going to involve wind.

"We should just go tomorrow afternoon," said Luna. She was

watching me shivering in the boat. "You look a little cold for sailing. Don't you have anything warmer to wear?"

I shook my head.

"Come on," Charlie said to me. "Live a little. What's the worst thing that can happen?"

"I can't really swim, Charlie," I said. "So the worst thing that can happen is that I drown."

"You can't swim?" said Suki.

"Not really," I said. I thought of my trip down the Otonabee River with Mr. Entwistle. "My last try didn't go very well."

"Well, we'll have to fix that."

"Can we fix it later?" I said. "Unless the water's warmer at this end of the lake."

So I got my bonfire after all. It wasn't so big that you could see it from outer space, but it did the trick. A few logs were set up as benches near the shore by the dock. They were arranged around a small circle of stones that kept the fire from crawling across to the neighbours' place. While I thawed out and dried my clothes, the others roasted marshmallows and talked sailing.

"You ought to try one," said Suki, as she plucked a toasted marshmallow from her stick.

"Oh, no thanks," I said. "I ate yesterday."

Charlie plunged his marshmallow right into the coals. As soon as it turned into a torch, he blew it out, ate the char, burned the next layer, then started chewing on the sliver of black marshmallow that was left on his stick.

"No, Zack doesn't eat sweets," he said between mouthfuls. "He likes roasted squirrel."

I could have killed him.

Suki glared at us. "What did you do with our squirrels?"

"I let them go," I said. "Honestly. You can come visit them anytime."

"They're living like rodent kings on our island paradise," Charlie added.

Suki pointed the sharp end of her stick at him. "You'd better not be lying."

Charlie grabbed the stick from her and started chasing her around the fire. I noticed he wasn't trying all that hard to catch her. Come to think of it, she wasn't trying all that hard to get away. Then the two of them disappeared around the corner of the cottage. I held my breath and listened. They didn't go very far, but they didn't come back, either.

And that left me alone with Luna.

She looked up from her seat and watched me soak up the heat from the fire.

"Why didn't you come by today?" she asked.

"By the Yacht Club?"

"Yeah."

I took a deep breath and let it go.

"Am I being too nosey?"

"No," I said. "I just . . ." *Can't tell you that I'm a vampire.*

Luna pushed another marshmallow over the remains of the last one, then hung it over the coals. "Stumped on question one. Wait till I get to the hard stuff."

"This *is* the hard stuff."

"Really?" Her eyebrows flashed up for just a second. "Well, this ought to be good. You out robbing banks or something?"

I stood and turned so that my back was to the fire. Luna was watching me. Her eyes sort of moved around my face. They were curious. And bright.

"I'm allergic to the sun," I said. "I sleep during the day."

"Really?"

"Yeah."

"You sleep all day?"

"Yeah."

"Every day?"

"Yeah."

"A creature of the night?"

"Pretty much."

She was looking at me to see if I was telling the truth. I pointed to her marshmallow. The bottom was starting to blister.

"Oh," she said. "Thanks." She turned it over and began toasting the other side. "So what do you do for school?"

"Don't go."

"Get out!"

I shook my head. "Not since Grade Two."

She pulled her marshmallow stick away from the fire, reached over and offered it to me.

"No thanks."

She waved it around a few times, like there was no way I could pass up a gooey ball of roasted sugar.

"No, really," I said, lifting my hand. "I don't want one."

She gave me a look like I was putting her on. Like living with no sun and no school was easier to believe than not wanting to eat a marshmallow.

"Suit yourself."

She tested it with her fingers, blew on it a few times, then carefully pulled it off and stuffed it in her mouth.

"So how do you get your vitamin D?" she asked. The marshmallow muffled the sound of her voice.

"Squirrels," I said.

She put her stick down and stood up so that she was right in front of me. "A wise guy, huh?"

"Not really," I said. "I haven't been to school since I was seven."

"I don't believe you," she said.

I smiled and shrugged. It was the perfect thing for her to say. It meant she thought I was normal.

While I continued to dry, she stepped over the log she'd been sitting on and walked over to the front porch. A towel was hanging over the railing. She pulled it off and slung it over her shoulder.

"I think I'm going to explode," she said. She was still holding the bag of marshmallows. She tossed them back beside the fire. "You warm enough for a swim?"

The correct answer was no. I was so cold I could have crawled right into the coals and made a nest for myself, but I didn't want to miss a chance to spend more time with her, even if it meant drowning.

"I think so," I said.

She started walking around to the back of the cottage.

"Isn't the water this way?" I pointed towards the lake.

"I'm just going to see if the others are interested."

She came back a minute later by herself. I had to put my hand over my mouth to keep my smile from showing. I was so happy I thought my lips were going to crack.

"Do I need a life jacket?" I mumbled.

"You mean you really can't swim?"

"No. I can't."

I started to walk towards the dock. Luna took hold of my elbow with both hands and steered me over to the shore.

"That part of the lake is better for drowning. This part is better for swimming."

Beside the dock was a narrow ribbon of sand that stretched along the shore. I pulled off my shirt, kicked off my shoes, rolled up my scrubs and waded into the shallow water. And what a thrill. I've never had a massage, but I imagine that swimming must come very close. I lay in the water looking up at the stars. Luna had one hand under the small of my back and the other between my shoulder blades. I just floated with the water pressing around me on all sides. Then she showed me how to keep myself from sinking. Sculling, she called it. It sounded like the kind of skill every vampire should have. And all the while we talked. She told me about her school. I talked about the ward. It took a while to convince her that I hadn't been joking earlier. I really couldn't go out in the sun and I'd never been to high school. She seemed to think I was lucky, but I thought she was the lucky one. All of her close friends were people she'd met there.

"So how do you know Charlie?" she asked me.

"My dad and his dad were old friends."

"When do you see him, if you don't go to school?"

"He visits me at night. Usually over the weekends, because it's pretty late."

"That's it?"

"Pretty much."

By this time I was lying on a flutter board. It fit under my stomach and kept me from sinking.

"Don't kick so hard," she said. She walked beside me in the shallow water. "You only move your legs so that they don't sink. It's your arms that pull you forward. Just like you're crawling."

"But my legs are so much stronger," I said.

"I think your arms will manage just fine."

I was starting to get the hang of it.

"You must spend an awful lot of time alone," she said.

I mentioned Nurse Ophelia. And Jacob and Sad Stephen, too. They checked into the Nicholls Ward a few times a year, so they counted.

"Still, that's not a lot of visitors," she said. "Not a lot of company."

"There aren't a lot of people who stay up all night."

"No. I guess not," she said. "Sounds like you need to meet a nice insomniac. Or a vampire."

I fell off the flutter board.

Luna laughed. She had a hand over her mouth, but it didn't do much to hide her smile. "I'm sorry," she said. "That was my fault."

She tossed the flutter board back on shore and went over the fundamentals of the backstroke. I liked this better. She had her hands underneath me again.

We talked about swimming, then sailing, and that led us to other stuff like hobbies and things we liked to do. The whole time she kept mentioning all the people she knew. I could hardly believe it, how she kept track of them all. It was mind-boggling. She must have known everyone in the phone book.

She brought back the flutter board and stuck it under my chest. Then she taught me how to do a frog kick. I liked it the best. Once I had that down, she took my hands and showed me how to pull myself through the water.

"This is the breast stroke," she said. "It's my favourite. Cup your hands, and sweep them around so that they make a heart, then push the water down to your feet."

I let her guide my hands for a few heart-shaped sweeps. Then she let go and I took a powerful stroke.

"I think you're a natural," she said.

I didn't think so. It seemed to me the flutter board was doing most of the work.

"Do you want to try swimming off the dock?" she asked.

I stood up and we walked out of the water together. She handed me her towel so I could pat myself dry.

"I'd rather warm up for a while," I said.

"Okay. Just hide that bag of marshmallows. They're going to be the death of me."

By this time the fire had died down a bit. It was hypnotic, the way the flames danced and changed colours. The embers, too. They shifted in the breeze from red to black to orange. I imagined cavemen must have spent a lot of time just staring at these things. It made me wonder why we didn't have a fireplace back at the ward. Infomercials about Miracle Glow had nothing on this.

"The coals are perfect," she said. She reached for the marshmallow bag, stuck her hand in and pulled one loose. "I'll just have one."

As soon as it was set on her stick, she turned it carefully over the coals.

"Do you have a girlfriend?" she asked me.

I shook my head. Males and females were separated at the ward, so I'd never had the chance to talk to any girls my age.

"Are you going to come for a sail tomorrow?"

"I'll be sleeping."

"Right." She nodded.

I noticed her first marshmallow was followed by a second.

"Well," she said, "if you find a cure by tomorrow, I'd be happy to rig us a boat and take you for a tour of the lake."

I smiled. If only . . .

On the way home, Charlie grilled me with questions.

"So . . . ?" was the first one.

"So . . . ? So what?"

"So what happened?" he asked me.

I told him about the fire and the swimming lesson and our conversation.

"That's it? You just talked?" He shook his head and looked at me like I'd just slept through my last day on earth. Then he started talking about baseball and getting to all the bases, and that I hadn't even gotten into the batter's box. I had no idea what this had to do with anything, but I wasn't really listening. I was thinking of Luna.

I'd never actually *met* a person before. A stranger. Not the way they do in movies where two people bump into each other on a bus or in a café and say things like, "Excuse me, is this seat taken?" and you just know they're going to get on famously. Meeting Luna was like that. I wondered if other kids ever felt this way, if it was normal. A week ago I'd never heard of her. Now she was stuck in my head so firmly . . .

Charlie interrupted me with a poke on the shoulder. "And no biting, either," he said. "You know what I mean?"

I hadn't been listening, which wasn't like me.

"I hear ya," I said. Then I went back to thinking about Luna.

Chapter 31
The Fate of All Vampires

Just as I had the night before, I snuck back down to the dock with my father's journal once Charlie was asleep. I was hoping I might find another entry with a little more detail about—anything, really. As long as it related to vampires. Why we have such a tough time of it. Where this whole thing came from. Why we can't be cured. Or maybe something about Vrolok and what his real name might be. I just needed more.

I skimmed a few pages, then came to a passage about Malta and Gozo. It didn't say where they were, but I could see that my father was hunting again.

Bad news confirmed by Mutada. B is now connected to three disappearances in Valletta. He appears to be spreading the contagion indiscriminately. Max and I are flying out tonight.

B must have been another vampire. One who was apparently doing a lot of biting. A few entries later, my father continued with this.

B found impaled and decapitated in Ta'Braxia cemetery.

There was more, but I stopped reading.

Impaled. The word stuck in my head like a shard of glass. *Impaled.* Like those people in my nightmare. There had been thousands of them writhing on those long stakes. Screaming. Bleeding. Dying. The memory was vivid, as though I'd really been there. And that strange man who had appeared beside me, laughing. His face was perfectly clear, too. Large green eyes. Wide face. Hard cheekbones. Dark hair and moustache. And the teeth. I wondered if he was real. Well, not real, exactly, but maybe a person I'd seen on television, or in a picture I couldn't quite place, someone ordinary that my mind had twisted a little so that he fit in with the rest of the nightmare.

A voice inside me said no. He wasn't a person I'd invented or recreated. And he was connected to that bloodstained field of dying bodies. The two belonged together.

Impaled.

Who ever heard of a vampire dying that way? A stake through the heart I understood. If you really wanted to go overboard you cut off the head too, and put garlic in the mouth, like Van Helsing did to Lucy in *Dracula*. But impaled? It seemed like a disgustingly cruel end, even for a rogue vampire.

I read on.

Of B's servants, we can find no trace. The lack of evidence suggests the Coven of the Dragon has been at work here.

The Coven of the Dragon? That sounded ominous. Like a secret society. I kept skimming, hoping to find more. Then my uncle's name caught my eye. And the letters *EP*, which I assumed at first were the initials of another vampire.

Max returned from Turgovishte last night in great dismay. Of the Coven of the Dragon, nothing can be confirmed. Like early stories about carriers, there is much rumour and few hard facts. In addition, our friends have concluded their research. If their findings are correct, the inevitable fate of all carriers is insanity, a condition they refer to as "Endpoint Psychosis" (EP). This confirms our worst fears—a carrier's madness cannot be prevented, only postponed.

I read it a second time, then a third. I kept reading until I'd practically memorized every word, but only two stuck out. *Endpoint Psychosis.*

I couldn't believe what I was reading. Did my father really believe that *all* vampires went crazy? Like I wasn't in *enough* trouble?

I started flipping frantically through the journal to see if he'd written any more about this. *Endpoint Psychosis.* When did it happen? Was I close? Was there any way to tell? My hands were shaking so much I had to set the journal on the dock just to keep the pages still.

I got to the end and had found nothing. I started flipping again from the back. Then again from the front. Nothing. Maybe this was how I was going to go crazy. I was going to get so worried about Endpoint Psychosis that I'd keep turning pages until my brain snapped in two.

I slammed the journal closed and slid it away from me. Then I flopped back on the dock so I was looking up at the stars. The sky was full of grey-blue clouds, but Cassiopeia was in full view, floating upside down in her orbit around Polaris, the North Star. I thought for a minute how cruel it was that she had been in my life longer than my father. It made me furious. Why hadn't he explained things properly? Why was his journal so vague? Why did he have to go off in the first place and get himself killed?

I balled my fists and tried to squeeze the frustration out of my body. My heart was pounding against my ribs like it wanted to escape, and who could blame it? If my father was right, I was going to go crazy. After spending eight years in a mental ward, I knew exactly what that meant—confusion and anger and pain. Or hopelessness and despair. I'd seen both. And because I was a vampire, it would be far worse. I would become a creature so terrible even my own father would have killed me.

I tried to slow my breathing so my body would stop shaking. It took a few minutes. Then I folded my hands under my head like a pillow and closed my eyes. The water was shifting gently underneath the dock. Normally, the subtle rising and falling would have calmed my nerves, but now it just made me nauseous.

For a time I just lay there, wrestling with my nervous stomach and listening to the sound of the bats hunting overhead. The needles of the trees made soft swishing noises that blended with the chirping of insects. My thoughts drifted and I found myself wondering about Nurse Ophelia. She'd vanished just after Mr. Entwistle crashed into my life. When all the trouble started. There was no way this was a coincidence. Her disappearance and my dilemma had to be connected. And Mr. Entwistle? He'd died by arson the day after saving me. That couldn't be another coincidence. Someone had to be responsible.

Maybe my Uncle Max would know. But he hadn't called back yet, so maybe he was gone, just like the others.

Thank God for Charlie. I wondered how much I should tell him. If I was in danger of going bonkers and biting everything in sight, I should warn him, at least. Or just go away by myself. That would keep him safe.

But I didn't want to go away. I'd spent enough of my life alone.

Mr. Entwistle had survived for over six hundred and fifty years. If that was true, then it *was* possible to stay alive and stay sane . . . if you could call him that. But Mr. Entwistle was gone, and his secrets were gone with him.

I thought back to the night of our escape, when he'd told me about his purpose: that he helped other vampires. Even the rogues. That must have been one of his secrets. And he didn't attach himself to things. And he drank. A lot.

Well, one of those things was possible for me. I could find a purpose.

I stood up and retrieved my father's journal. That would be my first purpose. I would finish reading it, all of it, not just the vampire parts, and learn all that it could teach me. Then I was going to find my uncle. That was goal number two. I had to find somewhere safe to hide, and then I could figure out how to deal with Vrolok. Find out who he was and if he had a weakness. That was goal number three. And I had to see Luna again. In fact, *that* was goal number two. My uncle and Vrolok could wait. As soon as I was done with the journal, I had to find a way to tell her the truth.

I looked up at the sky. Cassiopeia was still sparkling overhead. I felt a sudden swell of confidence, as if my Miracle Glow, fairy-tale ending was only minutes away. I smiled and started leafing through the journal to find my page.

No sooner had I started reading than a sudden coolness crept over the dock. A chill went through me, raising goosebumps on my arms. I looked out over the water. A fog was moving down the lake. It curled and tumbled like a living thing, clawing its way toward me. The wind picked up, lifting the back of my hair and causing the pages of the journal to flutter.

Something wasn't right here. I held my breath to listen, but heard nothing. The bats were all gone. The insects had stopped their chattering. The fog moved closer, swirling more violently now as it met the same breeze that stirred the pages of the journal and blew my hair down over my eyes.

The fog was moving against the wind.

I took a step backwards, and another. Then I heard it. The flapping of leathery wings.

I turned and ran. Trees and rocks passed me in a blur. So did the cottage. I followed the path straight for the shed, bounding with long, powerful strides. As I drew closer, I felt an icy cold against my skin, as if tendrils of fog were reaching out to snare me. I was panting loudly. The shed was close now. Just a few more steps. When I reached the door, I nearly tore it off the hinges. It snapped closed behind me and I fumbled with the latch. Then I held my breath and backed away. Although the window in the door was covered, in my mind's eye I could see the eerie luminescence drifting past outside, rolling, searching.

My lungs were burning so I sucked a quiet breath in through my teeth. I kept backing away until my foot hit the edge of my sleeping bag. Then I buried myself underneath and waited.

Chapter 32
Problem Child

Sometime during the early-morning hours I fell asleep. My dreams were frantic and confused. I couldn't find anyone. Everywhere there was shadow and fog and the sound of bat wings. I could feel an evil presence hunting me, but the more I ran, the closer it seemed to come.

It ended when Charlie ripped open the door of the shed the next day. I could hear his heart. It was doing a drum solo. He was so agitated, he actually pulled the latch right out of the door frame.

"We've got a problem," he said.

The sun was still up, and light was bouncing all over the place, so we had at least two problems. I buried myself under my sleeping bag and waited until he closed the door.

"Suki just called," he said. He made it sound like a bad thing. "The cops were there. They're on their way over right now. We've got to get you out of here. They could arrive any second."

I stood up and grabbed my shirt. Then I started looking for my father's journal. As soon as I'd found it, I lifted a corner of the garbage bag that Charlie had stapled over the window frame. My fingers started to burn right away, so I let it go.

"What time is it?" I asked.

"I don't know. It's evening, just after eight, maybe."

That meant the sun would be up for another half hour or so.

"What do I do?" I asked.

Charlie shrugged. "Can you wrap yourself up in that?" He flicked a finger towards my sleeping bag.

"Where am I going?"

"That's another problem."

"Can I talk to Luna?"

"And that's another problem."

"How did this happen?"

Charlie took a deep breath, then leaned back against the workbench under the window. "Their father read that article about you in the *Examiner* the other day. The one that said you're an escaped mental patient with psychotic tendencies. Who knew? Well, apparently he overheard the girls talking about you. Once he put two and two together, he detonated and called the cops. So we gotta get going. If the police catch you here, they're going to lock you away for about eight million years."

That didn't sound too appealing. But that wasn't what really bothered me.

"So Luna knows?" I asked.

"Yeah." Charlie nodded. "Sounds like she was pretty upset."

"I've got to explain."

Charlie shook his head. "No way. The girls, Suki . . . You've got to stay away."

I let out a deep breath. I felt as if my whole body was going to collapse. I looked at Charlie, and then at the floor, and then at the shelves. I don't know what I was expecting to see, like the key to my future was going to be written on a half-used can of spray paint. I was lost. The police were coming. The sun was still shining. I'd run out of hiding places. Funny thing was, I didn't care about that. I just wanted to talk to Luna. I couldn't have her believe all those things about me were true.

"Does your brother know I'm here?" I asked.

"No."

"Isn't there another place I can hide? Maybe at the other end of the island? I could sneak away as soon as the police are gone."

Charlie shook his head. "What are you going to do, make yourself invisible? Suki said they've got dogs with them. This isn't *The Hobbit*, Zack. This is for real."

"So what do we do?"

"We get in the boat and take our chances."

Charlie picked up the sleeping bag and handed it to me. I passed him my father's journal, unzipped one side of the bag and put it over my head like a giant cape. As soon as I was outside, it would be the only thing between me and the sun.

"Is that going to work?" he asked. "You aren't going to go up like a torch, are you?"

"We'll see," I said. I sounded braver than I felt.

I waited in the shed for Charlie to go down to the dock and get the boat ready. Then he whistled. That was the signal. I was supposed to take off.

I couldn't.

The light outside was just too bright. Why couldn't it have been cloudy?

Charlie whistled again.

I took a deep breath. Then another. I had to go, but my feet wouldn't move. The sun was out there. The sun was death. Painful death.

Charlie whistled a third time. I imagined him waiting in the boat. Then I imagined Luna at her cottage. If I stayed here, if I chickened out and hid in the shed, the police would find me and I'd never get the chance to set things straight.

Charlie whistled a fourth time. I pulled the sleeping bag tight around my shoulders, took a deep breath, then kicked the door open and ran outside.

Chapter 33
On the Run

I'd never been out in the full sun before. Even with the sleeping bag over my body and clothes protecting my arms and legs, I still felt like I'd just jumped into an oven. My eyes burned. My skin tingled. Everything was hot. Then I felt jabs, like pinpricks, spreading over my hands and neck. All the while, I ran as fast as I could. I kept my eyes on the ground, but even that was blinding. And so I didn't see the little boy until he was right in front of me.

He must have been one of Dan's kids. He just popped out of nowhere as I rounded the cottage on my way to the dock. I didn't hit him, or he would have landed somewhere in Saskatchewan, but I tripped and fell getting out of his way. The ground came at me quickly, so without thinking, I stuck out a hand to break my fall. The effect was dramatic. In less than two seconds, the skin turned red, blistered, then charred to black and cracked open.

I screamed.

Behind me, up in the cottage, someone started shouting. I pulled my hand back under the sleeping bag, but the damage had been done. My hand was a mess, and I'd been spotted.

A second later, Charlie was beside me. I could only see his feet. He was trying to help me up by the arm, but it was the bad one, so I just shouted, "Don't!" and ran down to the boat. I ate up the last fifty feet in about two strides. A moment later I felt the boat lurch as Charlie jumped in after me.

"What happened?"

All I could say was, "My hand." I leaned out of the boat so that the shadow of the sleeping bag was over the water. When I stuck my arm in, it made a hissing noise. It wasn't like swimming. It didn't feel like a massage. It was more like acupuncture. I got dizzy and fell back against the side of the boat.

By this time, Dan was calling for Charlie. I could tell by the sound of his voice that he was coming towards us.

Charlie didn't answer. He just gunned the motor, and we took off. I had no idea where we were going. I turned the sleeping bag into a cocoon and waited for the sun to set. I didn't say anything, I just gritted my teeth and rocked back and forth, doing my best to keep my hand from touching anything that would make the pain come back.

As soon as Charlie told me that the sun had gone down, I poked my head up from under the sleeping bag and looked around. My head was still buzzing. Or maybe it was the flies. We were in a swamp, with reeds and drowned trees in the water all around us. It was like something out of a Tarzan movie. Charlie had pulled the motor up so that the prop was sticking out behind the boat. He was using a paddle to push off the spongy bottom. The smell of rot coming up from the water was enough to singe your nose hairs.

"Where are we?" I asked.

"It's a bird sanctuary," said Charlie. "My dad calls it the Lost Channel, I guess because no one uses it any more."

"Where are the cottages?"

"You can't build in here. And you can't come in with motorboats, so we should be safe."

"Isn't this a motorboat?"

"If we get caught by the cops, that will be the least of our worries."

That made sense.

"So now what?" I asked. I had to speak through clenched teeth because my hand was still on flame-broil. "Can we go back to your place?"

Charlie shook his head. "No. The cops might still be there. We're going to feel awfully stupid if we go back and they nab us."

I was already feeling stupid, but I didn't say anything.

Charlie smiled. "I have a plan. I used to play hide-and-seek with my brothers all the time. You know the best place to hide?"

I blew on my hand. "In a cave?" I said.

"Look around, chowderhead. Do you see a cave anywhere? I mean in general."

I had no idea. Hide-and-seek wasn't too popular at the ward. Most patients couldn't remember what they were doing for more than ten seconds. And they got spooked super easy. Hide-and-seek would have looked more like hide-and-freak.

"The best place to hide from someone," Charlie explained, "is in a place they've already searched."

He paddled us out of the bird sanctuary and dropped the motor.

"So where are we going?" I asked.

"To see Suki and Luna. Where else?"

That definitely sounded better than a cave. And since the police had already searched there, it was probably safer than anywhere else. If he was concerned that the girls didn't want me around, he sure didn't show it. I was definitely more worried than he was. Of course, he wasn't an escaped mental patient with a warrant out for his arrest. But his confidence helped convince me things might turn out all right.

We drove with the lights off. It felt good to be moving, even if it brought us closer to trouble. It was a distraction from the pain in my hand.

We were lucky. The police were gone from Luna's part of the lake. We didn't see any of their boats. It was still early when we arrived at her cottage. Ten o'clock, maybe. All of the lights in the cottage were still on, so Charlie cut the engine and we drifted in to the dock.

"Are you sure this is a good idea?" I whispered.

"What have you got to lose? They already want to kill you."

Charlie stepped out of the boat and grabbed the rope to tie it up.

"What are you doing?" I asked.

"I'm going to knock at the door," he said.

I hadn't really considered what we'd do once we arrived, but I didn't think the front door was the best option.

Charlie motioned for me to get under the sleeping bag. "I'll see if Luna can come out. Just be ready. Their old man's pretty good with a shotgun. We might need to make a quick exit." I couldn't tell if he was joking.

He slipped up onto the front porch and knocked at the door. Suki answered. She took one look at him and folded her hands across her chest. I crouched under the sleeping bag in the front of the boat and watched.

"Well?" she said.

"Hey, it's me. It's Charlie. You don't have to look at me like that."

"Like what? Like you set my sister up with a crackpot?"

"He's not a crackpot. He's my best friend. And you were all wild about him until a few hours ago. You really think he's crazy? Come on!"

"He lied to us. You both did."

"That's a bunch of—"

"You *did*!"

"Zachary's got a lot of problems right now, but he's never been a liar. Never."

"Yeah, he said he lived in a mental ward. He never said he escaped! You let on like he was fine. It was in the newspaper. He attacked four police officers. Explain that one, Einstein."

I listened, but Charlie didn't say anything for a few seconds. I could hear the porch creaking under his feet as he shifted around.

"I can't explain it. But Zachary can. I know we can clear all of this up. Is Luna here?"

There was another long pause.

"Where is he?" Suki asked. "Is he here? Did you bring him here?" Her voice sounded like she was trying to yell and whisper at the same time.

"He's in the boat. He wants to talk to Luna."

"Forget it!" said Suki.

She backed up and started to close the door. Charlie stopped it with his hand.

"That's no good," he said.

Suki put her hand against his shoulder. "Not tonight, Charlie. Not tonight."

Then she closed the door.

Chapter 34
Explanations

There was nothing we could do but go back to the bird sanctuary. We waited there until just after midnight, then we headed back to the girls' place.

"Persistence is the key," said Charlie. He cut the engine and we drifted in, this time to the beach.

"I don't know about this," I said. "I have no idea what to say."

"Knowing what to say is a lot less important than making sure we go to the right window."

We snuck around the side of the house. Charlie pointed to a screened window on the second floor of the cottage. "That's the one, I think."

"You *think*? You're not sure?"

"Do I look like I designed the place? Here." He put his hand on my shoulder to get me to bend down, then he stood on my back and tapped the screen several times. Then several more. I heard a creak and a voice. It was Suki.

"Charlie!" She made his name sound like a swear word. "God, you're impossible!"

The screen slid open. I couldn't tell what Charlie was doing. It felt like Suki was trying to push him over. I heard a sound like kissing, so I started to back up. I wasn't here for this.

"Hey, hey!" he whispered.

I stopped.

"Wake your sister," he said to Suki.

"She's awake already."

"Well, come out then."

Charlie didn't wait for an answer. He just jumped down.

A half minute later Suki swung a leg out of the window and then lowered herself down so that we could catch her.

"You'd better have a good explanation for all of this," she said. She spoke to Charlie, but I think her words were really for me. She didn't look very angry, which was encouraging. Charlie grabbed her hand and pulled her towards the front of the cottage.

I stared up at the window. "Luna," I whispered. My heart was beating so hard, I think it was louder than my voice.

"I'm right here," she said quietly, circling around from the back of the cottage.

I turned. She glanced at me and glanced away. Her mouth was a flat line and her eyes were red-rimmed and watery. Neither of us spoke for a while.

"I heard you had a tough night," I said.

She nodded. "We shouldn't talk here."

We passed Charlie and Suki on the way down to the lake. I avoided looking at either of them. I thought Luna was going to sit down when we reached the end of the dock, but she turned and faced me instead.

"Is it true?" she asked. "Did you really do all of those things?"

I took a deep breath. *Here goes.*

"I ran away from the ward. I had to. I couldn't stay there another day. A friend helped me. We stole a car. Well, he stole it, and I was sort of along for the ride. I don't know how to drive."

I paused to make sure she was with me.

"They said you assaulted some police officers."

This was a tricky one, because I *had* assaulted a police officer, but not on purpose. I explained as best I could. I started with the three officers who'd pinned me in the parking lot of the Nicholls Ward. It was difficult, because I didn't want to mention any of the vampire business, so I couldn't say why I had to resist arrest. Fortunately, I had Mr. Entwistle to blame, since he'd really done all of the assaulting and I'd just watched. Then I told her about the fourth officer. The one I'd punched after he and his partner hit me with their van.

"It hurt so much," I said. "There was pain everywhere. When he touched me, I lashed out without thinking. Then I took off."

"You mean you got hit by a car and just ran away?"

"A van."

"Car, van, what's the difference?"

"I don't know," I said. "I've never been hit by a car."

That made her laugh. She was starting to come back.

"Why don't you just explain this to the police? It's not like they're going to toss you in jail."

I wasn't worried about jail. I was worried about Everett Johansson and Baron Vrolok, neither of whom I'd mentioned.

"I can't," I said.

Luna looked down at her feet, then out over the lake. The moon was bright, but hidden behind a thin layer of cloud that shone silvery-white along the horizon. We didn't speak for a moment, but we glanced nervously at each other and then out over the water. Then Luna noticed my hand.

"Oh my God! What happened?"

"I had a bit of an accident leaving Charlie's. The sun wasn't down all the way."

"The sun did that?"

"Yeah."

"You should put it in cold water."

I started to crouch down so I could dip my hand in the lake. She grabbed my other elbow with both hands.

"No. The lake water's got bacteria and stuff in it. You might get an infection. I'll get some ice water from the kitchen."

"Won't your parents hear?"

She laughed. "They might. But as far as I know, it's not illegal for me to get ice from my own freezer."

A few minutes later I was sitting on the dock with my hand in a pail of ice water. It was numb, which was an improvement. Luna sat beside me, looking at the lights of the far shore as they shimmered on the surface of the water.

"Here, let me check that," she said.

I pulled my hand out.

"It's a lot better than I thought. It looked black before. Must have been the light."

My hand was now an angry red. The blisters were gone and the cracks were all sealed over. I was healing, albeit a lot more slowly than if I'd fed. I put my hand back in the pail and looked up at the sky. With the clouds, it wasn't the best night for stargazing, but it was perfect for watching the bats hunt. I saw one do a half barrel-roll that ended with a dive and a mouthful of moth. I had to smile. It was impressive.

"What's so funny?" Luna asked.

"The bats." I followed the same one as he continued to stalk insects through the air. "They're unbelievable. That one in particular." I pointed. "He's an ace compared to the others."

Luna was looking in the same place I was, but she had no idea what I was talking about. The cloud-covered moon was like a giant night-light, but still she couldn't see them.

"I don't believe it," Luna said. I couldn't tell if she was impressed or irritated.

"How can you not believe in bats?"

She started laughing. "You obviously see much better in the dark than I do."

"Well, if you stayed up every night like me . . ."

She nodded. "I've heard that blind people hear and smell and taste better because their brains just adjust somehow. I guess it's the same kind of thing."

"Hmmm."

Her head flopped onto my shoulder.

"Did you get a bug bite?" she asked. "If you rub it, it just gets worse."

I stopped scratching my neck. I hadn't fed since I'd killed the deer. That was the night of the bonfire, almost two full days ago. I guess because I'd drunk so deeply, my hunger had stayed away for much longer than normal, but it was returning with the same impatience it always had. I took a piece of ice from the pail, wiped it across my forehead, then popped it into my mouth.

"Do you know what time it is?" she whispered.

I looked at the sky and then at the neighbours' cottage, where the twins lived.

"Almost one."

"And you know this how?"

"The kitchen clock."

Luna glanced over at the neighbouring cottage. "Zachary, they don't even have the lights on."

"I told you I see well in the dark."

"Apparently." She let out a deep sigh.

"Are you okay?" I asked.

"Yes. No. I don't know."

She stood up and offered me her hand. I took it, not because I needed to, but just so I could hold it. I'd never held a person's hand before, well, other than my father's. Then I stood so that we were facing each other. She was close enough that I could feel her breath on my neck.

"It just bothers me that you can't have a normal life," she said. She moved a bit closer.

"I'm not a normal person," I said.

"I got that much."

She was looking straight at me. I didn't know what to say.

"I have to go soon," she added. She was standing so close, I don't think even the wind could have snuck between us. I would have backed up a step, but then I would have fallen off the edge of the dock.

"You've never had a girlfriend, have you."

I shook my head. I started to say "No," but it got stuck on the way out.

I don't know how she managed it, but her hand was suddenly on my good arm. The way my legs were feeling I'm surprised it didn't knock me over. My heart started pounding so hard it was practically bruising my stomach. I felt dizzy. I could smell the blood coursing under the skin of her neck. It was right in front of me. I could hear her heart racing. She was still staring right at me. Her emerald eyes were beautiful. Soft and warm. Almost luminous. My hand rose to the side of her face and I heard her take in a quiet breath. *I could do this thing and I wouldn't have to be alone ever again.*

Luna closed her eyes and tilted her head back. I felt my teeth slide down through my gums and my mouth opened just a sliver. She was so close . . .

What was I thinking? I was a vampire. Cursed to endure a slow descent into madness. I shouldn't have been near her. I shouldn't have been near anybody.

"I can't do this," I said, pressing my lips closed.

Luna's eyes opened. I couldn't tell if she was confused or upset. She looked down, and then looked away, and then looked at me again. She started to back away, but I pulled her close and put my arms around her. I had to. I lifted my chin so that her head was cradled against my neck. Then I closed my eyes and just soaked up the feel of her. Warm skin. Soft hair. Her hands on the small of my back. It was the closest I had ever been to another person. It was wonderful.

"I wish I could explain," I said. "But I can't. I'm sorry."

I had a full minute of bliss. Of being alone with another person. It was the exact opposite of what I had experienced on the hunt. I didn't hear or see or smell anything around me. There was only Luna. Everything else had vanished.

And then the air went frigid and a deep chill ran through me. Everything suddenly felt wrong, the way it had in Mr. Entwistle's library, and the night before on the dock. There was no wind this time, not even a ripple on the water, but an icy cold made me shudder inside. I let go of Luna and sniffed at the air. I didn't smell anything unusual. I didn't hear or see anything unusual. Then I noticed the bats were all gone again, and a fog was beginning to rise from the water near the shore.

"We've got to get out of here," I said. I looked past Luna to see if I could spot anything in the shadows near the cottage.

"What is it? What's wrong?" she asked.

"I don't know. But you'd better get inside. And lock the door."

"You're making me nervous."

I pushed her gently towards the front steps. Then I heard a noise coming from behind the cottage. It was raspy. Like the sound of someone choking. Or being strangled. That was where Charlie and Suki had gone!

"Oh my God," I whispered.

A part of me that didn't think took over. I bared my fangs and bolted. I don't imagine you've ever seen a creature move so fast.

Just behind the cottage I found Charlie and Suki. They were lying on the ground. Their faces were glued together at the mouth. They were fine. Suki shrieked when she saw me.

"Get her inside," I said. "Hurry."

Charlie wasn't too happy about the interruption. "What's gotten into you?"

Then he saw my fangs.

"Get her inside and lock the door," I said. "Lock all of them."

"What is it?"

"Evil," I said. "I can feel it. It must be Vrolok. It isn't safe for you to be out here. You need to get inside."

A light came on in the cottage.

"And call the police," I added.

Suki ran for the door.

"Are you sure about the cops?" Charlie asked.

"Yes. Yes. Call them." I waved for him to go. "Just get moving."

I watched while Charlie followed Suki up the back steps. Then I thought I detected the faint beating of leathery wings. When I listened for it again, I heard another sound. This one made my teeth hurt. It was a scream, long and shrill. I followed it to the other side of the cottage.

It was Luna. She was standing on the porch facing the neighbours' place. And she was covered, head to toe, in blood.

Chapter 35
Helpless

Maybe you know this already: the human body contains about five and a half litres of blood. That might not sound like a lot, and I suppose it isn't. In a bathtub, it wouldn't look too impressive. But when it's all over the place, five and half litres of blood will blow your eyelids clean off. That much paint could cover half a football field. You can picture this, I'm sure. Half a football field painted red. Now change the image a bit. Imagine you're looking over a rocky clearing with a sandy shore on one side and a forest on the other. The bark of the pine and oak trees is covered. Blood is dripping from the leaves and needles. It's soaked into the moss and soil. It's pooling in tiny cracks in the rock. It's all over the porch steps.

And it was all over Luna.

I didn't know what to do. There was so much blood, you couldn't tell where it had come from. At least it hadn't come from Luna. She would have been empty. It must have come from somewhere else.

Luna started running down the front steps. I moved to follow, but as soon as I reached the bottom of the porch I saw the body. It had been stuffed under the stairs. Blood was everywhere. The sight of it and the smell stopped me dead. I'd never fed on human blood, but for eight years it was what my body had been craving, every day, day after day. It brought on a hunger so intense it was a kind of pain. Sharp and nasty. Maybe I'd have felt differently if I'd had a transfusion at the ward just before my escape, or if I'd just finished a brain cocktail or killed another deer, but that's not the way it was.

And so I did exactly what I shouldn't have done. I slipped under the shadow of the stairs to feed.

I recognized the body. It belonged to one of the twins. The blond. His brown eyes were glazed over in death. Blood ran in red ribbons down his neck, which I could see had been snapped and torn open. The flesh there was marked by dark bruises, and all of the vessels were exposed. The person who did this must have been a powerhouse.

I should have felt sorry for the twin, but all I could think about was the blood. How wasteful it was. And how angry it made me to see that it had been sprayed everywhere when I wanted it all for myself. So without a second thought, I drank every drop that was left in his body.

Blood for a vampire is life. Another day. Another week. Another month. Another year. You can't imagine how this felt, to drink life. I was undead, and then for a moment I was more than alive. Let's leave it at that. And that was when the police arrived.

Most vampires fear bright lights, which makes perfect sense. Nothing is more dangerous to us than the sun. So when that police boat appeared out of nowhere and turned its lights on me, I felt as if I were staring death straight in the face.

I am told that when people panic they have one of two responses: fight or flight. They either dig in like a wolverine and take on all comers, or they bolt like a gutless chicken. I discovered a third response that night, which is to stand still like a total idiot and not move a muscle.

Someone started shouting through a megaphone. He said they were the police and not to move. Well, I don't think they could have moved me with a battering ram. Other voices joined in. Some were coming from the porch behind me. Others were coming from the boat. I couldn't pay attention to what they were saying. I was too busy trying to hide my face from the light, so I remember only fragments. Things like "What's going on here?" and "Good God . . ." and "It's him" and "We're too late" and "Get them back inside."

Suddenly men were all around me with guns and lights and loud voices. Only when I felt someone grab me did I struggle. Then my whole body went stiff with pain. I found out later that they had used a Taser on me, like my father used when hunting vampires. It's a weapon that delivers a very powerful electric shock. Had I been Count Dracula or the Baron Vrolok, or even that vampire from the cereal box, I might have put up a better fight, but I had been raised on animal blood. "Bovine crap," as Mr. Entwistle would have said. Not the real stuff. It is human blood that takes a vampire to the next level. I had tasted it for the first time just moments before, and it might have done wonders for me, but I couldn't overcome so many full-grown men. Not when they had that Taser. Every time I moved, I felt the burn of electricity shoot through my body, paralyzing me with pain.

And so they chained my arms and ankles and stowed me away.

The boat ride was terrifying. There were so many lights trained on me, I don't think I could have blinked without the whole world seeing. All the time I heard two officers talking. One kept insisting that they "do it now," another that they "wait." I think they meant to kill me.

The same two officers lifted me out of the boat and onto the dock when we arrived at the marina. Each had a hold of one arm. They shocked me before we got out onto the wharf and again as soon as my feet touched the wooden planks. I was so scared, I think if they'd let go of me I might have turned into a puddle of goo and dribbled back into the water. I couldn't move. I couldn't run. There was only pain. Pain and bright lights, so I couldn't even see where they were taking me. I remember staring down at the gravel parking lot and at the feet of the police officers. It was easier than looking up at the lights. The stones made crunching noises under their shiny black shoes. And I remember when they stopped. A man was standing in front of us. He was leaning on a cane and had a long, pink scar under one eye. It was Everett Johansson.

When he saw me he grunted. There were bright headlights behind him so I couldn't see the expression on his face.

"Has he fed?" he asked.

One of the officers must have nodded, because I didn't hear them answer.

"Well, don't take any chances with him," Johansson continued. "If he moves, shock him."

Then he stepped to the side and opened the back door of a cruiser. I was pushed in, then the door was closed and locked. I was feeling very sick, as if someone had been kicking my stomach.

"What are you going to do?" I rasped. The men were still outside the car talking to Johansson, so I didn't get an answer. Then Johansson walked off towards the water and the other two climbed in the front seat of the car. I heard the engine turn over. Then we lurched forward to the sound of tires on gravel.

"Where are my friends?" I asked.

I was worried they were still back there with whoever had killed that boy. My instincts told me it was Vrolok. What chance would they have against him? A creature from a nightmare . . .

"Where are they?"

The two officers looked at each other. I got my answer when one of them reached back with the Taser. It looked like an electric shaver. Purple sparks crackled from the end of it. Pain followed, and for a few minutes I couldn't talk, so I just sat back against the seat.

As my strength returned, I tried to break my cuffs. It was no use. I was too weak. At least in the arms. But my legs were strong enough to snap the chain that bound my ankles. So I did. Then I turned sideways to try to kick the back door off its hinges, but the officer with the Taser reached back and jolted me again. He said something to me, but I couldn't make it out.

I realized a second later that he wasn't talking to me at all. He was swearing. Two bright lights were coming up behind us. They lit up the interior of the car so that everything looked white. The seat covers, the dashboard, the rear-view mirror. Everything. The officer who was driving stepped on the gas, but it didn't matter. Something slammed into the side of the car just behind the back wheel. My head nearly snapped from my neck as the back of the car skidded sideways towards the ditch. I could hear the tires screech. Then the car started to roll. I've never been on a roller coaster, but it couldn't possibly be as frightening. Or as fast. A car flips so quickly that you barely have time to panic.

In an instant, broken glass was everywhere. The top of the car smashed down against my head. My arms, which were still handcuffed behind my back, were practically wrenched from their sockets. Had I not been so strong, I think they would have ripped clean off. Fortunately we landed upright. I could feel my cheek swelling under my right eye. I think it had slammed into the door. And I must have had a cut on the top of my head, because blood was dripping down past my left ear. A loud noise was coming from the front of the car. It was the horn, which must have been broken, because it didn't stop. The driver's forehead was pressed against an airbag. I was guessing that he was unconscious. The officer beside him looked like he was out of it, too. His head kept shaking back and forth as though he was going to vomit.

Then I heard the sound of feet crunching on gravel. It stopped, and the door beside me began to groan. Metal was being bent. An instant later the door opened.

And there he was. My Uncle Max. He had come to save me.

Chapter 36
Flight

My uncle was holding a crowbar in his hand. He was dressed all in black. There was a belt around his waist with a whole slew of gadgets hanging from it. One of them was a gun. He looked like a commando. I wondered for a brief moment if my father had ever dressed that way when he was hunting vampires. It was like something out of a comic book.

He set the crowbar on the ground, then reached in to pull me out of the police car. When he leaned across my torso, for just an instant his neck was exposed. In the movies, that was where vampires did most of their biting. I'd never really thought about why, but after seeing that boy under the porch, I understood. The neck is the highway to the brain, and the brain needs blood, buckets of it. And unlike the brain, which is surrounded by a hard layer of bone, the vessels in the neck aren't protected at all. Blood there runs very close to the surface, so it's pretty much a bull's eye. When Uncle Max leaned past me, I was tempted to stretch out my teeth and chomp away. I was bleeding and bruised. My body wanted the good stuff so that it could start to heal. But I resisted. It helped to remember what he'd told me—that even vampires have a choice: to be good, or to be something that is less than good. I wanted to do what was right. I wanted to be good.

"Are you all right?" he asked me. "Is anything broken? Are you hurt?"

"I have a cut on my head," I told him.

He took me by the elbow and helped me carefully from the car. Then he inspected my scalp closely and made certain I wasn't cut anywhere else.

"We'd better get something on that. It's bleeding heavily," he said.

He took my elbow to steady me while he led me to his car.

"We'd better get those off of you first," he said. He was talking about my handcuffs. "Can you break them?"

I strained. My arms were aching, but I tested myself, just as Mr. Entwistle said I should. Still, I wasn't quite strong enough.

Maximilian reached down to his belt and removed a canister of something. I heard a hissing noise.

"Try again," he said.

I didn't have to work too hard this time. There was a loud crack and my arms jerked apart. The cuffs were still circling my wrists, but the chain between them was now broken.

"What did you do?" I asked.

"Liquid nitrogen," he replied. "When the metal's frozen, it's easier to break. Now wait here." He stepped quickly behind his trunk, opened it up, pulled out a red case and removed a wad of small, white squares. They were pieces of gauze.

"Hold these against your head," he told me. Then he motioned for me to get in the car while he walked around to the driver's side. "We've got to hurry."

And so I got in, and it was like stepping straight into a spy movie.

The car was unreal. I'd never been in an airplane cockpit before, but I'd seen them in movies, and I'll bet you this car had more dials, buttons and screens than a space shuttle. And it had two steering wheels. I knew this was a little weird. What kind of car had two steering wheels? And they weren't even wheels, really. They were like wheels with the tops cut off so that your hands fit on either side, like the controls for an arcade game, the kind you sit in.

There was no window behind me, just a solid wall of black. I wondered how he saw out the back. Then I noticed that in place of a rear-view mirror there was a small video screen. There must have been cameras in the back of the car, because you could see the road behind us. It was all tinted green.

In front of me on the dashboard was a screen covered with white lines. I figured out straight off that these were roads. A red light appeared on one of the lines. It was beeping and flashing and it moved quickly towards another light, a blue one that was sitting in the middle of the map.

"What's that?" I asked.

"That's either a police car or a car with a police radio," my uncle said. "Either way, we're getting out of here. Now buckle up."

I put the seat belt on. It was padded. Then he stepped on the gas, and the car whined like a jet engine.

"Will they catch us?" I asked.

My uncle smiled, then shook his head. "Not in this car." He coughed a few times into his sleeve, then pushed the pedal to the floor.

My head was forced back against the seat like I'd been shot from a bazooka. I'd driven a few times with Nurse Ophelia when she'd taken me out to the movies, or to bowl or whatever, but she never liked to break the speed limit. Uncle Max didn't break it either. He shattered it to bits. The road was winding, and I kept thinking we were going to fly off into the woods, but somehow he kept us from wiping out.

"Don't worry," he said. "The car has a vacuum in the bottom. The faster we go, the more firmly the car is held in place." Then he asked me how my head was.

I checked the bandages. That was when I noticed for the first time that my burnt hand was better. It must have healed when I drank the boy's blood. But my head wasn't doing quite so well. There was a long, red blotch on the bottom of the bandages. The blood had soaked right through.

"Keep it on," he told me. "It will probably heal before we get to my office, but if not, we'll stitch it up there." Then he pressed a button and a drawer opened up in front of me. He reached inside and pulled out a Kleenex. "Here," he said, "take some. Your chin is covered with blood."

I did my best to scrape it off. Once blood dries it's like paint. I'd have needed a chisel to get it all. There was blood on my shoes as well. And my scrubs. His car looked like it had just about every gadget you could think of, but I doubted a sink was one of them.

Uncle Max reached for the dash and started adjusting a dial. "I went back for you at the hospital," he said, "but I was too late. You'd already run. You can't imagine how relieved I was when I learned that Johansson didn't have you."

I told him about my trip through the ceiling, and that made him smile.

"You did well," he said. "But we were lucky, too. I thought Johansson was retired. I didn't expect him to be working so closely with the police. It must give him access to all kinds of information. We'll have to avoid the authorities for now."

"They can't all be bad," I said.

He shook his head. "No. You're right. But we don't know what Johansson might have told the others about you. And now . . ." He looked me over. "Now he's free to make up all kinds of nonsense. No, let me clear this up. I'll get you to a safe location, then I'll take care of the rest of this mess."

After I got as much of the blood off my face as I could, my uncle asked me what happened the night I escaped from the ward. I told him about Mr. Entwistle. About our escape from the police. And about his death.

"You have to find out if he's all right," I said. It seemed an absurd thing to suggest. Apparently, a whole building had fallen on him. How could he be all right? Unless his body armour was made on the planet Krypton, he'd probably been flattened.

Maximilian coughed quietly, but he kept his eyes glued to the road. "If what they printed in the paper is true, I think you should prepare yourself for the possibility that he didn't survive," he said. "Vampires are just as vulnerable to fire as normal people. And Entwistle kept some nasty company—"

My uncle stopped talking to have another coughing fit. He smothered his mouth with his sleeve, then cleared his throat. I waited for him to say more about Entwistle and what he thought might have happened, but he was apparently finished. I'd forgotten that the two of them were at odds, to say the least.

"Did you find out anything about Nurse Ophelia?" I asked.

My uncle shook his head.

I closed my eyes and let my head fall back against the seat. So Entwistle was gone. And Nurse Ophelia was still missing. She'd done more for me in the last eight years than everyone else in whole world put together. And I hadn't done a thing to help find her. Instead, I'd spent the last few nights thinking of myself and having fun. She deserved better.

"One thing at a time, Zachary," my uncle said. "One thing at a time. You can't do a lot for others when you're running for your life."

"I tried to call you," I told him. "I left a message at your office."

"And I got it. I called the number you left as soon as I could. When I didn't hear back from you right away, I started to get nervous. Your face has been all over the news."

I hadn't realized that he'd called me back. When I told him this, he looked surprised.

"It was later that night," he said. "About ten after eleven."

I wondered why Charlie and I hadn't heard the phone ring. We'd had Dan's BlackBerry with us all night. Then I remembered that when I'd left him the message, I'd given him the number for Charlie's cottage. That was the night of the island party, so neither of us would have been around at eleven. And Dan would have been asleep. He must have picked up the message the next morning, figured it was a wrong number and simply erased it.

"Don't be too hard on yourself," said Maximilian. "You're in good hands now. And I've just secured a deal that should keep us out of trouble. You're going to do just fine. I'm certain of it."

It was hard not to believe him. He looked like he was ready to storm the Batcave.

"Did you tell anyone?" he asked me. "About your condition?"

I nodded. "I told Charlie."

"Anyone else?"

"No."

"Did he believe you?"

"Yes." Then I told him about our conversation in his kitchen. And how I had stalked the deer. Finally, I told him about the body at Luna's.

"It was one of the twins," I said. "And he'd been strangled. I think it was Vrolok."

"What makes you think so?"

I told him about my encounter with the bat at Mr. Entwistle's house. And the fog. And how I'd seen them again at the cottage.

"So you've been there?" my uncle asked.

"Where?"

"Entwistle's house."

I nodded. "Yeah."

"Would you know how to find it again?"

"I think so."

My uncle seemed pleased by this. But it brought on another round of coughing. This was the worst bout yet. He actually had to slow down the car. When it was finished, he ran his tongue over his teeth. I could smell blood in his mouth. He must have been really sick.

"Is that the first time you've tasted human blood?" he asked. "Back at the cottage?"

I nodded. "Is that bad?"

He took a deep breath and checked a few of his gauges. Then he let out a big sigh.

"Yes, it is bad," he said slowly. "It is bad, and it isn't." And he explained to me how human blood made a vampire stronger, which I knew already. But he also told me that once you drank it, you craved it more and more.

"And therein lies the problem," he said. "You need it to be strong and so you will come to hunger for it. If you don't get enough, your desire might drive you to desperate lengths. You might even kill for it, if your hunger can't be controlled."

Well, I had felt the hunger, but I wouldn't kill a human being. Not ever. Or so I thought.

"I didn't kill that boy," I told him. "I found him like that. Maybe I shouldn't have fed . . . but I didn't kill him."

My uncle's head moved up and down slowly while he watched the road. "I know, Zachary," he said. "I know."

I relaxed when I heard him say this. I put my head back and watched the road.

"Do you think my friends will be all right?"

My uncle didn't have a chance to answer. A yellow light started flashing on the dashboard. He took his foot off the gas pedal and the car slowed just a little.

"What's that?" I asked.

"Someone's using a radar gun up ahead," he said. "Probably the police. I'll just have to slow down for a few minutes until we drive through their speed trap."

I checked the electronic map on the dash. Sure enough, a red light had appeared ahead of us on the grid of white lines.

The engine was quieter now that we weren't driving so quickly. I thought I heard something behind me. There was no back seat, just lots of trunk, but I was certain I'd heard a muffled voice.

"Is something wrong?" my uncle asked.

I nodded. "I thought I heard a voice behind us."

My uncle smiled, then reached up and pulled a wire from his left ear. He'd been listening to something. The earpiece was connected to the dash, and when he pulled it out, the sound of people talking came through the rear speakers.

"Is this what you heard?" he asked, turning up the volume.

I listened. "What is it?"

"A police radio. It's how I found out where you were. It and the radar detector will help us to avoid their patrol cars. I'm not taking any chances."

About a second later, we passed a police car parked along the side of the road.

"Will they come after us?" I asked.

My uncle looked over and smiled. "You don't need to worry about them."

"But you wiped that other car right off the road!"

My uncle nodded. "True. But no one saw us. So as far as anyone is concerned, we're just another car on the highway."

My uncle didn't speed up until the patrol car was miles behind us. Then he turned on an interior light and leaned closer. "Let me check that again, would you?" he said, nodding towards my head.

I lifted my hand so he could get a better look at my gash.

"It looks quite a bit better," he said. "I think the bleeding has basically stopped. You might want to get some rest now." He opened a compartment near his elbow that was hidden between our seats. Then he reached in a pulled out a small bottle. "Take one of these. It will help."

I looked at the bottle. The label said "Zaleplon," which sounded to me like a city on the planet Venus or something you would use to de-clog a drainpipe.

"They're sleeping pills," my uncle said. "If you don't feel you need one, don't take one, but I imagine that with all the excitement you've had in the last few days, it might help."

Had I known that I would die the next day, I would never have chosen to go to sleep. I would have stayed awake and asked questions about my mother and my father and what it's like to hunt vampires. And I would have asked to steer the car. I might even have suggested we stop somewhere along the highway so that I could just run for a while under the moon—run so fast that tears would spill out of my eyes. And I would have called Luna, or at least written her a note or something. But I didn't know. And so I swallowed two pills and fell asleep.

Chapter 37
Iron Spike Enterprises

I woke up feeling like a bag of cement. I was lying on a sofa. The room I was in could have fit neatly into an art or history museum. It was as big as the common room in the Nicholls Ward. Oil paintings and masks covered the walls, and busts and statues and carvings stood along the edges. There was even a suit of armour. And weapons, too. When I sat up and rubbed my eyes, I caught a glimpse of two crossed halberds. The wooden shafts were about six feet long, and the iron heads—a wicked blend of axe, hook and spear—had been polished to a deadly shine. When I looked more closely, I could see they were actually on the wall behind me, reflected in a mirror that hung on the opposite side of the room. And I guess I ought to mention that I could see my reflection, too. Because of the movies, some people think a vampire can't see himself in a mirror. It's a neat special effect, and I guess it ties in with this idea that a vampire doesn't have a soul. Well, I don't know anything about that, but I can tell you that I saw myself, and I looked like I'd been attacked by Mr. Entwistle's hairdresser. While I patted down my bed-head, I got up and looked around some more.

The room, long and rectangular, was obviously an office. Adjacent to the sofa was a desk that faced the expanse of the room. Sitting on one corner was a golden cup that must have been worth a fortune. On the wall just behind it was a large painting of a battle scene. Men in red with iron breastplates, long pikes and fin-like helmets were fighting against a bunch of men on horseback. There were muskets and cannons, and it looked like total chaos. I had seen it once before, but I couldn't remember where.

Then I spotted the windows. They sat on either side of the mirror on the wall opposite the sofa. The panels of glass were enormous, running from the floor to the ceiling. Even though no light was coming through them, I could somehow feel the sun shining from behind. I walked over to inspect them and noticed that they were covered with a thick layer of black paint. The only light in the room was coming from two candles, on either side of the couch.

I heard a knock and looked around. There was a door in the far corner of the room opposite the desk. It opened and my uncle came in. He was wearing a suit and looked the way he had when he'd first come to see me, like a man in charge of a bank.

"Just checking in," he said. "I trust you're feeling better?"

I nodded and told him I felt fine.

"Do you need anything?" he asked.

I was a bit dopey, and after getting tossed around in the back of a police car, my body wanted a little blood for repairs. "Something to drink?" I said.

"I suspected as much, but I don't have anything here at the moment. Once the sun goes down, we'll see what we can do."

I asked him where all the stuff in the room had come from.

"Oh, no one place, of course," he answered. "Some items were gifts. That bust of Napoleon, for example. And this cup." He held up the golden chalice I'd noticed earlier. "I received this just yesterday. A present to seal a new contract." Then he raised his hand to indicate the rest of his pieces. "Some I bought overseas while your father and I did our work. That painting I inherited from my parents." He nodded at the battle scene hanging above the desk, the one that was familiar to me. "It used to hang in their living room. You must have been there a few times as a young boy. And truthfully, some of this stuff your father and I took."

He looked at me and smiled. He must have seen the surprise on my face.

"Some vampires are old, Zachary. Not many, but those who survive the first few months of infection can live decades, even centuries beyond a normal human lifespan. And they collect things, as people collect things, to stay connected to the past."

I thought of Mr. Entwistle and his empty house. He was an exception, and he'd wanted me to know it. It made me wonder if a vampire's best hope of survival was to not be connected to anything at all.

Maximilian was looking at me carefully. When he knew he had my attention, he continued.

"Sometimes your father and I found ourselves in possession of old artifacts and paintings, things that once belonged to vampires. Since they technically weren't ours, we gave most of them away to universities or libraries or museums. But we also kept some for ourselves as a payment of sorts, because no one had any idea about the work we did. No organization paid us. No government. We were a secret to all but a few, and our operating costs were very high, so we took artifacts from time to time in order to sell them or keep them as a reward. I hope that doesn't sound inappropriate. I would hate for you to think of your father and me as thieves, just because we sometimes kept what belonged to those we killed." He crossed his arms and looked over the artifacts in the room as though he'd made them all himself. "Perhaps it would help if you thought of these as the spoils of conquest."

I nodded as though I'd understood every word, but between you and me, he didn't seem right in the head all of a sudden. Something about his tone had changed. It was nothing major. He just seemed a little more aggressive than normal. More excited. Like he was about to sit me down to explain his plans for world domination.

"We should have a talk," he said, and as he moved to sit behind the desk, he motioned for me to sit on the sofa. "You must have some questions. Now is the time to ask."

I sat back and thought for a moment. There were so many things I wanted to know about the secret world of vampires. Maximilian probably knew as much as anyone about Vrolok. About the Coven of the Dragon. And Endpoint Psychosis. But he wasn't just a vampire hunter, he was my uncle, and so he knew personal stuff, too. About my father and mother. I didn't know where to begin, so I decided to start at the beginning.

"How did they meet?" I asked.

"Who?"

"My mom and dad."

"They met at Trent University. Your mother studied anthropology, your father archaeology, and so as undergraduates they had a few of the same classes."

"How did she die?"

"Your father never told you?"

I shook my head.

My uncle looked down at his desk. He seemed uncertain about what to say. Then he reached to a console on his desk and flipped a switch. A light came on behind him. It was mounted on the wall, so his whole body became a shadow. One elbow was propped on his desk, and he rested his chin on his hand, between his thumb and index finger. I imagined that he must have spent long hours in this pose. I'd seen it before, back at the ward. It was a thinker's pose.

"There is someone who is better qualified to answer that question," he said, watching me. "Someone who would like to talk to you, if you're feeling up to it."

I nodded.

My uncle stood and stepped over to the wall behind his desk. He reached up and grabbed the light fixture. I noticed that his hand was shaking. When he pulled the light down, a panel in the wall opened. A secret door. He turned to face the opening.

"We are ready for you to join us now," he said.

Then the vampire from my nightmare entered the room.

Chapter 38
Betrayed

The vampire stood just inside the room. Although I had been watching him closely, I never actually saw him move. I would say that he drifted in, but it was more as if the room itself shifted. He was hidden in the corridor one moment, and standing in front of me the next. It left me feeling dizzy and confused. I imagine it's the way someone feels when they drink too much and can no longer trust their own eyes. In place of the fur cloak and gold-buttoned shirt of my dream, he was wearing a suit with long tails that reached past the backs of his knees. Underneath was a lacy shirt with a puffy collar and puffy cuffs. I would like to be able to tell you that it was a Victorian suit in the Balderdash style from 1857, but I don't know anything about that. To me it was just old. Old and purple. To one of his lapels he'd fastened the brooch, the one with the dragon holding a cross in its teeth, the one he'd worn in my dream. He saw me staring at it and a glimmer of amusement flashed in his large eyes. He stroked his thick moustache, then nodded to my uncle, who lowered his head very solemnly.

Uncle Max raised a hand and gestured towards me. "This is my nephew," he said. "Daniel Zachariah Thomson, son of the late Dr. Robert Douglas Thomson, famous archaeologist and vampire hunter, and my former partner. Zachary, this is a new business associate of mine. Former Count of Wallachia and the Grand Master of the Coven of the Dragon. His real name is Vlad. Vlad Tsepesh. You know him as the Baron Vrolok."

The vampire had been watching my uncle as he spoke. Then he turned his eyes on me. I couldn't move. It was as if Mother Nature had forgotten to equip me with any real tools for dealing with trouble. I wondered if this was a human failing. In nature programs, other animals could do all kinds of things when they were threatened. Squids squirted ink and scooted away. Chameleons changed colour. Possums played dead. Hedgehogs rolled into spiny balls. Lambs and rabbits shrieked. Skunks sprayed. Snakes bit. Dogs barked. Cats hissed. Stink bugs stank. The list was endless, really.

Well, if I could have chosen any response at that moment, standing face to face with my father's killer, I would have gone with the mountain gorilla. They go berserk and kill everything that moves. Unfortunately, that isn't what I did. I guess I was just too surprised. I'd never been betrayed before. I understood the word, but there is a huge difference between knowing a word and living it. This was terrible. I was cornered. My uncle was on one side, the Baron was on the other, and the sun was at my back. And it had all happened at a moment when I'd thought I was safe. So I was sort of frozen with disbelief. Like—how did I get here? Then I realized it didn't matter. Unless I tossed myself through the window, there wasn't going to be an easy way out.

The Baron looked me over without speaking. There was a power in his eyes that made it impossible to look away. He seemed to grow taller, more ominous. Then he spoke to my uncle, although his eyes still held me paralyzed. His voice was deep and seemed to come from inside my own head.

"My necklace, does he have it?"

"Yes," my uncle replied.

The Baron reached under his shirt and pulled out a necklace of his own. It was a golden crescent moon. Even though I had never seen it, I recognized it right away. It was the matching piece to the charm around my neck. And just like that, I knew how my mother had died. The Baron must have killed her—killed her and taken the necklace. The instant my mind zeroed in on this truth, a part of me just turned off. Sound disappeared. It was as though I was suddenly deaf. My vision started to narrow, as if I was seeing both my uncle and the Baron through a long tunnel. They were the only two things in the room. A surge of anger made my fists shake. I wanted death. To kill. In ancient times, they called this "blood lust." And that's when I ripped the halberd from the wall above the sofa and started swinging.

I would like to tell you that my first fight was a smashing success—that I was a mountain gorilla and didn't stop until everything around me was kaput, but that isn't what happened. The truth is, I was exhausted, still smarting from the car accident, and up against a true vampire, a creature who had fed for centuries on the blood of humankind and was stronger and faster than anything you've ever seen. So I didn't start a fight so much as I initiated what was to become a dreadful beating.

Vrolok became the kind of evil creature you'd expect to see in a horror film, a being unmoved by the suffering of others. He was fast. I could barely see his ghost-like movements. He took the halberd from me before I could even scrape the dust from his old purple coat. Then he tripped me to the ground, put a hand on my chest and pushed all the air from my lungs.

Through it all, my uncle watched with a face like a statue. I don't think he blinked even once. His eyes were focused on the two of us as though he needed to memorize everything that happened. But it was like he was watching us and *not* watching us, because his face just stayed blank.

When I said at the beginning of the story, way back at the Nicholls Ward, that my uncle had come to the right place, that he was nuts, well, I was right on the money. He really was crazy. He must have been. He'd just rescued me from the Taser-happy police, then looked after my injuries. Why? So I could get flattened in his office? It didn't make a bit of sense. And he didn't seem to care a pinch about what was happening. He didn't lift a finger.

The fight ended seconds later. I fastened both hands around Vrolok's wrist and tried to pry his arm away, but without any air, it was as if someone had flicked a switch and turned off the power. My strength vanished. The room started spinning and my eyes couldn't focus properly. Then I blacked out.

Chapter 39
The Coven of the Dragon

I don't know how long I lay on the floor. I drifted in and out of consciousness, and you can't really keep track of time when that happens. Some time later, my uncle came back into the room. He stood over me with his hands on his hips. I still couldn't see well. My eyes were watering and everything looked blurry.

"Get up," he said. Then he turned his back on me and walked behind his desk. There was a cigar in his hand, which he lit with something that looked like a miniature cannon. He took a big puff and turned to face the painted windows.

"Get up," he said again. "We don't have much time."

I wanted to tell him to leave me alone, but I was too tired, and when I opened my mouth to speak, the pain of moving made me gasp.

He looked down at me with the same blank expression he'd worn during my fight with the Baron. "In life, the only person you can really count on is yourself. Others will abandon you, betray you, disappoint you. You have to learn to depend on yourself. GET UP."

I couldn't believe that he was shouting at me after what had happened. It made me so furious I did stand up. Then I coiled myself for a charge. He probably had a gun handy, so I'd have to be quick.

"Don't be foolish," he said. He had a small black box in his hand. There was a switch on it. "One false move and I blow out the windows. And you know what that means."

I did. The sun would stream in and I would go up like gunpowder, so I straightened up as best I could.

"That's better," my uncle said. "Now, take a seat." He nodded towards the couch.

I shook my head. I wasn't sitting down. I wasn't going to do another thing he told me.

"Fine," he said. He took a haul on his cigar. The end of it glowed an angry orange. It lit up his face, and for just a split second he looked more like a devil than a person.

"That was incredibly foolish, what you did earlier. Reckless . . . mindless . . . stupid . . . I can't imagine what would have happened if I hadn't been here."

He paused. I knew he was giving me a chance to respond, but I had no idea where to begin. For starters, he was making it sound as if he'd saved my life, when he hadn't done a thing. And he was angry. I was the one who was half dead. What did *he* have to be so mad about? Had he forgotten that the Baron killed my mother and father? What was I supposed to do when I met him, snuggle up for a cozy hug?

"I didn't rescue you from Johansson to watch you get flattened in my office," my uncle said. "Another mistake like that, and it might be your last."

He took another puff on his cigar. The smoke brought on a series of coughs that shook his broad chest. Once he'd fought them down, he reached into the drawer of his desk and pulled something out. It took me a moment to recognize my father's journal. He stepped out from behind the desk and walked over to where I was standing.

"You left this in your friend's boat. The Baron brought it here. I flipped through it while you were sleeping. I've found some interesting passages I think you should read." He handed me the notebook.

I snatched it away and stumbled into the sofa. "You don't deserve to touch this," I said.

He blew smoke out through his nostrils. I guess he didn't care.

I stared at him. He stared back.

"Do you want me to read it for you?" he asked.

I looked down at the journal. There were yellow sticky notes marking several of the pages. I opened it to the first and glanced over the writing until I found a passage that had been underlined with a pencil. This is what my father had written.

Max is a true evolutionist . . .

And later, on the facing page, was this passage.

Because of his belief that the fittest will survive, and the confidence he has in his own abilities, he is willing to place himself in the most dangerous situations. I fear for him. At times, he shows a total disregard for his own safety. And yet, if he were not like this, we would never have achieved so many victories over those carriers who have fallen into darkness, who refuse redemption. And so, indirectly, he has saved hundreds, if not thousands of lives . . .

I shook my head. What was this supposed to tell me? Was I supposed to forgive him or something? Did he think it would explain why he had betrayed me and given me over to my father's killer?

I read the rest of the page and the one following.

"Why am I doing this?"

"Just keep reading," Maximilian said.

I found the next passage.

Max put forth the suggestion today that instead of merely monitoring those carriers to whom we have granted amnesty, we use them to hunt other carriers. I am reluctant to endorse this strategy. It seems a dangerous risk, given that we know so little about Endpoint Psychosis and what triggers its onset.

And that was it. He'd marked only those three entries. Well, perhaps my brain had been bruised, or maybe it was still disconnected from my wrestling match with the Baron, but I didn't get it. I looked up at my uncle. His eyes were dark and focused.

"Your father was a very conservative man, Zachary," he said. "Perhaps too conservative. The truth is, the best vampire hunters in the world are other vampires. You have the potential to be counted among them. But you must be able to prove that your mind is healthy. Uncorrupted by the pathogen. Another ridiculous stunt like the one you pulled earlier, and I won't be able to do a thing for you."

He went on to say other things, about Endpoint Psychosis and suicide and spreading the infection, but I wasn't really listening. I was thinking of my father. That he wouldn't have wanted me to bite Maximilian, which is what I wanted to do most at that very moment. I wanted to kill him. I'd like to think it was my hunger that made me think this way. I was a little short of juice, and after tasting human blood for the first time at Luna's cottage, my desire for more was making me furious.

When I looked up at him he must have noticed the change in my expression. That my rage was closer to the surface. Still, he didn't seem worried at all. Who would be? He had the sun as his ally. It was waiting to kill me, hidden behind a thin layer of glass.

"How much do you know about the Coven of the Dragon?" he asked me.

What did this have to do with anything?

"We don't have a lot of time," he said. "Answer me."

I shook my head. "Nothing, really."

My uncle pressed his lips together and nodded slowly. "They are an elite group of vampire hunters. They keep the pathogen from being spread recklessly by those who go insane. Baron Vrolok—Vlad—is the Grand Master of the Coven." He stared at me for a few seconds. I couldn't tell what he was thinking. That this excused the Baron for killing my mother and father and squashing me into submission?

My uncle turned and walked back behind his desk. He was practically shaking with excitement. "Your father and I tried for years to penetrate this organization. It is cloaked in secrecy. We only knew that it existed. And could move with terrible swiftness. On more than one occasion, your father and I started a hunt only to discover that the Coven had finished it for us. Always very thoroughly."

He stopped talking and opened one of the desk drawers. I expected him to remove something, but he didn't. He closed the drawer instead.

"And do you know how I made contact with them?" he asked.

He looked at me as though I was supposed to guess. Like I should have been as excited as he was. I barely had the energy to see across the room. Why should I care?

"I didn't," he said. "He came to me. Vlad came to me. He came with an offer, and I have accepted it."

He looked at me and started coughing. The coughing turned to hacking. He had a handkerchief in his pocket. He removed it and covered his mouth. When he pulled it away, I could see the crimson stain of his blood on the cloth. For just an instant, he looked like a wraith. Shrivelled and decayed. Then he straightened up and thumped his chest with the side of his fist. It helped him clear his throat.

"You're dying," I told him.

He nodded. "Yes. Yes, I am. But I'm taking steps to ensure that my work will continue."

Steps? What did that mean? I took my best guess.

"You want to become a vampire!" I said. "You want to enter the Coven of the Dragon. You want to work for *him*!"

Chapter 40
Abandoned

My uncle shook his head. He was still fighting with the disease in his chest. For all his strength, I could see it would soon get the better of him.

"I will not be working *for* Vrolok, but *with* him. Together, we will be unstoppable. Perhaps you have heard this maxim: *The enemy of my enemy is my friend.* Well, the Baron and I have many of the same enemies. Those, as your father says, who refuse redemption."

My hands were shaking. I almost dropped my father's journal. "But he's the worst—"

"No," my uncle interrupted. "No, he isn't. In time, you'll see how depraved the worst ones get. You don't—"

"But he killed my father. And my mother. Your sister. Your very own sister!"

"Well, he shouldn't have," Maximilian snapped. "Your headstrong father should have done a better job of protecting her. He failed, and we both paid for it. And taking off to Libya without me—it was foolish. Even so, he almost pulled it off. If you hadn't come along, Vrolok would have died."

"That's not my fault," I said, although I realized it probably was.

"Not your fault?" my uncle said. He snorted. Then he took another puff from his cigar. It seemed to calm him down a little. "No. Maybe not. But it *is* what happened. Vrolok survived. And yes, he did kill your father. And he killed my sister. But he was different then. Now he is back with the Coven. They would not accept him as a member if he wasn't mentally sound."

I started shaking my head, but my uncle ignored me and kept talking.

"Nothing can bring your parents back, Zachary. I know this must be hard for you to understand. But my work must go on. Since your father's death, I have been searching in vain for a competent ally. As the Grand Master of the Coven, Vrolok has a network of informants greater than most governments'. The Coven's eyes are everywhere. Places your father and I couldn't possibly have gained a foothold. Iran, China, Russia . . ."

He pulled out his chair and sat down. His eyes never left mine, even when he puffed his cigar.

"You asked me back at the Nicholls Ward how I had found you. It was an accident. I was searching for a different vampire. Even now, Vrolok's informants are gathering information to aid my search. This one has proven to be extremely elusive."

"Is it Mr. Entwistle?" I asked.

My uncle shook his head. "No. Entwistle is out of the picture now."

I took a step forward. It wasn't an aggressive move—I was still wobbly—but Maximilian raised the detonator to remind me who was in charge. Still, I had to do something. The expression on my uncle's face, it had changed slightly. Or maybe it was the tone of his voice. There was guilt in it. I could just tell.

"You killed him?" I said.

He paused, then nodded. "It wasn't intentional. I was trying to shut down an operation that provides blood to a number of dangerous vampires. Ones who have reached a point of mental decay that makes them unmanageable. Entwistle was trying to protect them. He has several houses in the city where he offers them refuge. You stayed in one yourself." He paused to take a deep breath. "He wasn't the intended target. He was just unfortunate. When he showed up, there was nothing I could do. The die was cast."

I watched my uncle's face as he spoke. He wasn't lying. Mr. Entwistle was really dead. All the hope just drained out of me.

"I don't understand why you would kill someone like him and help someone like the Baron. He's evil. Can't you feel it?"

My uncle butted the stub of his cigar in an ashtray. Then he folded his arms across his chest.

"You are wrong about the Baron. He's not as he once was. Despite his past crimes—and I know they are many—he is willing to redeem himself. To help control the spread of this pathogen. It is important work. More important than the life of any one man. Or any one vampire. You or your father, John Entwistle or anyone."

"So you don't care that he killed my parents? My father . . ." I was clutching his journal so hard that my fingers began to press through the cover. I wanted to add that Vrolok had killed me too, that he had ruined my life, but I couldn't speak.

"I am not going to be consumed by thoughts of revenge, if that's what you mean. I have to weigh the lives of your parents against the lives of those I will save by killing other vampires. As a member of the Coven, I will be in a position to do immeasurable good. As will you. I've told the Baron about you. We both think you have extraordinary potential. Few vampires live past the first year of infection. Did you know that? The fact that you have survived for eight years on your own is incredible. But it is not enough. You won't be accepted in the Coven unless you can prove that you can control yourself. And work with the Baron. And that means you must forgive him for what he's done."

My uncle stood up. Then he pulled down the light behind his desk to activate the secret door in the wall.

"Where are you going?" I asked.

"It's daytime, Zachary. You can feel that, can't you?"

I nodded. The sun was strong behind the blackened windows.

"This is the best time to hunt vampires. I am after one in particular. One that got away from your father many years ago. With the help of the Coven, that hunt will end today."

"And what is going to happen to me?"

"That is the Baron's concern now," my uncle said. "You may be my nephew, but that is less important than the fact that you're a vampire. As Grand Master of the Coven, it is the Baron who will decide your fate."

"What does that mean?"

"The pathogen you carry causes insanity in most people who get infected. Given your recent behaviour, your mental state is being called into question. So the Baron is going to test you. I suggest you prepare yourself. He will be here shortly."

He must have seen the look on my face when he said this, because he didn't head for the secret door. Instead, he walked over to where I was standing and put his hands on my shoulders.

"If I didn't have the utmost confidence in you, Zachary, I would never allow this." His grip was firm. He looked straight into my eyes. Then he nodded and walked to the doorway.

Just before exiting he turned back to me and made a fist. I could see the muscles in his arm ball tightly inside his sleeve. "You are your father's son, Zachary. And we will be great hunters together, you and I. Keep your head and you'll do just fine."

He looked me over once, then left. I heard the panel close behind him. And that was it.

I couldn't believe this was happening. I stumbled to the couch and eased myself onto the cushions.

I had been so hopeful after my uncle's first visit. A normal life seemed to be just around the corner. And now this. I put my head into my hands and felt my whole body shake. I couldn't make sense of anything. What was my uncle thinking? Was he bewitched? Charmed? If Dracula could make you do things you weren't supposed to do, why not the Baron? He was evil. How could Maximilian not see?

Endpoint Psychosis. The Baron was there. I wasn't. And still, my uncle trusted him to pass judgment on me.

Maybe that had nothing to do with it. Maximilian was dying. He was looking for a way out. And Vrolok was offering him just that. And more. Entry into an organization that would put him at the top of the food chain. A perfect place for an evolutionist, a man who believed in survival of the fittest.

I looked at the windows. The sun was still up. It would be for another hour. I couldn't leave. I couldn't stay. The parts of my body that weren't in pain were numb. I wanted desperately to talk to someone. To have Charlie cheer me up with a wisecrack, or to feel Luna's hand on my arm. I would have settled for a familiar face from the Nicholls Ward, even the Chicago Man, but I was totally alone.

It wasn't until that moment that I really understood what it meant to be an orphan. To know that there was no one alive in the world who had the power to save me. My father wasn't going to kick in the door. Mr. Entwistle was finished. My friends had no idea where I was. My uncle was right. There was only me. And I was a mess.

I had to get out somehow. Find a place to hide. I couldn't let Vrolok find me like this. I put my hand on the arm of the sofa and pushed myself up as quickly as I could. Too quickly. I got dizzy. My vision started to go spotty and I tripped over the carpet. And so I was kneeling on the floor when the Baron came back into the room.

Chapter 41
Reunion

Vrolok moved into the office dragging two long black bags, one in either hand. Unlike my uncle, who made me think of a stone statue when he walked, solid and purposeful, Vrolok seemed to shift from one place to another without moving, as though the room just bent and allowed him to be wherever he wished. It was soundless, and the sight of it was nauseating.

I turned my attention to the bags he was carrying. They looked like the kind of thing the police would put a dead body in. I could tell by the way they were moving that people were struggling inside. The Baron pushed each to the floor and I heard two muffled cries. The people inside, their mouths must have been gagged. I recognized that sound right away. I'd heard it before. During the drive with my uncle, noises just like that had come from inside his trunk. He'd covered it up with a bunch of hooey about the police radio, and I'd fallen for it. But it wasn't the police radio I'd heard. It was these two.

The Baron looked down and saw me on my knees. "Ah, a true penitent."

The words stabbed inside my mind. His voice seemed to come from everywhere at once so that you couldn't really tell where he was.

"Such faith is a rare thing in this age of skeptics. In a vampire, rarer still. Do they not call us soulless creatures?"

I had no idea what he was talking about. Then I realized that he thought I was praying. I probably should have been.

"You do well to concern yourself with such things," he said. "You will be meeting your God soon. I hope you will send Him my regards."

The Baron started moving towards me. I tried to stand up, but my head was reeling and I fell over sideways.

"It is just as well, my son," he said. "God cannot help you here."

He reached down, grabbed the front of my shirt and hauled me off the floor. With his other hand he snatched my necklace, then he tore it over my head and let me drop.

"This was a gift to my wife . . ."

He paused and stared at the window. It was exactly where the sun would have been. His expression was vacant.

My wife . . . The words echoed in my head almost too quietly to notice.

He saw me on the floor and seemed to remember where he was. When he spoke, the necklace dangled from his fist.

"Your father killed her. Then he stole this necklace and gave part of it to your mother. He had no right!" When he looked at me his eyes were black. His lips moved a little, revealing the long incisors underneath. I couldn't tell if he was smiling or snarling.

"I understand you have been talking to your uncle. A most useful man . . ." The Baron bent so that he was crouched down beside me. "But perhaps a little too trusting?" He reached out and brushed the side of my cheek. The touch of his skin made my insides squirm.

"You must forgive him for his weakness. Few men cope well with death. Only those of unwavering faith. Or those who have suffered much. He is neither. He seeks immortality. I have offered him this, in exchange for you."

He picked me up and set me on my feet. When he let go, I fell to my knees again.

"For what has happened, blame no one but yourself," he continued. "The day your father died, I should have perished. Burned to ashes. But fate brought you to me, and with your blood I endured. What an irony! To become that which your father once hunted. And to fall into the power of a vampire he himself would have destroyed had you not interfered. God is quite a trickster, is He not?"

He turned his back to me and drifted away. As soon as his eyes were off me, it was like I could suddenly breathe again. But the feeling of relief didn't last long. When he turned and fixed me with a dark stare, I froze again.

"Fate has bound us together, my son. I am your doom."

He then bent and picked up one of his hostages. With his other hand he ripped open the black bag so that I could see the person inside. It was Charlie! He was bound and gagged, and his eyes were wide with terror. I could see two small, red dots on his throat, as though he'd been bitten, and his skin was horribly pale. Vrolok pushed him to his knees, then grabbed the second bag and tore it open. It was Luna. She didn't look frightened. She was past that. She was in shock. Her clothes were still covered in blood. I could see the same red holes in the side of her neck. She glanced around the room with a face as white as chalk. I couldn't tell if she had any idea what was happening.

The Baron pushed Luna to her knees so that she was shoulder to shoulder with Charlie. "To see old friends, is it not wonderful?"

I raised myself to one knee. I could almost stand up. Almost.

He shook his head, as though I'd disappointed him somehow.

"You know the fate of most vampires. I see that. But no one recognizes madness in themselves. That is for others to discern. And so we have brought your friends along to test you."

He sucked a breath in past his teeth. The sound of it made my stomach tighten. He watched me with his bulging eyes and I felt them burning into my head.

"You were careless, you see." He scratched a finger under Charlie's chin. "You told this one you were infected." Then he glided past Luna and grabbed a handful of her hair. "And this one saw enough to divine the truth herself. Tragic, but fate isn't always kind . . ."

He raised one hand towards me. His fingers were long and gnarled with age, but I had felt them pressing down on my chest. They were strong. His eyes widened for just a second, and again I couldn't breathe.

"It isn't safe for humans to know this about us, and so I am giving you a choice. Consider carefully." He flicked a finger towards Charlie and Luna. "There were two halberds on the wall earlier. It was most kind of you to bring them to my attention. I had them fashioned into blunt stakes. There are three of you here. Two will be impaled for my amusement. It is for you to decide who will receive this honour."

The Baron stared at me while I crouched on the floor. I didn't whimper, but I couldn't stop tears from rolling down my cheeks. I pushed myself to my feet. I wasn't going to face him on my knees.

"Good," he whispered. "Good."

He waited while I got my balance. The whole time I kept wondering if this was really happening, if I really had to choose. My uncle's words kept coming back to me—that this was a test. It was about my mental state. What was I supposed to do? Argue? Fight? I looked at the Baron to see if there was something in his face that might give me a clue. It was a big mistake. His eyes dug into my brain. What he saw there made him smile, and that's when I realized that my uncle had been duped. My sanity was just fine. I didn't need a test to tell me that.

Neither did the Baron. This was about revenge. It was about cruelty. It was about evil and torture and death. And unfinished business.

The Baron nodded. "Quite right," he said. "Now make your choice. Who lives? And who dies?"

Chapter 42
The Test

I couldn't speak. My lips moved, but no sound came out. The Baron must have seen. Or maybe he just knew what I was thinking. He answered my silent question.

"Why? You ask why? Is the answer not obvious? Your father robbed me of a treasure beyond price. His debt has passed to you. You are here to suffer. And you will. But perhaps not in vain. You could save yourself . . ."

I shook my head. I didn't want his voice in there, telling me lies. He wasn't going to spare anyone.

"Of course I will," he said. "I am not without honour. And I believe God speaks to all of us in His own way. There were two halberds. Was that not a sign? Two long, wooden shafts for two blunt stakes for two slow deaths. It can mean nothing else."

I looked at Charlie, then at Luna. I wanted them to understand how sick I felt.

"You can let them go," I said. "They haven't done anything."

The Baron shook his head. "No," he whispered. "They haven't. But you have. You revealed yourself too carelessly." He looked at Luna and Charlie with contempt. "You must learn to see people for what they are. Food. A resource to be exploited. A source of amusement, perhaps. But never more than this. A hard lesson to learn, but a vital one, if you wish to join me and become a member of my Coven."

I saw his fingers twitch slightly when he said this, as if he was getting ready to slash something.

"Your father believed a vampire could be tamed. 'Redeemed,' he called it. A life spent pilfering donated blood. He was a fool. What kind of vampire sucks blood from a bag? We are predators. And a predator makes no apologies. You don't expect a wolf to repent for killing a *deer*, do you?"

The Baron stared at me. I couldn't look away. It would have been a denial of the truth. I had killed a deer in the forest, chased it down and fed. I had been a predator. And I hadn't felt the slightest bit sorry for what I'd done.

The Baron looked amused. He began to circle me. He drifted past one shoulder, then the other. "We are more alike than you realize. The spirit of the hunter is in us both. It stirs in your heart. I see it. Embrace your true nature, and together, we can transform you into something divine. Something eternal. All it will take is a little sacrifice, and a few more nights like the last one, when you found that gift I left for you."

I had no idea what he was talking about. Then I remembered the boy, the blond twin, whose body I had found at Luna's cottage. Was that what he meant? I saw him nod. He was right behind me, speaking straight into my mind.

"It was good, wasn't it? That first taste of human blood. Why deny it? It is ambrosia to our kind. And it is the only thing that can sustain you now." The smile on his face slipped away. The look that replaced it was one of exaggerated pity. "You are weak. That is why you suffer. And yet, only through suffering does one become strong. Don't you wish to be strong?"

The Baron stood in front of me and put his hands on his hips. His head tilted up as he spoke.

"I can make you so much more than you are. But you have to give up your past, starting now. So make your choice. Who dies? Tell me now, or I will have you all impaled."

I nodded, as though I finally understood what he was getting at, but I was careful to look down at the floor so he couldn't see into my eyes. I couldn't risk that he would sense what I was thinking. That there was a way out of this. I needed the Baron to get angry. So I did my best to irritate him. I made like the Chicago Man and started muttering incoherently. The only thing I left out was the tune.

"What was that?" the Baron said.

I mumbled again, making sure my mouth was moving but my head was down so he couldn't lip-read or look into my eyes and see that I was speaking gibberish on purpose.

"At me, pup," he hissed. *"Look at me!"*

He stepped forward, grabbed me by the throat and hauled me off my feet so that they were dangling above the floor. It hurt and I couldn't breathe, but it was working. I was so close. All he had to do was toss me against a wall, any wall. Then I could throw something at the windows. A statue. A candlestick. Anything. The sunlight would stream in and kill us both.

Instead, the Baron stared straight into my eyes. He glanced at the painted windows and smiled. Then he turned me around so that my back was against his chest. He wrapped the other arm around me so I couldn't move.

"Clever boy," he whispered. "Our weakness is known to you. And my strength, you sense that too, do you not? Indomitable. Eternal.

You desire this, too. You cannot hide it. You fear your end. But to hunt through the ages, your mind cannot be mired here. You must let go of all this." He waved a hand at my friends. "You cannot be connected to anyone but me. Only I will endure."

The Baron still had his hand around my throat. He let go so that his arms were around my chest in a bear hug.

"Because you are a vampire, because you are immortal, you think that time is not your enemy, but it is," he said. "Time is a thief. It will take everything from you. All of your friends, the ones you love, they will die centuries before you. All that you value will be stripped away. Music will change. Your language will change. Your country will change. Your religion. Everything will change but you. Cling to the past and it will drive you insane. I am doing you a favour. I am teaching you how to give up that which you care most about. You will thank me for it in time. When you are more evolved in your thinking. More detached and independent."

He held me up so that I was suspended at arm's length above the floor, then he set me down. By the time I had my balance, he was standing behind Luna and Charlie.

"You will choose," he hissed. *"Now."*

I was out of time. We were done for.

Then I heard a knock. Four quick raps. The secret panel opened and Maximilian stumbled in. I recognized him only by his suit. There was a black bag over his head and his arms were tied behind his back. He struggled to keep his feet, then tripped and fell against his desk.

The Baron dropped me. I heard another familiar sound—heels clicking on a hard floor. And that was when Nurse Ophelia walked in.

She wasn't dressed like a nurse when she came to save me. She was wearing a dress. An old dress. And nothing I'd ever laid eyes on was as beautiful as she was that day. Nothing. Not in any painting. Not in any movie. Not anywhere.

The Baron looked absolutely shocked.

"Ophelia . . . How is this possible?"

Ophelia looked at him and smiled. It was a smile unlike any I'd seen on her face. I can't imagine what she was feeling. Regret, maybe? Sadness? Disappointment? I don't know. But an instant later it was gone and her face hardened. When she spoke next, her voice was like granite.

"I have come to offer *you* a choice, *husband*."

Chapter 43
Choices

Ophelia and Vrolok stood face to face for a few seconds. Neither moved. Then the Baron drifted past me, but Ophelia raised her hand and he stopped.

I started backing away as quietly as I could. Luna was curled up on her side. I think she was shaking, but I couldn't really tell. I didn't want to take my eyes off the Baron in case he noticed I was sneaking off. Charlie was still on his knees, doing his best impression of a mouse in a reptile zoo. When I put my finger to my lips in the universal "Be quiet" sign, he shook his head. I didn't know if he meant "No, I won't make a sound" or "No, please don't come anywhere near me if that freak behind you is going to turn around and notice I'm still here!"

Then, while we both watched, stupefied, Ophelia reached down, grabbed my uncle by the shoulder and hauled him from the floor so that he was half sitting, half leaning against the side of his desk. She pulled off his hood. Blood was dripping from a welt on his forehead, but he ignored it. His eyes were alert and focused. I could tell he was thinking. Calculating.

"I am giving you a choice," she said. "Give up the boy and his friends and we will leave quietly and disappear. Then you and this worm can go back to doing whatever it is you do."

The Baron had his back to me, so I wouldn't have been able to see his face even if I'd wanted to. The tone of his voice was one of total disbelief.

"Ophelia . . . how?"

"How? How am I still alive? It's simple, really. I never died. Dr. Thomson didn't kill me. He let me go."

As soon as Nurse Ophelia spoke, I asked myself the obvious question. Why would my father have wanted to kill her? It made no sense. And then it did. Ophelia was a vampire, just like me! She always worked the night shift at the Nicholls Ward. She could see in the dark as well as I could, and she knew what to put in my brain cocktails. She could toss a boy into a trash bin. It made me wonder if she was the vampire Maximilian had referred to, the elusive one he believed had escaped my father.

"Dr. Thomson gave me a choice," Ophelia continued. "To hide and never again take a human life, or to be destroyed. I chose to hide. And I sealed my contract with a gift, as is the custom. I gave him *my* necklace. And after you killed him, I chose to look after his son, who is the most decent boy on the face of this earth, and if you don't agree to let him go, you're going to die in this room."

"So that is my choice?" the Baron said. "To let this boy go, or be killed by my *wife*?"

He sounded amused by the whole thing. But just like that, he changed, and his voice was so angry I'm surprised the light fixtures didn't shatter.

"You Judas! You had me believe you were dead!"

I was shocked that Nurse Ophelia could stay so calm in the face of his rage. His voice was an explosion. It made me wish I was on the other side of the planet. But when he spoke again, he sounded hoarse. Deflated.

"How I have suffered. You cannot imagine."

"I don't have to imagine," she said. "But I made a promise—to disappear and have nothing to do with you. And I have kept that promise."

"And what of your promises to me?"

"We both made promises," she said. "To love each other forever. To give up the old ways. And to be decent. But you broke your promises. You became what you are. What you were. You gave up your goodness, and so you gave away the only part of you that was worth loving."

"Oh, spare me the melodrama," he snapped. "We are vampires. You know what this means. To live—to be truly alive—we must hunt and we must kill."

"And since when did that include terrorizing children?"

The question hung in the air, unanswered, for a long time.

"So you would choose this boy over me?" the Baron asked.

Nurse Ophelia looked at him squarely, then her eyes slipped past him to where I was waiting. Her head shook slowly and she smiled such a perfect smile I could have cried.

"Vlad, you demented sadist, I would choose a sewer rat over you."

I cringed when I heard Ophelia speak. Then I felt Vrolok's hate and anger swell. I was overcome by the feeling that the most terrible things I could imagine were about to happen. The presence of evil that had nearly undone me at Stoney Lake filled the room until it was practically bursting.

Vrolok rose. He made no effort to disguise the malice in him. Instead, he unleashed it. It was foul. You could hardly breathe the air.

"There is a third option," he said. "I could rip this boy's throat out and feed his friends to the crows." Then he turned around to grab me.

Well, the look of surprise on his face when he saw me is difficult to describe. He'd forgotten about me, and I'd been busy. For a moment he was too confused to act. He had expected to find me curled up at his feet, exhausted and humbled, but I wasn't there. I was right in his face, chest to chest, eye to eye, tooth to tooth, and I was so angry, so ready to go berserk, that I'd have made the most insane mountain gorilla proud. My body was healed and I was strong again. Supernatural. And I can tell you, if the Baron had been given a choice right then and there to face me or dive into a pool of hungry sharks, he would have been wise to go find a bathing suit.

So while he stared at me in amazement, I wound up and threw a punch that nearly broke the sound barrier. And when it hit him in the jaw, he flew clear across the room.

Chapter 44
My Second Death

You have to be wondering how I managed this. Perhaps you've figured it out already.

While the Baron and Ophelia were having their argument, I was trying to convince Charlie and Luna to crawl out the door with me. But Charlie wouldn't move. He just shook his head like I was asking him to jump off a cliff. And I couldn't get Luna to even acknowledge that I was there.

"Come on," I whispered, "hurry!" But I might as well have been speaking Swahili. She didn't respond at all, even when I untied the ropes around her wrists and shook her gently by the shoulders. When I shook her again, she just squirmed back against the wall. So I had to come up with another plan.

This whole time, I was still listening to the conversation between the Baron and Ophelia. I didn't think he was going to let us go. And

I knew Ophelia wasn't going to leave us there. They couldn't both have their way, so things were going to get messy.

Well, there was no way I was going to let Ophelia face the Baron alone. He wasn't like that boy she'd tossed into the trash—a drunken teenager armed with nothing but a foul mouth. He was a killer. And my uncle—underneath that suit he was a piece of iron. If he got his hands free, he could certainly tip the balance. And so I did the unthinkable.

I bit Charlie and I drank until he died.

I hope you can forgive me for this. He was my best friend, and I loved him. I didn't mean to do it. I just needed enough blood to fix myself. I thought that if I took just a little, Charlie would be fine. After all, it was supposed to take more than one bite to turn someone into a vampire. But that's not what happened. I started drinking and I couldn't stop myself. The killing urge took over. And it felt so intoxicating that I didn't give my friend a second thought, not until he started having a heart attack. Then I looked into his face. I wish I hadn't. It was the most tragic thing I'd ever seen. His fear and confusion. It gave way to a terrible pain. He looked as though someone was pulling his insides out. His back arched. When he settled back to the floor, he was gone.

This should have crushed me. My best friend. And it was all my fault. But all I felt was rage. And power. I had tasted human blood only once before, and that was a very small dose—the body at Luna's cottage had been nearly empty. This rush was on a different scale. I gorged until my body swelled. Charlie's blood went to work right away. My exhaustion and soreness vanished. Dark bruises faded yellow and then disappeared entirely, as though someone had taken a cloth and just wiped them away. In seconds, I was filled with an energy that you have never possessed and never will. And so when the Baron turned around I was supercharged. He looked at me with total disbelief in his eyes, and then he was airborne.

This started an avalanche of events that fell so quickly, one after the other, you would have needed a vampire's eyes to sort it all out. The Baron hit the wall behind the desk and fell to the floor. An instant later he was on his feet, moving like a blur. He had a stake in his hand, the remnants of one of the halberds. The head had been removed from the shaft, so it looked more like a blunt spear now. Fortunately, another blur got in his way. It was Ophelia. She met his charge like a rock. The shaft of wood flew to pieces. Ophelia stumbled. The Baron tried to move past, but she grabbed one of his legs. I guess she knew more than one way to stop a man in his tracks.

The Baron raised his hand to strike her, but he didn't. "Insufferable woman!" he snapped.

I picked up a small statue to use like a club, but I didn't get to do anything with it, at least not right away, because the Baron's charge had stalled. Then I noticed that my uncle had somehow freed himself. His hands were loose and he was opening one of the drawers in his desk. I whipped the statue at him, but he ducked out of the way and it exploded against the wall behind him. He rolled to his feet. The little black box, the detonator, was in his hand. I met his eyes from across the room. He nodded, smiled, then flicked his head towards the door. "*Get out,*" he seemed to be saying. Then he threw the switch.

Pain. It started with the blast. A shock wave followed that knocked me to the ground. It made my ears bleed. Then glass showered everywhere, tearing through the skin of my hands and face. But none of this compared with the sun.

The windows were facing west. As the light of the setting sun streamed into the room, I caught a brief flash of my uncle as he tipped the light on the wall, the one that activated the secret panel. Then he disappeared.

I started to burn.

Someone took hold of my arm. It was Ophelia. She was running for the door. We were almost free when I jerked to a halt just inside the threshold. The Baron had crossed the room and taken hold of my other arm. He was screaming too, or maybe he was laughing, I couldn't tell, but I'd never heard anything that sounded so insane, so malicious. Not during eight long years in a mental ward.

And so a tug-of-war began. I was the rope, with Ophelia on one side and the monster on the other. It was excruciating. But Ophelia and I were close to the doorway and the dark hall behind. The Baron was standing directly in the sun. He wasn't going to last as long as we were.

I felt his fingers dig into my arm. All the while, he screamed his insane scream. Then he let go, and for just an instant, I thought Ophelia and I were going to make it to safety.

It shames me to be saying this, but in my panic, I had forgotten about Luna. The Baron hadn't. He must have realized he was close to death. His body was a torch. He needed blood, and she was the only source in the room, so he made straight for her.

Luna was still lying on the floor beside Charlie's body. I could see that she was bleeding heavily from the explosion of glass. I felt Ophelia pull me towards the door. She had hold of my wrist and was trying to get me into the hall and out of the sun. I twisted my hand away, then used her momentum to push her out through the door. She turned around as she fell. Surprise was all over her face. For a second our eyes met. She must have realized right then that I wasn't coming with her, because she reached out for me and called my name, and there was great pain in her voice.

I slammed the door shut and tipped a large statue in front of it so that she couldn't get back in. My skin started cracking. It was black. Charlie's blood was keeping me alive, but I didn't have long. I grabbed a picture from the wall and held it over me like a shield, then I crouched and ran for Luna.

She was kicking her way across the floor like a crab, trying to escape the Baron, who was crawling towards her. His clothes were on fire. The sun was setting, and so the last rays of the day streamed in. They had burned through the muscles of his legs, neither of which was working. I could see some of his bones as he dragged himself farther away from me.

Luna reached the wall and couldn't go back any farther. Her emerald green eyes were wide. Her shock was gone. She knew exactly what was about to happen. She was kicking at the Baron. His moustache and hair were gone and the skin on his face was burned black so that his head looked like a charred skull. He pushed her feet out of the way, put his hands around her shoulders and pulled her neck towards his mouth. Then he stopped.

He stopped with my hands around his throat.

After feeding on Charlie's blood, catching a half-baked corpse with fried legs wasn't all that difficult. I hauled him off the ground as if he were made of straw. He scratched at my face, but his strength was gone. Mine wasn't. Not quite. I held him at arm's length and looked him straight in the eyes. I can't tell you what I saw there. Insanity, perhaps? Pain? Or fear? There was so little left of him that was recognizable, there was no way to know.

The only thing that wasn't charred was the necklace he was wearing. I'd never seen the two pieces attached as they were now. The golden crescent fit perfectly along the edge of the full silver moon. Both reflected the fading orange light of the sun. It had nearly set, and the same rays that were stretching out to warm the bottoms of the clouds were streaming into the room, killing me.

There was little left to the Baron now. He weighed less than a child. Still, there was something in him, an awareness, a soul. I can't say. But he was still alive, or still undead. I thought of what my father would have done. And I thought about what Mr. Entwistle had told me in the safe house when we'd discussed the vampire problem. I looked out the window, then spun and threw him as far from me as I could.

I picked Luna up in my arms. I needed to take her somewhere she could get help. The pain nearly finished me. I stepped towards the secret passage, hoping it might take us somewhere safe, but I didn't have the strength. My legs buckled. I fell and dropped her to the floor. We landed in the shadow of the desk. She moaned softly and her eyes fluttered open. I would like to tell you that she recognized me, that there was understanding in her expression, but that's not what I saw. She was scared stiff. And who wouldn't have been? I must have looked like something straight out of a zombie movie.

I wished at that moment that there were some way to go back in time. I would have returned to the bonfire and started all over again. I felt cheated. Like this could have been a different story if I'd just done a few things differently. It seemed a terrible injustice—that I'd spent all those years alone in a mental ward only to die so soon after tasting real life for the first time. But life is like that sometimes. The things you want most are impossible and there's nothing you can do about it.

Life is also about choices. That's what my father believed. He chose to offer vampires a shot at redemption. He respected their right to decide for themselves whether they could give up the hunt. Nurse Ophelia had made her choices. To leave the Baron. To look after me when my father died. The Baron had made choices, too. Cruel ones. And Maximilian—he had chosen survival.

Me? I had one last choice to make. As my uncle had said: to be good, or to be something that was less than good. You see, all I could smell was blood. Old blood on Luna's clothes from the twin's body, and the fresh stuff that had leaked from the cuts on her neck and face. I was almost finished, and the hunger in me was more intense than the fire in my muscles and bones. All I had to do was pull her in and drink. She was weak, barely conscious. She wouldn't have been able to stop me. But she was alive. And she looked as though she was going to make it. Maybe. Once I'd started feeding, it would have been impossible for me to stop. And I would have needed all of her blood. It would have killed her, just like Charlie. So that isn't what I chose. I chose to be good. I chose to die.

I reached up. I was still holding the necklace. There wasn't much flesh left on my fingers and I nearly dropped it. I wanted her to take it. If anyone should have it, I thought, it should be someone who believed in giving people second chances, people like the young offenders she worked with. My father would have liked that. He believed in second chances, too. And I wanted her to know she'd be okay. That I wasn't going to hurt her.

I think she must have understood, because her expression changed. She took the chain that was hanging from my hand and held it up so that the moon charm caught the fading sunlight, just as it had caught the light of the bonfire that first night on Stoney Lake. The night I discovered real joy. She must have remembered too, because she smiled. It was the tired smile of a friend in pain. But it was still perfect, and it made everything all right.

And that was the last thing I saw before I died.

Epilogue

Life After Death

I have heard people say that religion was invented because people are afraid of death. They can't face the idea of not existing. They need to know that there is something after. Something more.

There is.

Many people have described it. Hearts stop beating and death occurs. Some people remember leaving their bodies. Most remember a tunnel of light. Then the heart starts up again and they come back. And they are never the same.

What I remember most about the tunnel of light is that I was not alone. I became a part of something much greater than myself. And I felt that it was good.

But you know that my second death wasn't my last. I'm not a ghost writer. I left the tunnel of light, or I passed through it, and I woke up in a warm bed. My chest was rising and falling in a comfortable rhythm. I could hear the familiar hum of electric lights. My eyes were slow to focus, but I saw beside me the faces of those I knew and loved.

Charlie. Then Ophelia.

"Hello," said Ophelia. There were tears in her eyes.

"Am I in Heaven?" I asked.

"Close," said Charlie. "You're in Peterborough."

"Charlie . . . you're alive . . ."

"Not quite," he said. He was sitting in a chair next to me. I felt the mattress shift when he lifted his feet and rested them on the end of the bed. "I'm undead. You bit me. Remember?"

Parts of that last day came back to me.

"But I killed you. I watched you die. It was awful."

"You're telling me. Painful, too. But I guess that's how it works."

He looked at Ophelia. She nodded.

"No one becomes a vampire from a mere bite," she said. "Even the old stories are consistent in this. The human immune system is too adept at fighting off the disease. Unless you drink a vampire's blood directly, you have to be bitten many times and lose a lot of blood before your system is overwhelmed. In Charlie's case, he was bitten twice. Once by Vlad, and then by you. But you drank too deeply and it was fatal, leaving the pathogen free to take hold and transform him. I suspect when Vlad bit you, it was much the same. Infection followed by extreme blood loss. Then death. Then life."

"I don't understand," I said.

Ophelia smiled. "You will, in time."

I remembered what my uncle had told me—that if you didn't understand something you needed more information, or you had to think about it a bit longer. I think I needed both.

"Why didn't the sun get you?" I asked.

"Who, me?" said Charlie.

"Yes," I said. "It was still up when I bit you."

He shrugged. "I guess it takes a while for your body to change. The sun was long gone by the time I woke up." Charlie had always been a late riser.

"Luna?" I asked.

Ophelia looked at Charlie. A sheepish expression came over his face.

"I woke up hungry—I mean, *really* hungry," he said. "So, she's one of us now."

One of us. I smiled. That meant she wasn't dead. I might see her again.

My lips cracked. I tried to moisten them with my tongue but it was too dry. My head fell to the side. I could see a red tube running into my arm. There was one in the other arm as well. Blood seeped into my charred body. But I needed more. Much more.

I looked at Ophelia. "Why didn't you tell me?"

She smiled, then reached out and put the back of her hand against my cheek. "Oh, Zachary, if only you knew what happens to most of us. There are no good endings. I hoped that you could be cured. I wanted to save you from what is coming."

I knew what she was referring to. Endpoint Psychosis. The descent into madness. It would happen to me. To all of us. Just as it had happened to the Baron.

"Where is he?" I said.

"Who?"

"The Baron. Did he make it?" I wanted to explain everything, but the right words were still scrambled in my mind. "I tried to save him."

"What do you mean?"

"I threw him through the secret door into the dark."

I felt the mattress shift as Charlie lifted his feet off and set them back on the floor. "Why?" he asked.

I didn't know what to say. I suppose I could have offered many reasons.

Maybe because my father believed in redemption. And Mr. Entwistle, too. Forgiveness, he'd told me. That was how you dealt with rogues. If there was even a small chance that they were somewhere watching over me, how could I disappoint them? I couldn't kill the Baron without offering him the choice my father would have. Or maybe it was because I'd spent my undead life in a mental ward. The Baron was mad. You don't judge people like that. You help them. But at the time, there was really only one reason.

"I don't want to hurt anyone," I said. "Never again."

I looked at Charlie. The memory of his death was clearer now. I had killed him. And the pain and confusion on his face was something I didn't ever want to see again.

I think they understood me. Ophelia reached up and put the back of her hand against my forehead as though checking my temperature.

"There was no trace of the Baron when I returned," she said.

I wondered what this meant. Perhaps the Coven of the Dragon took care of their own. Maybe Maximilian had come back for him. Or perhaps he had servants, like the vampires in the movies. The Fallen. Men like Everett Johansson who were ready to die in his service.

"Did I make a mistake?" I asked.

Ophelia checked the tubes running into my arm. "Time will tell, Zachary," she said, stroking my forehead again. "But for now, you need to rest."

That sounded like perfect advice. But it wasn't going to happen just yet. Someone was coming into the room. My vision was still too blurry to see all the way to the door. All I could make out was a tall, dark blob. As he approached, I could see he was walking with a limp. Then his face came into focus. What stood out most was the thick, pink scar under his right eye.

I struggled to rise, but Ophelia put a hand on my chest. "Relax . . ." she whispered. "It's okay."

"What is *he* doing here?"

Johansson barked a laugh but didn't say anything. He just hobbled over behind Ophelia and looked down at me.

"You don't need to worry about Everett," Ophelia said. "He and I have been working together for many years."

I couldn't believe it.

"How's our patient?" he asked. His voice sounded like sandpaper. "Blood supply okay?"

"We should be all right," Ophelia answered.

Johansson grunted, nodded once to me, then hobbled towards the door.

"My uncle said Johansson was one of the Fallen," I told her. "That he served vampires."

Ophelia smiled. "He does. He works for me."

This took a moment to register.

"But they kept shocking me," I said. I thought of the Taser the police had used the night they captured me on Stoney Lake.

"You must forgive the police for their excesses," Ophelia said. "After seeing you feed on that boy's corpse, can you blame them? It is not an easy thing, controlling a crazed vampire." She pressed her lips together in an arrangement that might have been a smile had it not been so full of regret. "I just wish you hadn't run away from him. I sent him to the ward to get you."

"Where were you?"

"Avoiding your uncle. He was getting dangerously close to me. And I didn't want to lead him to you. Not until I knew his intentions. I was also trying to get in touch with my husband. Not an easy thing, given that he and Maximilian started working together shortly after you ran off. In the end, I decided to risk a confrontation. I guess I arrived just in time. I should have come to the ward myself, but I didn't want to put you in danger. And it didn't occur to me that you would run from the police. As a rule of thumb, they're the good guys." She stood and smoothed out the front of her uniform. "But we're all here now. For better or worse."

She then excused herself and crossed the room.

"I need to have another word with Everett," she said at the door. "I'll be back in a minute."

I thought about what Maximilian had told me about Johansson. I'd assumed he served Vrolok, but he'd really been working with Ophelia the whole time. So my uncle had basically turned my life upside down to save me from a woman who was practically my mother. I was beginning to understand the whole *irony* thing.

I turned back to Charlie. He was a vampire now, a carrier, like me.

"Have you told your parents?" I asked.

He shook his head. "Nope. Not looking forward to that conversation." Then his face brightened up a little. "But on the plus side, at least it will explain why I lost my job." He laughed. Then he sighed and looked around the room. "What am I supposed to tell them? They can barely deal with me as it is."

I had no idea what to say to this. My instinct was that he should just tell them the truth. That it wouldn't stay hidden for long. But offering advice was beyond me at the moment, and I had other things on my mind.

"Tell me what happened," I said.

"When?"

"After I died. How did I get here?"

"Luna. She dragged you under the desk. I found you two after the sun went down."

"So she was still alive?"

"Barely. She was bleeding to death. There was only one way to save her. I had to kill her. So I drank. Man, the hunger . . ." He shook his head.

I understood.

"Then Ophelia showed up and took care of things."

"But I died," I said.

"Yes, you did."

"So how am I here?"

Charlie stood and leaned on the metal rail that ran along the side of the bed. "You were pretty crispy on the outside, but on the inside, you were still medium rare. Ophelia brought you here and gave you a blood bath. It seemed to do the trick. You started to heal right away. You still look like you've been sleeping in a sauna, but it shouldn't take too much longer to get you back to normal."

"How long have I been here?"

"Two days. Not even. A day and two nights."

"I don't understand how it's possible," I said.

"How is any of this possible? I can see in the dark now. And run all night. I'm faster than a rabbit. And that's just the tip of the iceberg."

"I know all about the iceberg."

"Oh, right."

"What happened to my uncle?" I asked. "What happened to Maximilian?"

"He's still a loose end waiting to be tied up."

"A loose end . . . ?"

"I wouldn't worry too much about it. Ophelia and Johansson are quite a team. And I'm a sailing instructor, remember? Tying knots in loose ends is supposed to be my specialty."

I didn't think tying up Maximilian was going to be that easy for anyone.

"Charlie," I said.

"Yeah?"

"You're a good friend."

"So are you."

"I mean it."

"So do I."

I tried to sit up in the bed so I could look at him more closely. I wanted to see if he had changed, but that was going to have to wait. It was all I could do to keep my eyes open.

"Oh," he said. "I almost forgot." He dug into his pocket and took something out. It was my necklace. He put it in my hand.

"Where's the rest of it?" I asked. The part that had belonged to my mother, the golden crescent, was no longer attached to my full moon.

"Where do you think, you goofball? Luna has it."

My heart went into overdrive when he said that.

"I'd like to see her."

"And she wants to see you, too," he said. "I'm sure Ophelia can arrange something." Then he looked me over. "On second thought," he added, "I'd recommend waiting a few days. Love may be blind . . ."—he shook his head—"but it's not *that* blind!"

Acknowledgments

Thank you to Janet Shorten for her early edits; Mark Swailes; Kathie Stevenson; my brothers, Charlie and Jake; my father, Robert Douglas; my wife, Joanna Richardson; and especially my mother, Julia Bell, for many invaluable contributions. Thanks also to Sharon McKay and her husband, David, for their interest and support; Catherine Marjoribanks for a fantastic copy edit; and to Lynne Missen, Patricia Ocampo, and HarperCollins Canada Ltd. for this wonderful opportunity.